A GOOD TIME

"How about one more?" he asked.

A pair of very alarmed eyes looked back at him. "One more what?"

"One more good time. You've already shown me you're not shy. The door's locked. Unless you're myopic, you know I'm ready."

"I'm shocked you would suggest such a thing."

"No, you're not. But you're scared. Coward. Wimp."

She lifted her chin in defiance; then she looked into his eyes and he looked into hers, and the air in the room heated twenty degrees.

He got up from the table, and this time she didn't raise her hand to stop him. "You look great in that lab coat," he said. "What's underneath?"

"Nothing sexy," she said. Her voice had grown hoarse. No surprise. So had his.

"I'll bet if I look long enough, I'll find something sexy."

"What I'm thinking has got to be unethical," she said.

"How about what you're feeling?"

"That, too." She was speaking barely above a whisper.

He kissed the corner of her mouth. "We're in an examining room, right? Examine me."

Second Opinion

Evelyn Rogers

LOVE SPELL BOOKS   NEW YORK CITY

To the newest heroes in the family,
Mark Edward Rogers and David Clemens Varner.

LOVE SPELL®

September 1999

Published by

Dorchester Publishing Co., Inc.
276 Fifth Avenue
New York, NY 10001

ISBN 0-505-52332-9

The name "Love Spell" and its logo are trademarks of Dorchester Publishing Co., Inc.

Printed in the United States of America.

SECOND OPINION

Chapter One

Charlotte Hamilton got through her divorce in far better shape than she thought she would. Two hours after the judge signed the decree, she was walking into the office of her ex's attorney to deliver a few final papers, congratulating herself on being so civil and civilized.

"Good afternoon," she said with a definite lilt in her voice as she dropped the papers on the attorney's desk. "I believe this concludes our business."

The attorney eyed her suspiciously from behind his desk. He wasn't used to seeing her in such a good mood, but until right now he hadn't given her reason to be.

Today she had reason to laugh out loud. During the yearlong separation, the meetings, the filing, and the final six months of waiting, not once had she indulged in an outburst of anger or display of pettiness, though she had felt very petty a time or two.

She had felt lost, too, and despondent, but that was to be expected, considering what she had once hoped to get out of the marriage. She certainly did not regret the fact that it had come to an end.

Charlotte had been raised to keep emotions private. Her parents and grandparents must be gazing down on her with pride. For them as well as herself, she was feeling liberated, feeling good.

The good feeling lasted until she turned to leave and Roger the Rat walked in. Her heart, joyously light a moment before, sank to her toes. Roger had that effect on her. It was one of the major reasons for the divorce.

He wasn't supposed to be anywhere near the office, not until long after she was gone. Not once in their five-year marriage had he done what he was supposed to do. Even now, freed of the union, he was still being a rat.

"What are you doing here?" they asked in unison when he halted beside her.

Charlotte observed him coolly. "There was a last-minute emergency," she said. "I was delayed."

"An arthritic hangnail?"

How like Roger to be sarcastic. He had never been sympathetic toward her geriatric patients, a natural enough attitude since he couldn't picture himself as ever growing old. Not once had he understood what those patients meant to her.

"What about you?" She glanced at the broad face of her wristwatch. "It's not even five o'clock. I understood you wouldn't be here until six."

"I've got an early dinner engagement," he said with a sniff. "Already I'm running late." Sniff.

Why she hadn't noticed the sniffing habit a long time ago, she had no idea. It irritated her mightily now. She would have suggested an allergist, but Roger Ryan's health was no longer her worry.

"You're meeting a woman, I suppose," she said, and then bit her tongue. The people he consorted with were none of her concern. Tonight, celebrating the final decree, he would probably be frolicking along the River Walk with a half dozen of his female friends. With his interest in deviant sex, there was no telling how many he would take on at once.

The attorney, as squat as Roger was tall and lean, continued to sit quietly, blinking like an owl behind his thick eyeglasses. She supposed it was a long-standing trait with divorce lawyers when their clients clashed.

11

"The dinner's with Redeye," Roger said.

Charlotte shook her head. Redeye was the fishing buddy who had taken her husband away from home a hundred times over the years; on the weekends when the men weren't actually fishing, he provided a convenient cover story for one of the Rat's trysts, or so she had eventually found out. She had been tempted to name Redeye as corespondent when she and Roger split, but since the divorce was uncontested, she resisted. Besides, she couldn't recall his real name.

If they ever ran into each other, she had a few substitute names she could throw at him, most that would shock even Roger.

She picked up the papers from the attorney's desk. "Here's the transfer deed to the house," she said, slapping the signed-and-notarized document into Roger's hand, "and the same for the car." She added it to the short stack. "They're both yours now, free and clear. Enjoy them in peace."

She meant it. She didn't wish Roger Ryan harm. She wished him gone.

He looked at her as if she had somehow insulted him, instead of turning over possessions that, in a community-property state like Texas, were legally half hers. They were worth a considerable amount, too. The elegant stone almost-a-mansion that they had purchased the third year of their marriage was in an upscale gated community fifteen miles north of down-town San Antonio; the car was a Lexus sedan.

She wanted no part of them, and it wasn't only because they weren't anywhere near paid for. Already she had received ownership of the beloved artwork her grandparents had left her, as well as the few items she had purchased after they wed. She also got a generous portion of all joint savings from the marriage, and she got her freedom.

If she was hurting inside, it was because of issues that had little to do with Roger's infi-delity; issues he would never understand.

The best thing she had done in the marriage was keep her maiden name. Perhaps, right from the beginning, she had sensed the movie-star handsome investment counselor she'd chosen as her mate would not provide the home and family she wanted above all else.

After five years, she wouldn't trust the Rat's opinion about what toilet paper to buy. She had been foolish enough to fall for a pretty face. She wouldn't make that mistake again.

Grabbing her purse from the desk, she turned to make her escape, but Roger was not about to let her get away without a parting shot.

"You realize, Charlotte, this marriage should have worked. The breakup is not my fault."

Her hand froze on the doorknob, and she glanced over her shoulder at him. This time she really looked at him, for the first time since he'd strolled into the room. As always, he looked impeccable in a gray Armani suit, every dark hair in place, even-featured, and tanned despite weeks of overcast skies. If his electric-blue eyes didn't look quite so bright as usual, it was probably because he was trying to evince pain.

"How do you figure that?" she asked, knowing she shouldn't. "You were the one who fooled around."

The knob turned in her hand, and she stepped away as the secretary peeked into the room.

The appearance of the sleekly coiffed head did not deter the Rat.

"I wouldn't have if there had been reason to stay home."

He looked her up and down, all five feet six inches, 120 pounds of her. She was wearing a camel-colored tunic-length jacket and matching knee-length skirt, a red silk blouse in honor of the Christmas season, and, of course, sensible shoes, all of it expensive, comfortable, and neat. When Roger's handsome features settled into a smirk, she knew he was about to find fault.

"You look good, Charlotte. As usual."

She wasn't comforted by the compliment. Roger wasn't through.

"But you were always a lousy lover," he said. "You gave me no reason to seek your bed."

Charlotte gasped, and the carpeted floor swooped and swayed under her. In that instant she realized how fragile her sense of well-being really was.

And she shattered like glass, not knowing what to say or how to react. Roger might as well have struck her. For all his infidelities, he had never done anything quite so low.

As if he could help, she glanced at the attorney, who had the good grace to lower his gaze. The secretary giggled. It was the giggle that got her. Something dark and furious bubbled inside her, and she forsook civility. Swinging her purse, she caught Roger in the arm.

"You bastard," she said.

He wasn't moved, either by the blow or the words.

"It's true, Charlotte."

She hit him again, she, the protector of life, who preferred to sweep cockroaches outside rather than send them to an insect grave. If she'd had the fingernails for it, she would have scratched his face.

Pettiness, she now saw, had its place.

He dared to smile, as if the final triumph was his. A lock of brown hair fell across her eyes; she blew it back in place. For a moment she seethed with a hate she hadn't known she bore.

The moment passed, leaving her breathing heavily, shockingly aware of the silence in the room. Maybe by the standards of others, the scene had been mild. For Charlotte, it was like the rampage of a barbarian horde.

She opened her mouth to speak, but she couldn't think of anything coherent to say, much less pithy and to the point. Which didn't stop her from babbling out a few epithets that made no sense, not even to her. But no amount of eloquence could have erased the fact that for a small period of time she had wanted to hurt him as he had hurt her.

For the son of a stiff-necked banker and a mother who had served on the board of every charity group in town, the Rat was amazingly low-class. Right now, she felt the same.

But knowledge of their shared character flaws was of no help. It certainly didn't erase the smirk on Roger's handsome, vacuous face. The best response she could manage was to run, shoving her way past the secretary and through the outer office, into the tenth-floor hallway, pushing frantically at the elevator button that was already lit, ignoring the stares of a couple of men waiting to go down.

Outside, twilight had descended over the city. A brisk wind almost knocked her over. Heart pounding, she pulled the jacket of her suit tight around her. Alone on the sidewalk, with the dark gathering around her, she lectured herself not to be weak. But how could a day that had started out good turn bad so quickly?

Roger the Rat, that was how. He had hit her where she was most vulnerable, her sense of self.

But she had the divorce. She had to remember the divorce. And that wasn't all. Ahead of her stretched a lifetime of helping others. She had a more than adequate income to get by, a beautiful place to live, and, that ultimate of American goals, a great new car. A lapse into self-pity, brought on by a momentary humiliation, would be a stupid indulgence.

Still, standing in isolation as people streamed around her, she felt stupid, and self-indulgent, and more than a little sorry for herself. Roger's words still stung.

Head down, she strode into the wind for the twenty-minute walk to her downtown apartment. Christmas lights sparkled from the River Walk below the street, reminding her the holiday was exactly one week away. With the lights came the sound of carolers on one of the barges that wound down the waterway.

Usually she loved the music. At the moment, joyous and lyrical as it was, it mocked her mood.

You were always a lousy lover.

You were lousy, too, she could have said.

But that wasn't necessarily true. By her

admittedly inaccurate count, he had close to a dozen women who would testify otherwise. The problem had been the things he wanted her to do. Kinky, she called them, beginning with the honeymoon. Adventuresome, he said.

Technically she had been a virgin, having extracted a promise from him that they would wait until the wedding night to "do it," as he adolescently phrased it. But they had done some heavy petting and there was nothing to suggest that when the time came for "it," she wouldn't match him urge for urge.

Until the moment in their Hilton bridal suite when he unpacked the handcuffs.

He had suggested her problem lay in the fact that as a doctor, she saw the human body from a clinical viewpoint. The suggestion was non-sense, of course, but once he got the idea in his head, he couldn't be swayed.

May he and his buddy Redeye meet up with a case of bad beer and spend a miserable night. The wish was definitely against the Hippo-cratic oath, but what the hell. This seemed the season for breaking rules.

The route to her apartment took her along the river. She descended the winding stairs to the walkway, determined to cut the normal twenty minutes in half. But the lights in the trees were so beautiful and the crowds so festive, sitting at the outside restaurant tables despite the cold, that she couldn't bring herself to hurry.

It would have done her little good. Half the tourists in Texas and a good portion of the locals must be strolling along in front of her, gawking at the lights. If she had any sense, she would take the nearest stairway and go back to street level. But something was keeping her by the river, something she couldn't define.

She spied the Hilton where her marriage had begun. What better place to visit at its end? She doubted if fate had directed her this way, but a celebratory drink would taste good until whatever was keeping her down here made itself known.

Making her way to the hotel's river-level bar, she claimed an empty stool at the far end of the long, paneled room, flipped a credit card on the counter, and ordered a Jose Cuervo Gold margarita.

"Straight up," she added. "And don't close out the bill. I'll run a tab."

To her own ears she sounded like Roger. She gave him credit. He'd taught her how to order a drink.

Next to her were a woman and her male companion, holding hands, touching knees and noses, unaware that anyone else in the world was alive. Sipping at the margarita, Charlotte caught herself leaning close in an attempt to overhear their whisperings.

You were always a lousy lover. They were the only words she could hear.

Ignoring the couple, she finished the drink and ordered another. She was thirty-five years old, for crying out loud. And she was walking home, not driving. If she wanted to get drunk, she had the right.

But she had never been much of a drinker, and the margaritas tasted very strong. Good, too. She licked the salt from the rim of the glass.

You were always a lousy lover.

Maybe what she needed was a good cry to get Roger's condemnation out of her mind. But she never cried. And it seemed a poor method for regaining her composure.

The margaritas offered a better way. Besides, she was supposed to be celebrating. Tears would get in the way.

She brushed her short brown hair away from her face. How did Roger know she was lousy? He hadn't been the greatest of motivators. Besides, they hadn't shared a bed in a long, long time.

Two years ago, with little discouragement from her husband, she had given up sex. He was playing around. He didn't need her and by then, she had found out that she didn't need him. Today, during the scene in the attorney's office, she had lost more than sex. She had lost her self-respect.

She let out a heartfelt sigh. Much as she hated to admit it, the respect of a man right now would do her ego a world of good. It didn't have to be a great deal of respect either.

She reviewed her assets. Maybe if she let her hair grow long, she might look more alluring. She would also be covering up the long neck that made her look like a giraffe. There was nothing she could do about the low-slung fanny that was much too large for the rest of her. Already she wore tunic jackets that came practically to her knees.

Besides, men were supposed to like big butts. The thought made her giggle. She hadn't thought the word *butt* since high school half a lifetime ago. But then, neither had she giggled.

She considered ordering a third margarita, but held back.

Lousy in bed, was she? Roger had hardly given her a chance. Why shouldn't she be great? She kept herself in good condition, never smoking, rarely drinking more than a glass of white wine, serving as an example for the Senior Olympics she helped to foster.

Except for the neck and the possible exception of the fanny, she wasn't so hard on the eye. Even Roger had complimented her more than once on her looks.

The devil take a man's respect. What she needed was a second opinion as to her sexual prowess. The thought brought on another giggle, this one much like the secretary's in the law office. She had never been good at meeting men. She could never pull off an affair, even a short-lived one.

Dimly she was aware of the couple next to her abandoning their perches. The woman was replaced by a man. She gave him a quick glance, and then another, and then an outright stare, shifting from his head of tousled sandy hair to his puppy-warm brown eyes to the finely toned gluteus maximus he had settled on the barstool.

He was wearing khakis and an open-throated, blue chambray shirt that looked far better than Roger's Armani suit. Or maybe it was the obviously muscled body underneath that she really admired.

Her physician's eye put him at five-ten, 165 pounds, two or three years older than she. His neck was wide and strong, and she suspected at one time in his life he had been quite an athlete. For a guy in his late thirties, he was still in excellent shape.

Hurriedly she returned to the eyes, noticing on the way the slightly crooked nose that must have been broken at least twice. He was not, she told herself, a pretty face, though he came very, very close.

All of her observations started rare poundings in various parts of her body, and not just her heart. She crossed her legs, inadvertently— or maybe advertently, she couldn't say—hiking her skirt halfway up her thigh.

The puppy eyes noticed and took on the glint of a hound on the scent. She lectured her insides to behave.

"I know it sounds like an old line," he said in a voice that mellowed her out, "but it looks like I've been stood up. Would you mind if I bought you a drink?"

"I really shouldn't," she said, and then, quickly, lest he change his mind, added, "but all right." This was no time to play hard to get.

After all, she asked herself, what could be the harm in sharing a drink with a stranger in a bar?

Chapter Two

Sam Blake had not picked up a woman in a bar in a long, long time. Women who came on too strong turned him off. Usually they had seen him on a television sportscast, or heard his radio show, and started picturing themselves as media groupies.

But this one seemed different, kind of lost and alone, nursing her margarita in the corner while outside a thousand parties had begun. She was pretty and shy with a hint of eagerness that got to him. For her, he might make an exception to the no-pickup rule. Should the opportunity present itself.

He ordered another margarita for her and for himself a soda and lime. There had been a time in his life when he drank too much. The drinking had never reached the point of being uncontrollable, but, still, he had liked the liquor far too much and he didn't want to go through that kind of worry again.

Besides, he could get high just by looking at the graceful curve of the woman's long neck and the way her short brown hair curled behind her ears and, yeah, he admitted it, he appreciated the way her bottom covered the stool. These days too many women believed they had to be skinny to be attractive. Not this one. She was just right.

Right for what? He didn't bother to come up with an answer, figuring one would occur if the need arose.

When the drinks arrived, he offered a toast to the season.

"I'd rather make it to the new year," she said with an intriguing edge to her voice, a combination of triumph and desperation that he had never heard before.

"Done," he said, clinking glasses. "To the new year."

"The new year," she said and took a deep swallow of her drink. He began to wonder how many she had already consumed.

But she seemed sober enough, her pale blue eyes wide and innocent and clear. He shoved the bowl of nuts toward her and she took a handful.

"The name's Sam, by the way," he said.

He could see her thinking that one over. Maybe she had a thing against guys named Sam. Maybe one had broken her heart.

"Charlie," she said.

"Huh?" he said, none too intelligently.

"Call me Charlie," she said.

"You don't look like a Charlie. Is that your name?"

"It's close enough."

"Okay, Charlie," he said, raising his glass, "here's looking at you. And a nice view it is."

She smiled, and he almost fell off the stool. The blue eyes got lost in crinkles and the smile took over her face. She was pretty when she was looking solemn, but she was a knockout when she smiled. For an unexplainable reason he got the feeling smiles didn't come to her readily.

"Do you come in here regularly?" he asked, then winced when she rolled her eyes.

"That's another old line, isn't it?" she said.

"They're the ones I know best."

She looked around her. "I was in here once. Five years ago. To be precise, five years ago last November 15. No, make that the sixteenth. It was the day after—"

She broke off and lapsed into reverie.

"It wasn't a serious question, Charlie. As you said, it was just a line. Something to break through the awkwardness of getting to know a stranger."

26

She nodded in acceptance of the explanation. Neither of them spoke for a minute. For him the silence wasn't awkward, but he wasn't sure about how she felt.

"Let me give breaking the ice a try," she said. "What do you do for a living?"

"That's a little serious for bar talk."

"Oh," she said, looking away as if she'd made a major social gaffe. "I didn't mean to pry."

"I do a little of this and that," he said hurriedly, wanting more than anything to put her at ease. Maybe he ought to cut out the preliminaries. Maybe he should just throw her over his shoulder and carry her up to the nearest available room.

She looked back at him. "This and that, you said."

"Yep," he said. He was really on a conversational roll tonight.

Actually, words were his business. He wrote a four-times-a-week sports column for the *San Antonio Tribune,* each one accompanied by a photo that was more realistic than flattering. There were also the occasional TV appearances, not to mention the weekly radio show. He kind of liked the fact that she didn't recognize him.

"Which pays better, the this or the that?" she asked.

"I've got a paycheck stub in my wallet if you want to look."

She blushed nicely.

"There I am prying again. You could be a street person for all I care." She leaned back and gave him a slow once-over. "Though you look far too healthy to be sleeping under a bridge."

She finished off the margarita and licked the salt off her lips, an act he would have liked to perform for her, the lips under consideration being full and pink and moist.

"It's just that I've never done this kind of thing before," she said.

He leaned close and got a whiff of Chanel No. 5. Class, pure class. But it didn't keep him from whispering in her ear, "What kind of thing do you mean?"

He felt the shiver that went through her. It traveled all the way through him. A little more of this kind of stuff and he would have to get his jacket from the coatrack behind him and throw it across his lap. The last thing he wanted to do was frighten her off.

Whoever and whatever she was, Charlie was definitely not a 90's woman, though she was sitting on a barstool in a 90's kind of way.

She fanned the collar of her red silk blouse, and the jacket of her suit fell open wider. He got no more than a hint of breast size, which seemed nice rather than massive, but there was always the bottom that covered the stool. Her thighs weren't bad, either, and as long as he was crude enough to notice such things, neither were her ankles and calves.

Put them all together, and he came up with a length of leg that was spectacular.

She was wearing sensible brown shoes, gold studs, and a gold watch with a face that could be read across the room. Everything that he saw, he liked. He wondered if maybe he wasn't falling in love.

The thought came out of nowhere. He shook himself and came close to ordering a beer. For crying out loud, at the most, this was a bar pickup, not a lifetime commitment. Lately he had been discontented, restless, edgy, but it wasn't because he was lonely for female companionship. He had all of that he wanted. It was just that he hadn't wanted it in a while.

Until Charlie.

A silence fell between them. He didn't find it uncomfortable, but apparently she did because she shifted about on the stool. He watched each movement from the corner of his eye.

"Do you come here regularly?" she asked. It was the same question he had put to her. He liked it that she was mimicking him.

He smiled. "That's an old line."

"It's the kind I know best." She played with the nuts, taking them out of the bowl one by one and lining them up on the bar. "Actually, I don't know lines very well. You'll have to feed me some more."

"Okay. How about, 'what's a nice girl like you doing in a place like this?' Of course you'll have to change the sex and ignore the fact that this is a very respectable bar."

"As long as I don't have to ignore the sex and change the fact." She lifted her thick black lashes and stared at him. "That was supposed to be a joke."

He grinned. "Charlie, I think you're flirting with me."

She nodded. "How am I doing?"

She asked the question solemnly, as if his answer mattered very much. Something was going on here, but he didn't have any idea what it was. All he knew for sure was that he was not the one in control.

Maybe she was a 90's woman after all, or better yet, Y2K.

"You're doing fine," he said. Too fine. "Excuse me a minute, will you?" He went to the coatrack and came back with his jacket, which he rested across his lap as he settled on the stool.

She seemed so innocent, he wondered if she would know what he was covering. She studied the pattern of salt around her glass with such thoroughness, he decided she did.

The good news was that she didn't grab her purse and flee.

"I work with the elderly," she blurted out. "I wanted you to know something about me."

"That sounds like serious stuff. What do you

mean work with them? Like in a retirement home?"

"Something like that. I'm with them so much, it seems strange talking to someone who has his own teeth."

He gave her a big grin. "Are you sure these are attached?"

"I'm sure. Believe me, I can recognize the difference, no matter how skilled the dentist is."

"What else did you notice?"

"You're in great shape." He got the feeling she was fighting hard to keep from looking at his lap. "Were you ever an athlete?"

"Several decades ago I played baseball for the University of Texas."

"I don't know much about sports."

"Except for a cranky uncle, I don't know much about the elderly."

"Are you married?" she asked.

"No. Are you?"

"Definitely not." The response came out as an explosion.

"You're divorced," he said. "Don't look surprised. I can tell. I went through the same thing a long time ago, right out of college."

"And you haven't been tempted to try marriage again?"

"No. How about you?"

"Never. I'm not very good at it."

He leaned very close and ran a finger down her cheek. "Not good at what?"

31

"At—" She cast him a pensive look. "You really are flirting with me, aren't you?

"I'm trying my damnedest."

"Don't give up. You're getting there."

He didn't ask where *there* might be. He didn't want to dash all hope.

"Any children?" she asked.

He shook his head. "And you?"

"No."

She seemed far too solemn for her own good. It was time for Sam the Sportsman to appear. Using the only tools at hand, he began to play with her nuts, lining them up in various orders. She watched awhile and when he had lulled her into security, without warning he flicked one at her. She flicked one back, and they were promptly in a battle. Within a couple of minutes, he had all the nuts scattered around her end of the bar.

She surveyed the scene. "You're very competitive," she said.

"Very. It's a family trait."

"Mine was very reserved."

He'd figured as much. "Was?" he asked.

"They're all dead," she said, not sadly but in a reportorial kind of way.

"That can be tough this time of year."

"I've been alone a long time. I'm used to it."

Something inside him responded to the bravado in her words. No children, no family, but she wasn't asking for sympathy. Damned if he didn't like her all the more.

The bartender picked up the empty bowl. "You two kids want some more toys?" he asked.

Sam shook his head, and to her he whispered, "I've got all I want to play with right here."

She shivered and closed her eyes. "Me, too."

Sam felt like he was losing his mind, either that or going through one of the most amazing, exciting experiences of his life. If a dozen violins suddenly burst into soaring music, he wouldn't have been surprised.

One of the tables in the bar opened up and they quickly claimed it, ordering a couple of appetizers when they were settled in. Over the next hour, while she downed another margarita and a half, they talked movies—he liked technothrillers, she went for foreign films— and books, surprisingly, he was the one who liked fiction while she preferred fact, and music, where they became hopelessly lost in an argument over rock, jazz, and Bach.

As they talked, the noise level in the bar increased and they had to move close to hear each other. The truth was Sam kept lowering his voice until she was practically in his arms. He congratulated himself for remembering an old trick.

He was tempted to tell her about his writing plans, and ask her about her dreams, but that was serious talk. He was serious, all right—he had never been more so—but talk was only slightly involved in his plans.

Eventually he told Charlie a couple of off-color jokes, which she didn't pretend to misunderstand. Neither did she laugh uproariously, but she did smile and that was all he could ask.

He wasn't sure which of them suggested seeing about a room, but some time around ten he was talking to a friend who worked at the Hilton and arranging for one of the accommodations they held back for emergency drop-ins, the emergency usually being a celebrity who needed a room. As a sportswriter, Sam was hardly that, but he did have a standing among sports buffs, especially those who liked to place an occasional bet and asked for whatever inside information they could get.

He came back to find she had put the drinks on her credit card. But that didn't mean she was calmly accepting the situation. She looked so nervous, he thought she might back out during the elevator ride. But a party of revelers crowded in with them, and she was stuck at the back, eyes staring straight ahead. He doubted she saw anything or anyone. At least she didn't pull her jacket over her head to keep from being seen.

First on, they were the last off, arriving at

their floor in silence. He guided her to the door of their room and gestured for her to go in first. She did and snapped on the light, muttering something under her breath about an opinion, or maybe it was a second opinion, which made no sense to him.

But he promptly forgot it, hardly being in an analytical mood.

The room was spacious and grandly furnished, with a balcony that overlooked the River Walk. Sighing, she tossed her purse on the quilted satin cover of the king-size bed.

"I'm healthy, in case you're wondering," she said.

"So am I," he said, then pulled out his wallet and dropped it beside her purse. "I'm also prepared."

The color drained from her face. "You're going to pay me?"

"I was referring to condoms. I have several of them in there."

The color came back with a rush.

"Oh," she said, and then, recovering, "I guess you like to be ready. Should the opportunity ever arise."

"I bought them for a date, Charlie. A long time ago. They didn't get used."

She looked to the right and left, then looked down and smoothed her skirt. "I wonder what could have happened to all that alcohol in my blood."

"You're sober."

"Not completely. But close enough to realize what's going on."

"Good," he said. Conscience made him add, "You've never done anything like this before, have you? Are you sure you want to go through with it?"

As usual, her response was totally unexpected.

"You're changing your mind, aren't you?" she said flatly. "I knew you would."

"No way, Charlie."

Dropping his jacket, he took her into his arms and kissed her, lightly, just to get a taste. He picked up hints of lime and tequila and salt, and more than a hint of Grand Marnier.

He also picked up the taste of paradise, telling himself it was the writer in him that brought such an extravagant word to mind.

She took off her jacket and dropped it on the floor beside his before throwing herself into his arms.

Paradise, he decided, was not too strong a word for what the woman named Charlie promised.

Chapter Three

Hugging Sam was like hugging a man for the first time. Charlotte grabbed hold of shoulders, arms, shirt—anything and everything she could reach fast—and held on tight. What she wanted to do was to rip off his clothes for a better look at his contours, but she limited herself to clinging. If she let go, he might change his mind and bolt for the door.

She came close to whimpering. They weren't in the room five minutes and already she was handling this wrong. But if he really did try to leave, in the mood she was in she would probably resort to begging.

So much for a come-on in a bar. She truly was a fraud. And a pitiful one at that.

The possibility also existed that if he stayed, she might be the one to run. Mixed with all the excitement inside of her was a definite feeling of panic.

She gave herself a mental slap. He would not leave, and neither would she. Here was her chance to prove herself a complete woman. And she had a complete man to help her. She ran her hands down his arms, then moved to his neck, burrowing her head into the warm crook of his shoulder. He was complete, all right.

Sam types didn't come along very often—virile, attractive men with a sense of humor and insight into a woman's feelings. At least that was the way she read him. Whoever had stood him up tonight was a fool.

She felt his warm hands against her back, strong hands around her waist, probing hands cupping her bottom and holding her firmly against his erection.

Okay, so he wouldn't be leaving right away. As long as he stayed, so would she.

She shivered in anticipation. While she was shivering, she was stroking—the back of his neck, his shoulders, his arms. The guy was solid. The possibilities for the night were endless, the human body being a truly glorious creation. Knowing the scientific names for its parts didn't make it any less magnificent.

Sam kissed his way to her lips.

"On or off," he growled against her mouth.

On or off what? She was going to blow this whole scene yet.

"The lights," he said, when she didn't answer right away.

Oh. "Off. That way we can leave the draperies open and see the lights outside."

"We may not be looking outside."

She managed to hold his gaze for a minute. "Maybe we won't."

He gave her a wink, then broke away and headed for the light switch. Insecure mess that she was, she had to fight against following.

In the few seconds he was gone, she occupied herself with the buttons of her blouse. With the bright lamp turned off, the soft colors of holiday lights filled the room and gave a sense of magic to the night.

He eased back in front of her, bringing with him the warmth of a summer sun. "Let me," he said, stroking the slope of red silk over her breasts. A pair of nipples thrust forward in invitation. His thumbs accepted the challenge, and she had to hold on to his wonderfully broad, firm shoulders to keep upright as he gently rubbed back and forth against the tips.

"You'll have to tell me what you like," he said.

"Everything."

This was a strange response from Charlotte Hamilton, celibate M.D. She knew of one man—the only one she'd ever made love to—who would be laughing if he could hear.

The thing was, she meant what she said. Sam was going slow, kissing her eyes, her throat, while his thumbs kept up their assignment at her breasts. Gentle as he was, everywhere he touched burned. She couldn't imagine him hurting her or humiliating her in any way. Except if he grew bored and left.

The assessment was based on instinct, that and an almost pitiful eagerness, both of them mixed with a more than adequate portion of alcohol. She had lied about not feeling its effects.

Tugging the blouse free from her skirt, he finished the unbuttoning, slipping the red silk off her shoulders, and stared at the red lace bra underneath. His sharp intake of breath sent her breasts swelling and spilling over the top. Maybe it was the way the outside lights played across her body that brought his quick breathing. Or maybe not.

She began to feel good about herself. Watching his eyes, she decided to test him further. Unzipping her skirt, she let it fall to the floor and kicked off her shoes. She was wearing matching bikini panties and thigh-high hose. All of her underwear had been purchased for the day of the divorce. She had even painted her toenails a bright red.

All of it was also supposed to be hidden. Sam's eyes did not miss a thing.

With agonizing slowness, his gaze moved up to hold hers.

"You're a beautiful woman, Charlie," he said in a voice she scarcely recognized. "You like everything? I'm not sure I can do everything, but let's give it a try."

Without a word, she went back into his arms, tugging at his shirt, her normally skilled hands turned clumsy as she struggled to undress him. He would never believe she was a physician and surgeon. But who cared? It was something about her he would never find out.

For a moment she wondered what her patients would think about her now. They saw her as competent, caring, reserved, the last person in the world to wear thigh-highs and red bikini panties. When Sam returned his hands to her bottom, she forgot everyone but him. She didn't even wonder if he found her buttocks too large to cup. If he didn't complain, she wasn't about to put the thought in his mind.

Thrusting one leg between his, she moved her thigh up and down against what could euphemistically be called his sensitive area. His khakis had been starched, but they were limp compared to the stiffness she felt against her leg.

41

He growled. She took the sound as encouragement. Her head reeled, and she knew it was only in small part from the margaritas. There was a very hard, very large part of him that influenced her more.

He kissed the side of her neck and whispered, "We're in trouble, Charlie."

Her heart stopped. "Why?"

"There are only three condoms in my wallet."

She let out a long, slow breath. The last year before she and Roger gave up sex altogether, that would have been a six months' supply.

He let her go long enough to clear the bed, then tumbled her backward onto the sheet. After a long, thorough kiss, he backed off and undressed. She watched without a hint of shyness. She'd seen enough naked men in her lifetime to kill shyness, although most of them ranged from sixty-five to a hundred and one, not any of them were put together like Sam.

From his devilish brown eyes to his slightly tilted smile to his strong neck and shoulders, tightly muscled biceps, flat abdomen, and narrow hips, all the way down to his ankles, he looked like an "after" poster in a health spa, the kind that didn't overemphasize muscles. She couldn't see his feet, but she imagined they were poster perfect, too.

Two thin scars on either side of his right knee might have marred the perfection in anyone else, but, like his crooked nose, on Sam they looked good.

His body hair was sparse and pale, reflective of his sandy hair—except at the base of his abdomen, an area she had saved for last. There the hair grew dark and thick. She gave a closer look. Bingo. Poster perfect, again.

The magic of the lights had nothing to do with her assessment. The man was put together right.

Lifting one leg at a time, she slowly rolled down her hose and tossed them aside. He watched in silence. Talk wasn't necessary. He did watching the way he did everything else: He made her hot, he inspired her to brazen acts.

Giving her time to do nothing more than remove her bra, he lay beside her and took her into his arms, and she forgot about what he looked like or whether her bottom was too big or even whether she would disappoint him in some way. This wasn't a test, this was an immersion into sensual pleasure. She asked herself exactly why she was doing such an insane and risky thing, but when he brushed his tongue against hers and touched her breasts, she forgot the question, much less the answer.

When he ran his hand up the inside of her thigh and stroked the damp parts of her panties, she forgot how to think. When his fingers eased beneath the red silk, he taught her with one stroke the power and the beauty of sex.

She was the one to remove the last article of clothing that separated them, but she was hardly in control. With the sounds of singing and laughter drifting in through the balcony door, he played her like a harp, plucking the right strings in the right rhythms, caressing, resting, kissing, stroking, holding her tightly or loosely, whichever the action of the moment called for, and always, always driving her out of her mind.

There wasn't a place on her that he didn't touch, and more often than not trail his lips. She tried to keep pace, doing the same touching and kissing everywhere on his body she could reach, but like the flicking of the nuts, he had her beat.

He took a long time to reach for the first condom. But he used it fast. She wasn't sorry in the least. And she wasn't disappointed in her response. Between the two of them, they made the bed rock.

For the night, she took on another persona, a passionate woman who not only welcomed suggestions for unusual positions and experiments but came up with a few of her own— when he allowed. She figured they weren't new to him; he had probably made love on a stack of towels in a bathtub a hundred times. But not her.

She had thought she knew all the nerve endings of the human body, but Sam introduced her to a few more.

All of the books she had read on sex—and she had read quite a few—failed to describe what a man's tongue felt like as it rasped along a woman's inner thigh. They failed also to mention the different tastes of a man's skin, from his wrist to the back of his neck and down to the inside of his knee.

The books also neglected the importance of laughing. Sam made her laugh with a corny joke, and then he squelched the laughter with a touch, a kiss. He made her see fireworks, he made her hear music, he wrapped her in a world of sensuality.

Tough man that he was, he also used up the condoms far too soon.

"They were like the proverbial three wishes," he said as he cuddled her next to him beneath the bedcovers sometime in the wee hours of the morning. He had closed the draperies a couple of condoms ago, and they were lying in the dark.

She rested her hand on his chest, feeling his heart, and caught herself estimating the rate.

"Three wishes?" she asked, then dared to add, "Did you get what you wanted?" She held her breath as she waited for his response.

"Oh yes," he said, nuzzling her neck. "More than you can imagine. You're quite a woman, Charlie, but then I expect you know that."

"Yes," she said, smiling, "I really think I do."

"We need to talk," he said.

Her heart stopped. "We've been talking."

"Not seriously."

The last thing in all the world Charlotte wanted was a serious talk with Sam. She lectured herself not to panic. She must remain the coolly experienced, sophisticated woman he thought her to be.

"Later," she said, then let her voice trail off with another whispered, "Later," and he didn't push the point. Gradually her heart began to beat again. She could handle the situation. She had no choice.

Exhausted, sated, and very, very pleased with the way the night had gone, right up to the talk about talk, at last she fell asleep, stirring once at the unfamiliarity of lying in a man's arms, then settling down and letting the sound of Sam's even snoring lull her back to sleep.

Nobody, she told herself just before oblivion came, had ever been better in bed, and she meant not only Sam but herself.

Sam woke with a start and took a minute to get his bearings. Light broke around the edges of the wall of closed draperies, and details of the previous night came back in a rush.

Charlie. The name brought a very satisfied smile to his lips.

He felt on the bed beside him, but she wasn't there. He eased all the way over to the far edge of the king-size mattress. She was definitely gone. But the sheets weren't completely cold. She hadn't been gone long.

He searched the bathroom and the floor around the bed for signs she had ever been there. Except for a pile of towels in the tub and the neat way she had folded his clothes on a chair, he found nothing in the way of evidence.

There was, of course, some stiffness and soreness in a few too-long-neglected parts of his body, proof the parts had been well used. He thought about the woman who had done the using. Considerate, responsive, inventive in her passion, she was just about perfect. She even laughed at his jokes. He was in love.

Or he could be if she gave him the chance.

He had to see her again, get to know her better, give her a chance to know him. He was thirty-eight years old. It was long past time he found a good woman and settled down. If she wanted it as much as he, they could even start a family, which would have the added benefit of hushing his mother about what a wasted life he led.

And then reality struck. His mother had better not start counting grandchildren yet. He didn't even know Charlie's real name.

Sitting at the side of the bed, he rubbed at his head and cursed himself. How could he let her get away?

He couldn't. He wouldn't. But how was he to find her again?

He was standing under a hot shower when the answer came. The solution lay in the same place the relationship had begun: the bar.

Sans toothbrush and shave, he made himself as presentable as he could and hurried downstairs. It was almost ten o'clock. He never slept this late. But then he'd never had a night like last night.

The bartender was checking stock for what would no doubt be a very busy Saturday. Unfortunately, the bartender was not the one who had waited on them. When Sam asked how he could see the charge slips from the previous evening, the bartender rolled his eyes without a sign of sympathy.

"Impossible," he said. "They've been turned in. Besides, if it wasn't your card, you couldn't see them without a court order."

But Sam had something more effective than any paper from a judge. He held four tickets to next week's sold-out Alamo Bowl game between Texas and Florida. He went to the business office to do his negotiating. In half an hour he came out with the information he sought.

But it was information he would rather not have received.

Making his way into the hotel restaurant, he sat at a corner table, drank a cup of coffee, and stared at the slip of paper in his hand.

Charlotte Hamilton.

It simply couldn't be. Charlotte Hamilton was the name of the woman Roger had called the cold-as-a-bass bitch doctor of the Alamo City. There was nothing cold or bitchy about Charlie. The name must be a coincidence.

But she was divorced, and now that he thought of the way she had confessed to it, the condition was still new, still raw.

On every one of their fishing trips, Roger had found a way to complain about her.

"She kicked me out of bed," he'd whined a couple of years ago. At the time, Sam hadn't viewed the comment as whining, but now that he thought about it, it was.

"She hates you, Redeye," he had also said. "She thinks you're leading me astray."

Sam had pleaded innocent to the charge, then and now. Roger didn't need any help playing around. But it wasn't Sam's business to judge him, or interfere in a man's relationship with his wife.

Or so he had thought. But that was before he

had met the cold-as-a-bass bitch. If that was who his mystery woman was. He wanted to believe otherwise. Roger's ex. It was too much coincidence. A writer would never get away with putting something like it in a book. And yet he knew that was who she was.

He groaned just as the waitress walked by.

"Can I get you something, sir?" she asked.

A gun to shoot himself would not have been out of line.

"More coffee," he said instead.

He stared at the slip of paper, wishing the letters would rearrange themselves into another name. But he had used up his wishes last night with Charlie. He caught himself smiling at the memory. No matter who she was, he had to see her again.

And what would he say?

"I was waiting in the bar for my friend so we could celebrate his divorce," he would say.

"What a coincidence," she would say, and then her eyes would narrow. "What was his name?"

Sam would have to respond, "Roger Ryan. We go fishing a lot together."

"You're Redeye," she would say, and that would be the end of that.

He would bet a week's salary, including one with a couple of TV appearances, that Roger had come in last night, spotted Charlotte and his buddy huddled together, and made a cowardly retreat. Which meant that Roger knew something was going on between his ex and good old Redeye. Which meant Roger was another problem to deal with.

Again Sam groaned, but he kept the groan quieter. He shouldn't have accepted Roger's invitation. He should have been back in his apartment starting the book he kept telling himself he wanted to write. It was the story stirring in him, his take on modern-day professional athletes, that had led to his recent discontent, and not, as he had wondered last night, his need for a woman.

Or so he was telling himself today.

But if he had been home at the computer, he wouldn't have met Charlie. No matter how difficult the situation was between them, he knew it was Fate that had brought them together, Fate with a capital *F*, Fate with a twisted sense of humor and a decidedly cruel streak. Somewhere Fate was laughing at him now.

Tossing a five-dollar bill on the table, he left the restaurant and went home to plan his strategy. He would have called it his game plan, but that would have belittled the importance of his quest.

Charlie was more important than any game he had ever played. She brought out the tenderness in him, the corny jokes, the feeling of being completely at ease with another person, a feeling he had never experienced before.

51

She also brought out a permanent hard-on, the likes of which he hadn't experienced even when he was seventeen.

The trick would be letting her know how he felt. Fast. The woman was a doctor. She would know special ways of inflicting pain.

Chapter Four

Charlotte settled a tired, aching, but very satisfied body into her arctic-white Corvette convertible and leaned back against the headrest of the firethorn red leather sport seat.

The Corvette sat in the Central City Condominiums covered parking garage, next to her dependable '89 Ford station wagon. She used the Ford for driving. But this was a contemplative 'Vette type of morning, the best morning of her life.

All was well, everywhere she touched, and she didn't touch only the car.

Eyes closed, she stroked the leather-padded steering wheel, but it wasn't the wheel that brought a smile to her lips, much as she admired it and everything else about her extravagant purchase. The reason was Sam. She must have smiled more in the last fourteen hours than she had in the previous five years.

She also cringed a little, but that was a small price to pay for the memories she had brought with her from the hotel early this morning. Sore as she was, she had walked all the way to the condominiums, where she now lived. Automatically she had gone to the celebrate-the-divorce car she had purchased three months before. She viewed the ridiculously expensive vehicle as her own private cocoon.

Here she could think. Here she could dream. She added a third reason for the unusual habit. Here she could call up her most private and personal memories.

Flicking the lights on and off, she thought of the gleam in Sam's eyes as he saw her naked for the first time. Well, not exactly naked. He had really liked her new underwear. She planned to put every piece of it away, preserving it as a reminder of last night.

Stretching out her legs, she wiggled her toes inside her sensible shoes, and she remembered how Sam had played with those toes and encouraged her to ease them slowly up his leg. Or maybe she had come up with the idea. No matter, the idea had been a good one. It pleased him and it demonstrated how supple she had kept her body.

Suppleness had come in very handy more than once.

With a sigh, she went through the routine of checking out the clock, the temperature, the windshield wipers, the radio, the CD. When the latter went into play, Bach's "Toccata and Fugue in D Minor" soared through her end of the garage. She adjusted the volume. Not everyone was a fan of Bach. Sam hadn't been familiar with the music, claimed he didn't want to be; someone named Eric Clapton provided the apex of musical experience for him. But he had been open to other suggestions, and she had been more than content.

Years ago, she had dubbed her husband—her ex-husband—Roger the Rat. The only other man she had ever slept with she would always think of as Sam the Man.

They had teased each other and they had pleased each other. Before slipping out of the room a little more than an hour ago, she had planted a kiss on his forehead and whispered a heartfelt, "Thanks."

He hadn't heard, not consciously, but he had grinned in his sleep and she thought that on a subconscious level he knew what she said. He wanted talk? *Thanks* would have to suffice.

He was the best thing to come into her life in as long as she could remember. She would be eternally grateful he had walked into the bar and chosen the stool beside hers. She would also be glad never to see him again. He had shown her what a mutually satisfying sexual relationship with a man could be like; she had shown him and herself that she could be an equal in making love.

That was what she needed and what she got. She would be a fool to ask for more. Her heart would be heavy for a while with a sense of loss. She'd had experience with loss—her parents long ago, and her grandparents' deaths much more recently. She had survived those very real tragedies. She'd also gotten through the death of her marriage. Loss was definitely something she understood.

With Sam she would regret the way she had left, probably regret it forever. But she'd had no choice. Far too clearly, she knew her shortcomings. And now she knew her strengths.

She turned off the music just as the intense young couple from 4A walked behind the car, Justin and Denise Naylor, an architect and his teacher wife. Sometimes she heard them arguing as they hurried past her car. Today the discussion was over what they were to buy his mother for Christmas.

Spying Charlotte, they waved and she waved back as they scurried on. It was six days before Christmas; they needed to hurry. Justin's mother lived in Fort Worth, and the package had to be mailed. Funny the things one could pick up about others just by being quiet.

On their heels came the two restaurateurs who lived on the floor directly above her. She knew them as David and Bill; she had never heard their last names, but she knew they owned and managed the new tea room that had opened on one of the quieter stretches of the River Walk.

They, too, waved and called out "Merry Christmas" before heading toward their black Cavalier. David cast a look of longing at the Corvette before slipping behind the wheel of his sedan.

As if part of a parade, next came the flamboyant artist Cerise Lambert and her lawyer husband, Fernando. The Lamberts had hosted a building party two weeks ago; theirs was the only other condominium besides her own that Charlotte had entered. Where hers had stark-white walls decorated with dark pre-Columbian and Mexican Colonial art, the Lamberts had chosen shades of red with lots of crystal and mirrors to reflect the recessed lights. Too, the red walls were hung with gorgeous samplings of Cerise Lambert's abstract paintings.

Fernando Lambert came over to Charlotte's side of the car. "When are you going to let me drive this beauty?" he asked in what had become a ritual every time he saw her behind the wheel. She was, she knew, considered somewhat of an eccentric around CC Condos, but a harmless one who offered no one threats.

Usually she shrugged and put him off with a noncommittal reply. Today she smiled. "How about right now?"

His eyes widened. "Am I hearing you right, Dr. Hamilton?"

"Please, call me Charlotte."

The eyes narrowed speculatively. "Of course, Charlotte. And be careful of what you offer. You may find yourself getting a yes."

Her smiled died. He had figured out what had happened to her last night. She knew it. The hours of lovemaking must show on her face. Her cheeks burned and her heart began to pound.

And then she got control of herself. He couldn't know. No one could. And no one ever would.

After the Lamberts departed, she saw one other resident she knew, an unmarried blond beauty who never seemed without male companionship. This morning she had a gray-haired must-be-a-professional man on her arm, his head tucked low as if he were avoiding recognition. Charlotte gave him only a cursory glance. He looked vaguely familiar to her, but that was probably because he had been at the condos before. The blonde was striding by with head high, looking very proud.

When they were gone, feeling bold, Charlotte

actually turned on the motor. It purred contentedly. And so did she. One of these days, she told herself, as she turned off the engine and got out, she would actually get the nerve to put the car in gear and drive it out of the garage.

On the way up to her third-floor apartment, she saw no one else. Either everyone was already out at the malls or was sleeping late on this brisk, clear, beautiful Saturday morning.

The first thing she did was strip and look for signs of last night, as if Sam had left fingerprints on her skin. Nothing showed. The changes were all inside.

Next came a long, hot shower; she used the scented bath gel that had been a gift from her friend Louise Post. Afterward, she lathered a matching lotion all over her body and eased into cotton underwear, khaki slacks, and a blue silk shirt. Except for the fabric of the shirt, she was dressed a great deal like Sam. Only her khakis weren't starched, and she was all softness underneath.

Everything she did was performed slowly, methodically, as she went about returning normalcy to her life. After much debate, she decided to wash the red silk undergarments and thigh-highs before tucking them away. She was standing at the bathroom sink when Louise knocked at the door and walked in.

"You really ought to keep that door locked," Louise called out as she tracked her down.

A short, full-bosomed, green-eyed redhead, her lawyer friend was as outspoken as she was loyal. There was no use telling her she ought to wait until her knock was answered before opening the door. Glib as she was, Louise would probably turn the comment back on her.

Louise was a year younger than Charlotte but considered herself decades wiser, especially in the ways of men. Counsel for the city's biggest insurance company, she was determinedly single but she claimed that hadn't hurt her male/female education. Having gone through a long string of frog dates, she was positive that out in the world of dating there was not a prince to be found.

Charlotte could have told her differently. But she never would.

Louise spied the underwear in the sink. "Are you taking in laundry now?"

"These are mine. I bought them to wear for the divorce."

"Hmmm," Louise said. "I'm sorry I couldn't have been there with you yesterday, but work kept me tied up."

Charlotte tried to look regretful, as if her dearest and closest friend had been missed. She, too, had been tied up for a while.

"You told me you probably couldn't make it to court. I was fine. Great. Better than I've ever been in my life."

Louise gave her a sharp assessment. Charlotte concentrated on finishing the wash. Maybe she had put a little too much enthusiasm into the reassurance. Maybe she ought to keep her mouth shut.

Hanging the garments on a rack she had set up in the bathtub, Charlotte went into the kitchen and offered to make breakfast. Suddenly she was famished. Except for a few nuts, a smattering of nachos, and three sticks of fried cheese, the closest she had come to nourishment since lunch yesterday was the salt on the margarita glass.

As a physician, she knew she shouldn't have ordered the salt.

As a physician, she also knew sleeping with a stranger was as foolhardy as anything she could have done.

But Sam had said he was healthy. She had discovered nothing about him to prove otherwise, and she had examined him as closely as any patient she had ever seen. Not, of course, with the same purpose in mind. And the only instruments available had been parts of her body, including her lips and her tongue.

"Charlotte," Louise said sharply. From the tone and pitch of her voice, it was clear she had said it more than once.

Charlotte was standing at the sink spreading half a stick of butter on a piece of bread.

"Sorry," she said as she began to scrape off

the butter. "I was thinking about yesterday."
She spoke the truth.

"This divorce really has you rattled."

"Maybe," she said, straying into the area of
equivocation. "But Roger and I had truly separated a long time ago. The judge merely made
it official."

Under Louise's watchful eye, Charlotte set
about making the toast, sectioning a grape-
fruit, and poaching a couple of eggs in the
microwave. She considered serving the meal
on the balcony that overlooked the river, but
instead chose the warmer dining area off the
kitchen.

She cleaned her plate and ate Louise's egg as
well, along with half her toast. Her friend
talked all the while about the traveling they
could do. Charlotte nodded as if in agreement.
Louise liked to go abroad once a year, but
Charlotte was not the least interested in
accompanying her. She could not abandon her
patients for so long. They needed her, as much
as she needed them.

They were the focus of her life. Brooding
about herself was out. Selected remembering
would be like a chocolate eclair, an indulgence
for only the most special of times.

Over the next week, Charlotte kept herself busy
with work, staying close to her senior citizen
counseling group, some of whom became

despondent over the holidays. Two especially had her worried, an eighty-five-year-old man who admitted to depression because of his wife's dementia and a widow who had just turned seventy and who insisted far too regularly that her life was great.

On Christmas Day Charlotte and Louise indulged in a lavish champagne buffet at the Adam's Mark Hotel, and on New Year's Eve they attended the San Antonio Symphony's Night in Old Vienna concert, following it up with an hour of watching fireworks over the Alamo, along with a hundred thousand others who crowded into downtown.

Memories of Sam were gradually growing dimmer, except for sometimes in the middle of the night when she felt the loneliness of her bed. These were the moments when her body ached for him, and she came as close to crying as she ever had.

But she was not a woman given to tears.

And, glorious as he was, Sam had not been a forever kind of man. Some things in life were simply too good to last.

On a gray Wednesday morning in mid-January, she arrived late at the office, having been detained visiting a hospital patient who had suffered a heart seizure. A specialist had been consulted, but Charlotte knew the elderly woman would appreciate a visit from her.

Using her private entrance, she was putting

on her lab coat when Gloria, her very competent nurse, accosted her.

"Something must be going around. We've got an office full of patients coughing and grumbling."

Ah, January. It was the gloomiest month of the year.

With a sigh, Charlotte looked down the hallway at the four closed examining room doors, each with a folder stuck outside.

She took them in order, offering firm hands, kind words, and in a few cases a prescription for medication. She was of the less-is-better school concerning antibiotics; most of what she prescribed was very mild.

Mostly her patients needed someone to listen to them. That, she could do.

It was close to noon when Gloria handed her another chart. "You've got a new patient in number one."

"What's his problem?" she asked, starting to open the folder.

"You'll have to ask him."

Something in Gloria's voice caused her to look up.

"Anything unusual about him?"

"You might say that." She stepped back to watch as Charlotte opened the door to room number one.

"Take your time," the nurse added. "We've got a few more patients scheduled, but nothing that sounds like an emergency. Besides, they're all chatting away out in the waiting room, comparing symptoms. They'll be diagnosing treatment any minute, so, like I said, take your time."

It was a long speech for Gloria, and a little out of place, coming in the hall where the patients might overhear. And what was with *take your time?* Gloria liked to keep things moving along. Her second nurse, Claire, was the one to dawdle.

When Charlotte stepped into the room, the first thing she saw were the bare feet dangling at the end of the examining table. Good, strong feet, not gnarled or wrinkled or sprouting gray hair. The calves came next. They matched the feet; if anything, they looked better.

Then there were the knees, a little bony but still nice. The right one, she noticed, was bounded by a parenthesis of years-old scars.

The bottom of the white paper gown lay across a couple of great-looking thighs. Thighs she had touched. Thighs she had kissed.

With a shudder, she fell against the edge of the counter. By the time she got to the slanted smile, the crooked nose, the puppy-warm brown eyes, she knew exactly why Gloria had told her to take her time.

Sam the Man had come to call. And he was doing it without a stitch of clothes.

Chapter Five

Sam could not have asked for a better response. The look of approval as she moved her eyes slowly up to his, the warmth of recognition, the stunned silence that followed, all showed she was very much moved by seeing him again.

The only improvement he could have made was to have her throw herself into his arms, the way she had done in the hotel room. Later, he hoped.

It wasn't a hopeful hope. Later, she would know who he was.

"Hi, Charlie," he said, grinning. Might as well grin while he had the chance.

"Just a minute," she said. "Don't say another word."

Opening the door of the examining room, she looked up and down the hall, then obviously spied whomever she was looking for. "Hold all calls, please. I do not want to be disturbed."

Hot damn.

She locked the door.

Double hot damn.

Then she turned and went to lean against the counter, her arms crossed over her breasts. It was body language for *don't get any ideas*. Sam could read her body very well. He couldn't hold the grin. It didn't go with the frown on her face.

"How did you get in here?" she asked.

"The usual way. By appointment. I had to wait a long time. You're a very popular doctor, did you know that?"

"But I'm a geriatrician. You're not old enough. My receptionist would never have let you in."

"She gave me a hard time, at first. And Gloria protested, too."

"You're on a first-name basis with my nurse?" She sighed a helpless sort of sigh, and her shoulders sagged. "Of course you are. You're Sam the Man."

"You call me Sam the Man?"

"I name people. My ex is Roger the Rat."

Sam wasn't ready for Roger to intrude. He changed the subject fast.

"I missed you," he said. "Did you miss me?" He started off the end of the examining table, but she held up a hand to stop him.

"Stay right where you are. Pretend I just walked in. Never mind how you got here. Just tell me why. You're certainly not sick."

"You mean I'm in good shape."

"Don't fish for compliments."

Sam winced at the *fish*. Fish he associated with Roger.

"I've already complimented you more than enough," she added. "That's all you're going to get."

"You may be done, Charlie, but I'm not. You are the most wonderful woman I've ever met. While I was waiting in here for you, feeling more than a little foolish, I have to admit, I told myself to go slowly. I didn't want to frighten you or say anything you wouldn't believe."

"If you don't want to frighten me, you might try going away."

He ignored her. "When I'm around you, I can't go slow. Everything shifts to fast speed, heart, lungs, things you can't see, and things you can. You know the parts. And I don't mean from an anatomy book."

She pushed back her hair. "Don't talk dirty."

"You've heard my dirty talk." He tried another grin. "This ain't it."

He watched as the expressions played across her face, signs of her remembering. He could have watched that face until the end of time.

Maybe he shouldn't tell her right away. But what the hell.

"I could watch you till the end of time, Dr. Charlotte Hamilton. I could—"

Again the hand went up. Then she used it to cover her eyes. "I'm dreaming this. It can't be happening."

"I can prove I'm real."

She dropped the hand. Her fine blue eyes glittered. "Don't you dare. You haven't told me why you're here. When I left the way I did, that should have told you that I didn't want to see you again."

"You were shy."

"Come on, Sam. Shy was one thing I most certainly was not."

"Frightened, then."

The fine blue eyes rolled. "Face the truth. I was through, finished, done. That was all. We had a good night together—"

"Good?"

"—a great night, but the sun came up as it always does and I went on my way. I know it's the man's place to do that, but I saved you the trouble. Admit it. If I had stayed, we would have talked awhile. Maybe exchanged phone numbers. Then you would have left, and I never would have heard from you again.

Unless you found yourself hard up for a good thing."

"Hey, doc, give me a little credit. Give yourself some, while you're at it. You're wrong. Whatever is going on between us is far too strong for a one-nighter. It needs to be explored."

"Nothing is going on between us."

"How about love?"

That stopped her. It stopped him, too. He hadn't planned on bringing out the big guns right away. Well, maybe one big gun, depending on how things went. Sitting practically naked in front of a woman like Charlotte got a man prepared.

"Love?" she asked. It was actually more of a squeak.

"It's possible. It's more than possible. On a possibility scale of one to ten, I'd put it at a very strong eight."

"You're demented."

"Love can do that to a man."

"Ha!"

"Don't laugh. I'm being very honest with you." Almost. He wasn't telling her who he was. "I've never felt about anyone the way I do about you."

"What about your ex-wife?"

"Nowhere close. I want to explore the feeling. I want to know how you feel about me."

She set aside the folder holding the information about him. "I guess I'll have to take the man's part here," she said.

He crossed one leg over the other. He noticed that she noticed. She really had him twisted inside out. Now she had turned him into a flasher.

"Man's part?" he asked. "Pardon me for mentioning it, but I don't think you've got the equipment. What kind of doctor are you, anyway?"

"I didn't mean that literally. Isn't it the man who usually kisses the woman off?"

"I'll kiss anything you want, Charlie. But then, I already have."

Her sigh was definitely a show of exasperation. At least she wasn't indifferent.

"Let me put it another way. And don't you dare make a joke of that comment. The man usually says it was great while it lasted, sugar, but it's time to leave. That's what I'm telling you."

"You're calling me sugar?"

"I'm trying to tell you good-bye. Leave. Go away."

Her gaze drifted down to his crossed leg, which, former athlete that he was, he managed to shift higher. The way she was inspiring him, he could have wrapped it behind his head. She was definitely looking up his robe. She did the man part very well.

His strategy in coming here was to be reasonable, to explain how he felt, to put things on an emotional, a philosophical, a factual basis, anything to let her know he was serious. But she was getting physical. He couldn't entirely object.

If she got a really good look, she would know he didn't object in the least.

"Look," she said, "what we had really was a one-night stand."

"You always were good with old lines."

"The phrase may be old, but it's hardly a line. I needed to have a good time. A brief good time. I'm no good with relationships that are expected to last for even a short while. I told you I've just gone through a very painful divorce."

"I don't recall the painful part. I thought you were glad."

He *knew* she was glad, both from how she had acted and from what Roger had said.

"I was glad. But I wanted—"

Her voice trailed off. Something in her tone, a sadness in her fine blue eyes, twisted his gut. She sounded lost, unsure of herself, or as close as she had come since he'd first sat down beside her in the bar. He kept his mouth shut. It did not seem like the moment for a smart-ass remark.

What it called for was a gentle caress. Or a thousand. As many as she would allow.

She visibly shook herself. "Whatever I had

wanted out of the marriage, I didn't get it. And that hurt. This is very embarrassing. I know you're not proposing marriage or anything like it. But you want us to see each other again, and I can't do it."

He watched her carefully, saw the pain in her eyes. She wasn't lying about having been hurt. Damn Roger to hell.

But she was wrong about her and long-term relationships. He knew it in his heart.

The challenge was to convince her. He would have to take this one step at a time.

"You say you wanted a good time. Did you get it?"

"I told you not to fish for compliments. You know I did."

"And one time will serve you for the rest of your life?"

She twisted her hands in front of her, looked at him for a moment, then looked away. "It will have to."

"Do you mean one time with me or with anyone?"

"I'm not looking for anyone else. You were it."

She sounded bereft and wistful and stubborn, all at the same time. Charlie was a complicated creature, but then he wouldn't have her any other way.

Her complications inspired him to craziness.

"How about one more?" he asked. The suggestion was not only crazy, it was also a gamble, but he had been known to take a chance or two in his life.

A pair of very alarmed eyes looked back at him. "One more what?"

"One more good time. You've already shown me you're not shy. The door's locked. Unless you're myopic, you know I'm ready. If you're not in the same frame of mind, I can take care of that in a minute. Okay, maybe two. I don't want to brag."

"I'm shocked you would suggest such a thing."

"No, you're not. But you're scared. Coward. Wimp."

She lifted her chin in defiance; then she looked into his eyes and he looked into hers, and the air in the room heated twenty degrees.

He got up from the table, and this time she didn't raise her hand to stop him. "You look great in that lab coat," he said. "What's underneath?"

"Nothing sexy," she said. Her voice had grown hoarse. No surprise. So had his.

"I'll bet if I look long enough, I'll find something sexy."

He put his hands on her shoulders and rubbed his thumbs against her neck. She swayed toward him, but her hands remained clasped at her waist.

"What I'm thinking has got to be unethical," she said.

"How about what you're feeling?"

"That, too." She was speaking barely above a whisper.

He kissed the corner of her mouth. "We're in an examining room, right? Examine me."

He reached inside her labcoat, tugged her blouse free of her skirt, and slipped his hands up under the hem to caress her breasts. He would have unhooked the bra first, but he didn't want to move too fast.

She sagged against him. He let go of her breasts long enough to unfasten her skirt, and when it fell to the floor, he kicked it aside. Lifting her by the waist, he set her on the counter. Her legs parted enough for him to wedge himself between them. His paper gown crinkled against her thighs.

She eased out of her shoes; they fell beside the skirt with a thud. The fall sounded like a gun signaling the games to begin.

"I take it we're going to go all the way," he said.

"Hush," she said. "We don't have much time."

Here was the Charlie from the hotel, except that she wouldn't look him in the eyes. Sam did what the doctor ordered. He shut up.

She wrapped her arms around his neck and

put her tongue in his mouth. He would have said something about it being a very nice tongue depressor, but she wouldn't appreciate the joke. Besides, he was fast falling out of the mood for levity.

The panty hose were no joke. He hated the things. Pushing him away, she slid down to the floor and took them off, but she kept on everything else. She was naked from the waist down. Her coat parted just enough for him to see her pubic hair. That was when his gown hit the floor.

"You're already wearing a condom," she said, her eyes nicely round and warm.

"Ever hopeful, that's Sam the Man. I had a while to wait before you came in. It was something to do."

"I'm as bad as you are," she said with a shake of her head. "I'm glad you've got it on."

She shoved him backward to the table. He got the idea she wanted to be on top. He couldn't come up with a reason why not. She proceeded to prove herself more agile than he, straddling him in an instant, her knees balanced on either side of him, the coat billowing around her like a cloud as she rested her chest against his.

She had him so ready, he barely got inside her in time. No time for foreplay here. He needn't have worried. They climaxed at the same time. She buried her cry in his shoulder, biting him at the same time. He was so busy swallowing his own sounds of pleasure, he didn't object.

Mostly he was holding her tight, letting all the whirling and the swirling take him up into the stratosphere, then slowly bring him back down. Part of him had emptied his fluids, but the rest of him overflowed with a pleasure and a sense of joy that made him feel like the king of the earth.

He hadn't been wrong about his feelings for her. They were as strong as they were crazy. If this wasn't love, it was the closest he had come to it in all his life. He couldn't bring himself to let her go.

Charlotte leaned her head against Sam's shoulder and tried to slow her breathing. The teeth marks she'd left on him met her eyes. At least she hadn't broken the skin. But that was the only positive thing she could think of. She couldn't believe what she had just done. Dumb, dumb, dumb. That's what it was.

It was also wonderful. Glorious. As thrilling as anything they had ever done. She could never let him go.

But of course she had to do just that. She glanced down at herself. For crying out loud, she was still wearing her coat. The laboratory coat that distinguished her as a physician. That definitely had to be unethical. She could never again enter this room.

She heard footsteps in the hall outside, and an elderly voice say, "I know the way, Miss Gloria. You just make sure Dr. Hamilton knows I'm here."

Walter Farrow had arrived for his monthly checkup. He didn't need one so often, but at eighty-five he thought he did and he was paying his own bills. Walter was one of her special cases, a strong man who hated the closing years of his life.

He depended upon her very much. He ought to see her now.

"Don't worry, Mr. Farrow. I'll tell the doctor," Gloria said, so clearly she sounded as though she was practically in the room.

Everyone must know. She and Sam hadn't raised their voices, but she couldn't believe the sounds of their lovemaking hadn't communicated what was going on. The examining table hadn't really rocked, but it had rolled a time or two.

"They didn't hear us," he said. "I promise."

He knew what she had been thinking, as accurately as he had understood what she was feeling. She didn't like it. It gave him power over her.

She had to pull herself together. But first she had to get off of him.

Easing away, she made sure the condom did not spill its contents. Pulling her coat closed, as if he didn't already know what was underneath, she gestured to the waste receptacle by the table.

"Put it in there."

"The condom?"

She rolled her eyes. Always a joke.

She watched as he read the warning on the top of the can BIOHAZARDOUS MATERIAL INSIDE. He seemed to find that amusing. At any other time, so might she.

She turned her back on him. "Put on the gown and get your clothes. There's a rest room across the hall where you can clean up."

"Marching orders so soon?"

She closed her eyes for a second. "Please. I've got to handle this, and I can't do it with you standing around like that."

He nuzzled the side of her neck. "That's my Charlie. Ever the romantic."

If he only knew. Romantic was the one thing in all the world she would like herself to be. Right now it was the last adjective she would use to explain what she had done.

"We really have to talk," he said. "I know in the hotel room I said the same thing, but now, seeing who you are and who I am, we really have to talk."

He sounded serious. Dead serious. But there was nothing they could talk about that had not

79

already been settled in her mind. When she didn't respond, he did what she asked, grabbing up his clothes and heading for the small room across the hall. Once she was alone, she hurriedly dressed, splashed cold water on her face, and smoothed her hair, using the reflection in the metal paper towel dispenser as a mirror.

We really have to talk. The only thing she could possibly tell him was that she had been wrong. Making love with him once had not been enough. But twice was definitely too much—too much only because of the circumstances, but he didn't have to know that.

She spied the folder with the information about him inside. Opening it, she started to read. Name: Samuel Blake. Age: 38. Occupation: Sportswriter. Something stirred at the back of her mind.

Samuel Blake. Sam Blake. He had been a baseball player at UT. His knee had been injured, forcing him to quit the team.

Her husband's ramblings came back to her, the few details he had told her about . . .

It couldn't be.

But Sam had said something about who she was and who he was and that was why they had to talk. Surely not. It couldn't be.

If it were, if the unthinkable were really true, she was handling being a divorcée far worse than she had handled being a wife.

Rushing into the hall, she threw open the door. He'd put on his shirt and was pulling his pants up to his knees.

"Tell me you're not Redeye," she said.

"I'm not Redeye."

But she saw from the look on his face that he was.

"You bastard!"

"I was going to tell you. That's why I came here today."

"Hah! Did you and Roger plan this? Did you have a good laugh?"

She didn't wait for an answer. Slamming the door, she tried to ignore the stares of Gloria and Claire, who were standing a few feet away in the hall.

Sam came out of the rest room still pulling up his pants.

"I didn't know who you were in the bar. I promise. I was supposed to meet Roger, but when he didn't show up—"

She cried out and covered her ears, but unfortunately she could still hear him.

"I had to see you again. I'd never been with a woman like you."

If those were titters she heard from the hallway, she didn't think about them. All her anger, all her humiliation was because of Sam.

"Marry me," he practically yelled. "I just decided. We've got to get married. There's no other way."

She dropped her hands and stared at him in disbelief. The commotion brought heads popping out of the examining rooms. But she was too far gone to pay them any heed.

"I don't want a husband," she cried with more anguish and honesty than he could ever realize. "I just got rid of one. All I want is sex!"

Chapter Six

Over the next hour, pitching possibilities back and forth, Sam came to the brilliant conclusion that he was caught in a dilemma.

Charlie wanted sex. So did he, big time, all the time, more than he had ever wanted anything in his life. But that was all she wanted, or so she claimed. Greedy male that he was, he was after more.

After today, the day when the ugly truth of his identity had come out, he wasn't sure she would accept even sex from him. Immodesty helped remind him she wanted it, but he wasn't sure wanting was enough. Therein lay part of the problem. The eight-block downtown walk from her office to his did not take a sufficient amount of time for him to come up with a solution.

While he was walking, he wasn't always thinking about the problem, either. Sometimes he remembered her moving in on him at the examining table. Sometimes he pictured his last view of her as she ran down the hallway and slammed into her office. The heads poking out of the examining rooms, along with those of the nurses, had turned to her, then back to him.

At least by then he'd been able to zip his pants. It lent decency if not dignity to his what's-a-guy-going-to-do-with-a-woman-like-that shrug.

Were they thinking about the proposal of marriage he had blurted out? Probably not. Charlie had upstaged him with *all I want is sex*.

It wasn't a declaration that would bring a complaint from most men. But he wasn't like most men. She had to see that. Whether she knew it or not, she wanted a lot more from him than sex. She was crazy about him. The trick would be getting her to realize it.

All right, so the proposal had been unplanned, unrehearsed. But it made sense. She had said something about not being good at long-term relationships. That was because she had never really had one. Not with him. And that was the only relationship that really counted.

If any two people were meant for each other,

it was Sam the Man and Dr. Charlie. They could set new records for lovemaking.

Entering the *Tribune* Building's double doors, he waved to the receptionist, started for the elevator, then decided to take the stairs instead, taking them two at a time, all the way to the third floor. Some athletes swore off sex before a game, claiming it depleted them of their energy. Sam could have climbed the Tower of the Americas after the session in his doctor's examining room.

The picture of her coming on to him, half naked under her lab coat, was the kind of memory to invigorate a man, sort of like a perpetual twelve-volt battery. Sam the Energizer Man, that was him.

Striding through the sports department, he waved at the sports copy editor, Jim Grayson, who was standing in the center of the copy desk's doughnut-shaped rim.

"Good column on the NBA salaries," Grayson called out across the desk.

Sam nodded, but he was thinking, *Good column? Hell, that was a great column. Everything today is great.*

He was hanging his jacket on the coatrack in his office, expanding on the greatness idea, telling himself the dilemma would not be permanent, when Roger Ryan walked in. Roger was the one person in all the world Sam did not want to see. One look at him and the great-ness of the day took a downward turn.

"Hey, Redeye," Roger said, slapping him on the back. "Old buddy, I owe you an apology."

Sam started to protest, then settled for a shrug. Maybe he was owed an apology, but then again, maybe not. Since mid-December, the circumstances between them had definitely grown murky. It was a good thing their paths had not crossed.

Or had they? After learning Charlie's identity, Sam wondered if Roger had seen them together in the bar. No, he'd long ago decided, otherwise his less-than-subtle fishing buddy would have called him by now.

"Before Christmas," Roger said. "Remember?" He pulled out a cigar and began to unwrap it.

"We're nonsmoking now," Sam said as he moved behind his desk and sat down. Was Roger leading up to something? Probably not. He wasn't big on guile.

"Since when have you been one for the rules?" Roger asked.

Since I bedded your ex-wife, old buddy. The rules say she has to marry me.

Would Roger care? Sam was in no hurry to find out.

With a sniff, Roger stuck the cigar in an inside coat pocket. "What the hell. Anyway, I was supposed to meet you for a celebration dinner after the divorce. Don't tell me you forgot. I promised to pick up the tab at the Stetson Room. Biggest steak we could order, remember?"

"Seems as if I recall the evening. You never showed."

"I did drop by, but the damnedest thing happened. I was on my way into the bar when I saw Charlotte sitting on a corner stool. She was tossing back margaritas like the place was running out of tequila. Drowning her sorrows, I figured. She must have realized what got away."

Sam should have let the comment go. That would have been the smart reaction. So naturally he asked, "What did get away?"

"Her meal ticket. Her sex machine. Me, of course." Then he chuckled. "Redeye, you're quite a kidder. You know what I mean."

Sam gritted his teeth. "I think I do."

"Anyway, I decided it was not a good idea to join her. She'd been pretty unpleasant at the lawyer's office. That's what she's good at. Being unpleasant."

"Roger, there's something I ought to tell you." *Before I punch your face in.*

Roger regarded him with care. "Something's bothering you."

"To tell the truth—"

"I know what it is. You didn't show up either, did you?" He sniffed and grinned. "I knew it.

87

When you didn't try to get in touch with me, I figured something had come up. It's okay to call the house now, by the way. She's long gone. Gave up rights to it, and the car, got herself one of those condos downtown. Even bought herself a 'Vette."

"A Corvette?"

Here was something he hadn't known. He pictured Charlie behind the wheel, tooling down I-10, the wind whipping her hair, dark glasses covering her expressive blue eyes. She would be smiling, laughing, too, feeling great, her fine eyes lost in the crinkles of her smile, and all of it because she was driving to him.

For the ride, she had chosen her lab coat. And nothing else. He was beginning to get a real thing about that coat.

"You like Corvettes?" Roger asked.

It took a lot of willpower to leave her image and come back to the office and to Roger the Rat. Damned if he wasn't thinking of him the same way that Charlie did.

"They're too expensive for a newspaperman's salary. I'm surprised she has one. I thought you were the one coming out ahead financially. Her meal ticket. Wasn't that what you said?"

"She's probably up to her fat ass in debt."

Sam snapped a pencil in half and rose from his chair.

"Naw," Roger said, oblivious to the fact he

was a quarter of a second away from getting his nose smashed. "Forget the debt. She's a doctor. I'll bet she's been holding out money for years. When it comes to holding out, Charlotte is the world champion."

Sam settled back and warned himself to calm down. Here was another dilemma, this one moral more than situational. He had been Roger's fishing buddy for years. That was the only connection they had, but still it was strong enough for them to be friends. Complaints about the former Mrs. Ryan had come often, but he'd never paid them much attention. He corrected himself. Complaints about Dr. Hamilton. The fact that she had kept her maiden name was one of Roger's milder gripes.

Things had changed. All of Sam's allegiance was with Charlie now. But of course Roger didn't know that. And he wasn't saying anything worse than what he'd said before. So maybe smashing him in the nose was not such a great idea, morally speaking.

Unless he made reference to one of Charlie's body parts again. Sam thought about a few those parts. They were perfect. Nothing anywhere to criticize. And they were his as much as hers. No one was going to slam them when he was around.

"Sam," someone was saying, and then sharper, "Sam!"

The image of Charlie's parts faded.

"Roger, uh, sorry. I'm a little preoccupied at the moment. I've got some thing on my mind."

"You've got a woman on your mind. I can see it on your face." He looked like he'd just landed a champion striped bass. "Don't try to deny it. I've got an instinct about these things."

"I guess there's no fooling you, is there?" Sam said.

"Nope. Not where women are concerned. I was wondering how long you'd keep your pants zipped. It's not natural—"

Moral dilemma solved. Roger had to go.

"Out," Sam said. "I've got things to do."

"You don't do any work. You're a writer."

Sam came around the desk and opened his office door. "Out."

Roger grinned. "She must be some woman, Redeye. Imagine that. Sam Blake with a hook in his mouth. With something in his mouth, that's for sure. I never thought I'd see the day. What did she use for bait?"

"She's none of your business." Not anymore.

"Aha, I was right. There is a woman. You can't fool old Roger Dodger when it comes to the opposite sex. Who is it? Someone I know?"

Here was the time to confess all, get the truth out in the open. But he'd had enough of Roger to last until next Christmas. And telling him what had happened would be betraying Charlie, though he wasn't sure exactly how. What he did know was that if she learned about his indiscretion, she would probably come after him with a scalpel, and he didn't think she would be aiming above his waist.

He nodded toward the door.

"Okay, I'm going," Roger said. "Anytime you want advice about how to handle her, ask me. Just remember, don't make the same mistake I made. Steer clear of marriage. It's a trap. There's nothing in it for men like us."

With a wave and a smirk, his fishing buddy— his former fishing buddy—strolled out. Sam started to slam the door. Naw, that would be childish. He slammed it anyway.

Looking through the plate-glass window that gave him a view of the sports department, he saw Grayson glance at him questioningly. Sam shrugged, went back to his desk, and took a stab at working on the next day's column. He had written it already, but it needed tightening. And then there was Sunday's to worry with. That was the beauty and the beast about column writing. There was always another one waiting to be created.

Now if he were working on his book . . .

But that was a dream job. Reality was the blinking cursor on his computer and the deadline schedule on top of his desk.

Maybe what he needed was a new take on the world of sports. From the perspective of a non-sports person. Maybe a woman. It was a terrible idea. He liked it. He needed someone to interview, someone sensible, smart, dedicated to a world far removed from athletics.

Not that she wouldn't be healthy, fit, and very, very agile. Someone who could come up with an acrobatic routine on top of an examining table that would put the Russian gymnastics team to shame. He could think of only one someone who would meet the criteria. But she probably wouldn't be home for a while.

He remembered all those heads popping out of examining room doors, patients yet to be seen. She must have done some fast explaining on the *all I want is sex* remark. If the patients had been blunt enough to ask. In Sam's experience with senior citizens—mostly with his seventy-six-year-old uncle, who hated that term—fear of bluntness was seldom a concern.

Ah, if only he could have heard what his beloved said to them.

For the next hour he puttered over words, shot the bull with a couple of writers who dropped by, then cancelled his regular Saturday tennis game with one of them, in case something else worked out for him.

And finally he picked up the phone. Along with learning Charlie's identity and the location of her office, he had also found out where she lived and the telephone number of her unlisted line.

A woman answered. She wasn't Charlie.

"May I please speak to Dr. Hamilton."

"Who's calling?"

He thought that one over. "A patient."

Hesitation. "May I have your name please."

"This is a confidential matter. I promise you Dr. Hamilton will want to talk to me."

"You don't sound like one of her patients. You sound like a crank."

"That's what she's treating me for. Crankiness, that is. She says it's only temporary, but I'm not sure."

"Then contact her answering service. Another doctor's taking her calls."

"Nope. My problem is too personal. I speak only to Dr. Hamilton."

"So call her at the office. Her hours are—"

"I know her hours. Is she all right? Is that why you're not putting her on the phone? She's fallen. She got attacked walking home."

"There is nothing wrong with the doctor. How did you get her number anyway? If you call here again, I'll put a trace on this phone."

"You and who else?"

"Me and the phone company. I'll also charge you with harassment."

She started rattling off something about the Texas Penal Code. A lawyer. Damn. Sam hung up. He hadn't handled that very well.

Fearless suitor that he was, he called again.

"Look," he said when the same voice answered, "I'm not a patient, well, I was, in a way, but that's not what I mainly am. Charlie's my friend. I'd like to ask her for a date." He swallowed. He sounded like a kid. "There's the Mud Festival this weekend. You know, when they drain the river for cleaning and elect a Mud Queen and King, and they walk down in the—"

"I'm well aware of the festival. Who are you? No one calls Charlotte Charlie. Did Roger put you up to this?"

Sam bristled, as much for his beloved as for himself. "Don't you think Charlie can get a date without someone putting a man up to it?"

"I think she doesn't need any more trouble from men."

This was a testy creature he was dealing with. And a lawyer on top of that. Probably didn't even like men.

He gave up. "Just tell her the patient with the biohazardous material called. She'll understand. Tell her, no, ask her to call me at work. The number is—"

But Charlie's testy lawyer friend had already hung up.

Sam dropped the phone in its cradle. A direct telephone assault had not worked. Especially since she had a female inquisitor answering the phone.

The one thing he felt sure of, and it brought him a great deal of pleasure, was that Charlie hadn't told the Grand Inquisitor anything about him. He refused to believe it was because she was ashamed of what they had done.

The one thing Charlie hadn't exhibited, either in the hotel room or at her office was shame. What they shared was joyous. She knew, as well as he, that they would share it again.

"All I want is sex."

At least her confession was a start.

Chapter Seven

Charlotte chopped nervously at a cucumber and scraped the uneven pieces from the cutting board into the salad bowl, on top of the mangled lettuce and shredded mushrooms that had gone before. She didn't want a salad. She didn't want anything to eat. She didn't care if she never ate again.

Maybe tomorrow she would feel better. Today had not been a good day.

A nagging voice at the back of her mind reminded her it had not been all bad. In fact, some of it had been very, very good. A tingle of remembrance shivered through her. She was picturing a hard-muscled, tight-skinned male stretched out on her examining table. He should have looked out of place, but he had looked right at home.

The exam she gave him had been nothing short of spectacular. And without a stethoscope.

The tingle turned to a shudder. What was wrong with her? What had she become? Here she was thinking about the good of the day, when it was all tangled up with the bad. It was getting so that she couldn't tell the opposites apart anymore.

Louise walked into the kitchen. Louise with her short, full-bosomed figure, Louise with her red hair and stubbornness to match. Charlotte could be stubborn, too. Centering a stalk of celery on the cutting board, she took aim with the chopping knife.

"Who was that on the phone?" she asked, not bothering to keep the irritation out of her voice. It was bad enough Louise had decided to screen her calls. "The Rat might realize what he's done and start calling," she had said, not being much of a Roger Ryan fan. As long as she refused to answer the phone in the same room, the least she could do was report on the calls without being asked.

"A crank," Louise said.

Charlotte's heart skipped a beat. There was only one crank she knew. She knew him very well.

No, it couldn't be. Along with losing all her standards, she was getting paranoid.

"Both times?" she asked, then had to clear her throat and ask again.

"A determined crank. He called himself a patient, but I saw right through that." Louise strolled over to the counter and picked up a carrot stick, giving no sign she noticed Charlotte's immoderate distress. "He mentioned something about biohazardous waste, at least that's what it sounded like. Then he also said something about a date—"

Charlotte caught herself about to smile, and her self-esteem sank lower than ever. There was nothing humorous in what Sam had dropped into the waste receptacle. How could she think of him with anything close to charity? He was Redeye. He was worse than a rat. And he brought out the worst in her.

She felt Louise's eyes studying her. She chopped furiously at the celery, mincing the tiny slices until they were mush. Louise continued to watch. She forced herself to slow down.

"You know the guy?" Louise asked.

Charlotte scraped the mush into the sink and dropped another stalk on the cutting board. "I know him." It was the mother of all understatements, but it was all she was going to admit.

Louise leaned against the kitchen counter and crunched on the carrot stick. "So tell me what you know."

"There's nothing to tell."

The lie came easily, too easily to a woman

who had always considered herself truthful and honorable. Since Sam had come into her life, she was picking up nothing but bad habits.

Not only was she getting them from him, she was coming up with a few of her own. Today would go down as the worst of her life, the day she hit rock bottom on the medical-ethics scale. She should have at least taken off her lab coat before jumping his bones.

But she hadn't been thinking clearly. The knife flailed away.

"Charlotte," she dimly heard someone say. The knife slipped and caught the tip of her thumb. Sucking on the cut, Charlotte gave up on the salad and backed away from the counter. Away from Louise's watchful eye.

Louise eased a wineglass from the rack under the kitchen cabinet and filled it from a bottle of Pinot Grigio that had been chilling in the refrigerator.

"Sit," Louise said, thrusting the glass in Charlotte's hand and gesturing to the dining table at the end of the kitchen. "I'll finish up here. You tell your best friend in all the world what's going on."

Charlotte backed up and collapsed into the nearest chair. Louise was formidable when she assumed her in-court voice, while she, guilt-ridden wanton, at the moment felt very vulnerable.

"Nothing's going on." The response was

weak, but then it was a lie. Charlotte did better with the truth.

"Ha. You haven't been yourself since the divorce."

"I don't know who myself is. I'm having to redefine myself."

"You're an attractive, intelligent, successful professional who is free to go anywhere and do anything that she chooses. There are no limits to how far you can go in your career. That is what means the most to you, isn't it? Your career?"

"Of course."

Charlotte put as much force as she could into the agreement, which wasn't difficult since this time her answer was the truth, but she still got a suspicious glance for her efforts.

"I know you're not much of a drinker," Louise said, gesturing to the untouched glass in her hand, "but a little wine won't hurt."

Not long ago Charlotte had thought the same about a margarita. Maybe if she had stopped with one, her life would be simpler now.

No, she couldn't blame the tequila. And besides, if that evening hadn't happened, she would have gone through the years thinking herself a cold, passionless woman, a failure at a part of life that was basic, instinctive, vital for the propagation of the species. She was a doctor, for heaven's sake. She knew the importance of sex.

As of last December 17 and edging into the wee hours of December 18, she also understood its appeal. Then, of course, there was today, January 12. She grew warm just remembering what she and Sam had done. A deep swallow of the chilled white wine did nothing to cool her off. She was forced to finish the glass.

She caught Louise looking at her, the bottle still in her hand. With a sheepish smile, Charlotte held out her glass for a refill.

"I had a rough day," she said by way of explanation.

"You were fine until the phone call."

"No, I wasn't. Not five minutes before the call came, you told me yourself I seemed distracted."

"Distracted, yes, not spaced out."

If Louise thought she was spaced out now, she should have seen her reserved physician friend yelling out "all I want is sex," then attempting to wave away the remark to a series of far-too-worldly and far-too-interested septuagenarians who had forgotten their ailments, so concerned were they for her.

And then there were the nurses Gloria and Claire.

Not to mention the memories of what had brought on the remark.

How dare Sam yell out a proposal of marriage? Besides, he wasn't just Sam, he was the despicable Redeye. Why she should have trouble remembering that fact, she had no idea. Sex was not more important than honor, than dignity, than pride.

The doorbell rang. She jumped. It couldn't be. It just couldn't be.

"You sit right there," Louise said, eyeing her the way she probably did opposing counsel. "I'll get it."

She came back holding an envelope, staring at it as if she were about to rip it open. Charlotte half expected her to hold it up to the light.

"It's for you," she said. "A young man from Alamo Messenger Service delivered it. Want me to read it first? It might be obscene. These days, you never know."

"I'll take my chances," Charlotte said. It wasn't much of a chance. She already knew whom it was from.

She traded her wineglass for the envelope. Inside was a three-by-five card. The message it contained was brief: I DIDN'T KNOW WHO YOU WERE WHEN I SAW YOU AT THE HILTON BAR. OUR MEETING WAS FATE. I MUST SEE YOU AGAIN. LOVE, SAM.

Charlotte thrust the letter deep in the pocket of her khaki slacks. "It's from a patient," she said.

Louise scratched the side of her nose. "A very unusual patient," she said, looking as if she wanted to wrestle Charlotte to the ground for the card.

"Believe me, he is."

"He? You've got an admirer among the geriatric set?"

Charlotte pictured Sam sitting at the end of the examining table in his paper gown. Then she pictured him lying there without it. With a groan, she buried her face in her hands.

Geriatric? Not with a body like that.

"I can't have supper tonight," she said. "I've got a terrible headache."

"You need a vacation."

A vacation was Louise's answer to everything. Each year she trekked to a different place in Europe, bringing back gifts for Charlotte from the regions she visited. Tonight the Provencal herbs purchased last year in Narbonne had been destined to season the chicken breasts, which were in the refrigerator waiting to be cooked on the grill out on the balcony. The weather was mild; the glass-topped patio table had already been set.

All that had been planned before Sam's call, when Charlotte believed that if she kept busy she could postpone dealing with the details of the day.

It took another groan and a semi-sob that wasn't a total fake to convince Louise she really wanted to be alone.

"Roger's got you upset."

"I haven't seen or heard from him since the day of the divorce."

"That doesn't mean he's not at fault."

Charlotte would have liked to blame him the way Louise did. For close to five years, since right after the honeymoon, she had gotten in the habit of putting him on the guilty side of every difficulty between them. But where Sam was concerned it was mea culpa from beginning to end.

In her heart she knew Sam had not conspired with his fishing buddy to humiliate Roger's ex-wife. Not that she would admit it out loud right away. Blaming him for being Redeye was a way to keep him at bay.

After Louise's departure, Charlotte threw the salad makings in the trash and tried sitting out on the balcony in the dark, but she heard sounds of laughter drifting up from the balcony below, laughter that seemed to be mocking her.

She recognized the woman's voice; it was that of her beautiful, unattached blond neighbor, who seemed very attached at the moment to a man with a deep chuckle. When a man and a woman were alone together, they had a laugh different from the one when others were around. It was almost a mating call. It was possible she and Sam had sounded much the same.

She listened to them for as long as she could stand, which she estimated to be five seconds. Then it was inside for a hot shower and into her high, wide bed for a session with the book she was reading: *Growing Gray with Aplomb,* a best-seller pop-psychology publication concerning aging, one of many that had become popular in modern America. Occasionally, she scanned them to see what was being said concerning the age group she cared about so much.

Whatever the message in this one, she wasn't getting it. Which could be because after several tries she hadn't gotten past the table of contents.

The phone rang. She jerked so violently, the book flew out of her hands. She stared at the receiver; it refused to grow quiet. With a sigh, she picked it up. This could be her medical answering service letting her know about an emergency.

"If you hang up, I'll keep calling," a low, rumbling male voice said.

Charlotte white-knuckled the phone, sinking low in the bed, refusing to say a word, but, then, neither did she hang up. She felt as if she were paralyzed, mesmerized, caught in a mindless kind of trance.

But she also would have arm-wrestled Godzilla to keep hold of the phone.

"Did my message arrive? Did you read the note?" Hesitation. "Forget I asked. I followed the Alamo Messenger truck to make sure the driver found the right address."

Sam had been outside her condominium. She wondered how long ago. She glanced toward the wall of windows that opened onto the river side of the building. Maybe he was outside now, calling on his cell phone. Maybe, like Romeo, he was prepared to scale vines up to her third-floor balcony.

Maybe she had lost her mind. This was the scenario most likely to be true.

"I just wanted you to know that today was the most remarkable experience of my life," he said. "Better than the hotel room because . . . well, maybe not better, since nothing could be, but definitely close on the spectacular scale."

Spectacular. It was the same word that had occurred to her. The coincidence was hardly soothing. The truth was it terrified her.

"I'm thinking about calling for another appointment," he said.

He meant it. She knew he did. The trance gave way to panic, and she shot up in the bed. "Don't you dare."

"You could give me a regulation exam this time. I've been feeling very strange lately. A checkup is just what I need. I promise to be good."

"Sam, this isn't funny."

"No, it's not. Don't you want to hear my symptoms? Heart palpitations, sudden rise in body temperature, inability to concentrate at work. I'm off my feed, too. That's not like me at all. Pardon me if I'm blunt, but I also have erections at the damnedest times. So what do you think is wrong?"

A mental image of Sam's last-named symptom sprang to mind. It took a few seconds to make it go away.

"I will not dignify that question with a serious reply."

"So try this one. What do you think of the Little Church at La Villita?"

"What has the church got to do with anything?" Even as she asked the question, she knew the answer, and she sank a little lower in the bed.

"It's right downtown," Sam went on, "between your place and mine. I live downtown, by the way, did you know that? No more than two miles from you. So what about the church? Have you ever attended a wedding there? The place is small, but—"

"You're frightening me, Sam. I mean it. For all I know, you're some kind of nut."

"Is that your professional opinion? Is *nut* a term you learned in medical school?"

She kept quiet, listening as he took in a deep breath. When he spoke, it was no longer jokingly but rather with a sobriety that frightened her all the more.

"I'm sorry, Charlie. I didn't mean to make fun of you, or to scare you. God knows that's the last thing I want. Maybe I am a little crazy right now, but it's because I want to see you again, to let you get to know me, to start our relationship the way any normal one would start, with a casual meeting, maybe dinner and a movie, some talk. Most couples could take up to a year to share what we shared our first night. If they are very, very lucky."

He fell silent, and she knew that, like her, he was thinking over the details of that night. She was honest enough with herself to admit she would cherish the memory and at the same time run from it for the rest of her life.

"Please listen to me. Very, very carefully." She spoke from the heart. "We don't have a relationship, not an ordinary one, and not a bizarre fantasy one, either. What I did was totally out of character. You don't know me, not the real me."

"And you don't know the real me. I come with credentials. Steady employment, nice folks, friends . . . okay, forget the friends. My father's an elementary school principal, for God's sake. My mother works in the office at the electric company. I've got a sister and two nephews in California. Uncle Joe lives here. He's a retired accountant. I'll admit he's a little cantankerous, but I figure, what the hell, he's lived a long time. He also figures income-tax returns for a few old friends. I'll bet I can get him to figure yours."

Charlotte tried not to listen to what he was

saying, tried not to care, but the truth was she was hanging on to every word.

But she couldn't let him go on. He was breaking her heart.

"You sound like a wonderful catch. For somebody else. Don't call here again. Not tonight. Not ever. I've made a terrible mistake. Please, please, just go away."

Dropping the phone in its cradle, she waited for another ring, but all was quiet in the room. The seconds crept by, but the quiet remained. Her hands shook; she squeezed them tight. Ten minutes passed before she could draw a close-to-calm breath.

All the while she was seeking composure, she was picturing Sam with his family, the kindly father who worked with young schoolchildren, the secretary mother, the tax-preparer uncle. They probably doted on Sam. He came with credentials, all right.

And what could she have told him in return?

"I was an only child. My parents were adventurers, wildlife photographers. I didn't see them much. When I was eight, they died in a plane crash in the Serengeti Plain, and I was raised by my grandparents."

Sam would be full of sympathy, but he would be thinking, *Serengeti Plain? What were they doing there when they had a little girl to take care of?*

Charlotte had an answer. It hadn't satisfied

her as a child, but it did when she became an adult.

"They came by their wanderlust naturally. Like me, my dad was orphaned early and moved around a lot. On my mother's side, Grandfather was a collector of pre-Columbian art, and Grandmother was an archaeologist. They spent a lot of time in Mexico. When they could, they took me with them, but eventually they had to put me in a boarding school. While I was in college, they died on a hiking trip at Copper Canyon south of Chihuahua, Mexico. They were on their way to visit the Tarahumara Indians at the canyon's base."

She had a colorful background, all right. Her upbringing sounded more glamorous than it was. The lot of them, parents and grandparents, had been withdrawn, introspective, reserved. And they had taught a watchful little girl to be the same.

Thinking of them made her feel lower than ever. Sleep felt hours away. She tried, but she couldn't read, couldn't bring herself to turn out the light. Easing out of bed, she pulled on her serviceable terry-cloth robe and roamed both floors of the condo, something she hadn't done since the night she moved in.

Upstairs was a wide loft area she had turned into a television and music room, and a large second bedroom with a full bath. She seldom came up here except to put a CD in the stereo.

She ended up where she had been before, looking at the paintings hung on the spiral staircase. They were small religious scenes that had been painted on wood somewhere deep in Mexico hundreds of years before. They were also the primary legacy of her grandparents.

It was at times like this, in the dark, reflective hour after midnight, when she best understood herself. She had decided on her geriatric specialty because of her past. It was as if her patients represented both her parents and grandparents, the loved ones she had not been able to protect from harm. No one, not Sam, not even Louise, could begin to know what her patients meant to her.

If she tried to tell Sam, he would disagree, or worse, say he understood when he couldn't possibly. What a mess she was in, just when she had been so certain she was uncomplicating her life. What kind of troubles had she stirred up?

For two whole years she had gone without the touch of a man, except for an occasional public kiss on the cheek when Roger thought someone was watching. Now she was close to becoming a nymphomaniac.

It wasn't a word she used loosely. It wasn't a condition she viewed with pride.

Nymphomaniacs were anything but reserved.

And what about Sam? He wasn't crazy, wasn't a threat to her safety. This was something she knew in her heart, and she didn't need particulars about his life as proof. Given the way she had behaved, he was reacting in a totally sane and, she had to admit, very flattering way. Eventually he would get over his temporary obsession, which was the most his feelings could be.

In the meantime, it seemed his conscience was bothering him. Otherwise, how could he possibly propose marriage? He didn't know her. He certainly couldn't love her. As she had tried to tell him, she was not the lovable kind.

One thing that seemed as strange as any other facet of the situation was the fact that he, a friend of Roger's, the oft-cursed Redeye, should show a conscience. Put in the same situation, Roger wouldn't lose a second's sleep.

Louise was right. She needed to concentrate on her career. If she allowed Sam into her life, even on the fringes, she would make more mistakes than she had already managed. She could not begin to imagine the depths to which she might sink.

Besides, Sam Blake was not a man to remain on the fringes for long.

All I want is sex.

As she climbed back into bed, the memory of her own words mocked her. She pulled the covers over her head. The worst thing about her outburst at the office hadn't been that others

had heard it, or that it was Redeye she was
addressing at the time.

The worst thing was that everything she said
was true.

Chapter Eight

Charlotte made it to work the next day with bleary eyes and a stiff upper lip, greeting Gloria with a professional nod as she came through her private door.

"Good morning, Dr. Hamilton," Gloria said in an equally professional voice. "It looks like we'll have a fairly busy day." And then she ruined it all by adding, "But it probably won't be as busy as yesterday."

Despite her words, her tone was innocent. Innocent, too, was the smile Claire gave her as she passed her in the hall. Charlotte's stomach knotted from all that innocence.

Still, she could do little else but behave as if

nothing out of the ordinary had happened the previous day. Easing out of her suit jacket, she slipped into the lab coat with a shiver that was barely detectable and threw herself into her tasks.

Over the next few hours Gloria and Claire continued to perform their duties with expressions a little too smug for Charlotte's peace of mind, but there was nothing specific she could complain about. While they were being smug, the nurse's aide, Barbara Anne, an enthusiastic twenty-something who attended college part time, walked around with a half smile on her face.

Yesterday she had forgotten all about Barbara Anne. Yesterday she had been insane.

What was she supposed to say to them today? *Quit looking happy*. They would have thought she had truly lost her mind.

Only Jolene, the receptionist and book-keeper, was business as usual. But that didn't mean she wasn't thinking about yesterday and the virile patient who had kept the doctor occupied for an inordinate amount of time, or about the declaration said doctor had shouted to the world.

But they were all too polite, too much her supporters, to say a word. She did notice, however, no one had put a single patient into examining room number one. She wasn't about to ask why, although there were a number of people in the waiting room who could have used the space for their office visit.

In truth, she was glad the staff hadn't. She could barely bring herself to glance at the closed door.

And then noontime came, the four women were taking turns grabbing a quick lunch, and she found herself alone in the hallway outside the dreaded room.

Eventually, she had to go inside, if for no other reason than the room would be needed in the afternoon to relieve her barely adequate facilities. Might as well do it now. Easing through the door, she closed it quietly behind her. The light was off; she stood for a moment in the dark, remembering, breathing in the scent of Sam, listening to the echoing sound of his voice, before she snapped it on. She should have left it off.

Someone had placed a single long-stemmed red rose on top of the paper that covered the examining table. Someone who knew what had taken place there.

If someone in the office knew exactly what had led to her outburst, that meant everyone knew, just as she had feared. She had tried to be quiet, but around Sam she was seldom in control. Commemorating the event like this was their way of letting her know that what had happened was all right with them, or if not exactly all right, they did not condemn her for it.

The condemnation she was handling herself.

Putting the rose in a milk glass vase Jolene kept at the back of her desk, Charlotte went about her work. No one mentioned the flower, and the room was once again put into use. All was as it was, or as close to it as she could get.

Obviously they saw her embarrassment and took the incident for what it was: the aberration of a newly divorced woman trying to find her way.

Over the next week, when she wasn't busy at work, she was dodging shadows and jumping at ringing telephones. Rather than walk to and from the medical building or even drive, she took taxis, choosing to leave both her station wagon and most definitely her sports car in the condo garage. Sometimes when she got home she sat in the Corvette and gave long lectures to herself about regaining control of her life.

During the long seven days, she heard not a word from Sam. Something she had said must have convinced him she wished to be left alone. Admitting to an absurd sense of abandonment, she also felt an enormous relief.

On a Wednesday afternoon that marked exactly one week since Sam's visit and subsequent phone call, with the weather balmy and a restlessness eating at her, she made a few late hospital visits, then chose to walk along the river to the tea room that her condo neighbors David and Bill owned and operated.

Bistro Tea was located on a quiet stretch of the river, beneath a small street-level hotel. There were two ways to enter, through the hotel and down the stairs to the restaurant or through the riverside door. Frequently she stopped by on her evening stroll home to pick up food, not being one to enjoy dining in public alone any more than she liked cooking for just herself.

This evening, with the cozy, low-ceilinged room less than half full, she decided to stay and enjoy the ambiance. In addition to great light food and imported teas and wines from around the world, BT, as it was called by the regulars, featured linen tablecloths and napkins, soft lighting, and classical background music.

The walls were hung with the abstract paintings of their mutual neighbor Cerise Lambert, wild splashes of color and light that shouldn't have worked in such an old-world atmosphere, yet worked very well.

And there wasn't a fern in sight. Both David and Bill said they hated ferns.

She was seated at a secluded corner table with a view of the river, studying the beverage list, trying to decide on soup, salad, or sandwich, letting the mellowness of the place soothe her, when Sam Blake walked through the riverfront door.

She buried her head behind the menu. This wasn't his kind of place. He was a sportswriter. He ought to be in a sports bar.

Peering around the edge of the menu, she saw him just inside the door, laughing and talking with Bill. While his tall, well-padded partner David ran the kitchen, short, spare, birdlike Bill took care of other aspects of the business, including greeting and seating the customers. Right now he was doing a great job of greeting Sam. They were acting as if they were old friends.

To her dismay, even David, wearing a big white apron across his spreading middle, came out of the kitchen to say hello to Sam. David had never done that for her.

Sam was wearing khaki slacks and a brown sweater over a lemon-yellow shirt. His sandy hair was cut shorter than she remembered, close on the sides and sort of casual wind-blown-style on top. In addition to the change in hair style, he also looked thinner, but that could have been her imagination. She wasn't used to seeing him dressed.

When he cast a glance around the room, she ducked back behind the menu. He must have seen her. He would certainly be at her table any second. She steeled herself to tell him she wanted to be alone.

He didn't show. Hearing the low rumble of his voice from nearby, she peeked out again.

He was standing ten feet away at a table where two women were seated. Two young, attractive women. They were smiling up at him and he was smiling down at them.

Without even trying, she was able to pick up general greetings, but she was unable to determine if the meeting had been planned. Obviously they all knew one another, knew one another well. One of the women gestured to the empty chair between them. Sam sat, and Bill brought him a bottle of wine to inspect.

"Looks great," he said "Three glasses. Anything this pleasurable ought to be shared."

Why did his voice have to carry? It was as if he were throwing it her way. But that was ridiculous. He probably hadn't even seen her.

Which was, of course, exactly the way she wanted it.

She drummed her fingers on the table. He was already drinking and her order hadn't yet been taken, though she had been there first. The injustice burned inside her, but she reminded herself she was a mature adult. He had known what he wanted. She did not.

He had also claimed he wanted her, wanted her as the only woman in his life forever and ever, the mother of his children, the woman with whom he would glide into old age. How long had the offer lasted? Not even a week.

But then, of course, he was Roger's friend. And he was a man. She had never considered herself a man-hater, but right now she found the opposite sex a definite irritant.

When the waiter came up, she ordered a bottle of wine just for herself, a Chardonnay, well chilled of course, along with a salad of mixed greens and feta cheese under a sprinkling of corn-relish dressing and a spinach-and-salmon quiche. Her next chore would be to get a portion of all that food down.

Reluctantly she gave up the menu and stared with ferocious concentration through the window at the tourist-packed barges gliding by on the river. The passing lights were festive, the people smiling, all was well with the outside world. Which made her feel worse than ever. Maybe she should have left before ordering, but that would have been a cowardly retreat. Since meeting Sam, she had let the possibility of his presence alter the way she lived. Now that he was a reality, she couldn't let herself run.

The decision was a good one, a smart one, a brave one, but she regretted it with all her heart when a shadow fell across the table and she looked up into a pair of puppy-warm eyes.

"Charlie," he said, "good evening. How are you?"

She felt like a warm puddle in the chair. A puddle with a pounding heart and a stomach tied in knots. It was a purely physical reaction to a very physical man. She hadn't been sleeping well or eating well or even getting the exercise she needed, but her libido was working just fine.

A functioning libido, she was learning, could be a very inconvenient thing.

"Why, good evening," she said a little too loudly. "I thought that was you over there. But you seemed so cozy, I didn't want to intrude."

Far too catty. She should have said *busy* instead of *cozy*, or maybe *occupied*. Or pretended she didn't notice him, though when he walked through the door the half dozen other women in the room had given him at least a cursory glance.

"You're dining alone?" he asked.

A dozen lies popped into her head. She settled for a truthful, "Yes." She wasn't ashamed of eating by herself. She simply preferred reading while she ate, and she never had any reading material with her when she was on her way home.

Unless it was a professional publication, but somehow browsing through the *New England Journal of Medicine* was not her idea of entertainment to make the gastric juices flow.

"Why don't you join us?" he asked, nodding in the direction of his two female companions.

"In a ménage à trois isn't that taking on one too many?"

She bit her tongue. She had never before

even thought ménage à trois, much less said the phrase aloud.

He pulled a chair close to her side and with a grace and control far too familiar, lowered his finely toned glutes onto the seat. She took in a deep breath, as if to show indignation at his boldness, but all she got was a whiff of Sam. He smelled better than anything BT might serve.

His brow furrowed, and he looked at her straight on, forcing her to look away.

"I thought a ménage à trois was some fooling around involving a married couple and a third party. We're not married, Charlie, as you very well know."

Her eyes snapped back to him. "Of course we're not married. And we're never going to be."

His answer was a smile. A small one, it took one corner of his mouth at a time, twisted his lips, and deepened the lines in the brown skin at either side.

An unbearable silence lengthened between them.

"What's that cologne you're wearing?" she asked, wondering where the question came from. What he smelled like was no concern of hers.

Here was an opportunity for him to look victorious, as if he had bested her in some way.

Instead, he treated her question with a serious-
ness it most certainly did not deserve.

"Obsession. And it's aftershave, not cologne.
My mother gives me a bottle every year for
Christmas. She thinks it will help me attract a
woman, so that she can have grandchildren
here in town. She has only my sister's two boys
in California. She's ready for more."

So his mother wanted babies. She wasn't the
only one. Charlotte fought the tightness
around her heart.

"So you wear it for breeding purposes," she
flipped out.

"I wear it to please her. For purposes of
breeding, I like a more natural odor. Yours, for
instance." He inhaled deeply. "I don't detect
perfume tonight. At the hotel I noticed Chanel
No. 5, which is good, very good. Classy, like
you. I want you to wear it again. But tonight I
like your natural erotic scent."

For all the innuendo in his voice, he might
have been talking about what she had ordered
to eat. Still, the words were enough. Particularly *erotic*. A shiver ran from her well-
scrubbed scalp to her hidden scarlet-tipped
toes.

While she was busy showing she wasn't the
least affected by anything about him, the
waiter brought the Chardonnay for her inspec-
tion. Without a glance at the bottle, she pointed
to her glass. The waiter looked at Sam, at his

chair pulled out at another table, and then to the wine.

"Mr. Blake is leaving," she said. "I believe he has chosen his own wine." And the company with which to drink it.

She watched the pouring with all the attention she would give to brain surgery. When the waiter was gone, she was about to take a sip, playing it cool, pulling off a delayed show of aloofness, when Sam leaned close and brushed his lips against her temple.

She jumped, miraculously not spilling a drop of Chardonnay, and, heaven help her, she leaned into the momentary kiss. So much for aloof.

"I've missed you," he whispered, and it was puddle time again. Except that this time she wasn't a warm puddle; she was hot.

Sam must have recognized her condition. Beneath the protective covering of the table-cloth, she felt his hand rest on her thigh. Unfortunately, instead of the slacks she usually wore, this evening she had on a skirt. When his fingers worked their way beneath the hem, she thanked providence that she was wearing panty hose. Not that they would prove an impediment to him.

Sam the Man was inventive as well as determined.

"Stop it," she hissed into her glass. "Get your hand off my leg."

"Where would you like me to put it?"

Pitiful creature that she was, she came up with an answer that was not only specific and close to clinical, it was also insane.

"Please," she said, closing her eyes, "I'm not a tart."

But that was exactly how she felt. Her denial was as much for herself as it was for him.

"I know you're not," he said. Giving her inner thigh a squeeze, he removed his hand. "It's just that you have this thing for me and can't decide what it is."

She set aside her wine, closing her eyes for a moment, deciding it was time for another try at honesty. If, that is, she could forget the remaining warm imprint on her leg.

"I know what it is. I've declared it to the world. It's a case of arrested adolescence, that's all. I had a very reserved upbringing. I married Roger while I was still in school, not long after my grandparents died. For the first time in my life I'm free and on my own. Unfortunately, with that freedom I've made some mistakes—"

"I'm not a mistake."

He touched her chin and turned her to face him. Before she could pull away, he brushed his lips against hers, very softly, with no more pressure than a breeze. But it was enough to rob her of every coherent thought.

"I'm your destiny," he said. "And you are mine."

Just as she started to sway toward him, he pushed back his chair, waved to the women at the other table, and left the room, striding toward the stairs that would take him up to the hotel and out to the street.

Unless he was arranging a room for the night. A room for two, no luggage, no questions asked. Such arrangements he managed very well.

But she knew he wasn't doing any such thing, not tonight. Sam wasn't subtle. He would have told her what he was about.

She felt the women staring at her; she couldn't imagine what they must think. More than anything, she wanted to hug herself, to squeeze into nothingness the turmoil he had stirred inside and, worse, the sense of loss because he had gone.

Seeking refuge behind the glass of wine, she took a sip and choked. Trying to look casual and unconcerned, she spied the waiter approaching with her salad. Too late. Whatever ambience BT usually held for her had fled along with Sam.

"Please, could you box this along with the quiche? I'll be taking it with me tonight."

"Of course, Dr. Hamilton. And the wine?"

"Cork it. I'll take it, too."

While she waited for her food and the bill, she stared at the lights twinkling along the banks of the river. But she was feeling Sam's lips brushing against hers and his fingers stroking her thigh.

And she was picturing the way he looked and the way he walked and the way he sat and every detail about him she could recall, feeling miserable and exhilarated at the same time.

So he wore Obsession, did he? As far as she was concerned, the aftershave was perfectly named.

Chapter Nine

Sam had handled Charlie wrong. All wrong. The instant he touched her thigh, he knew it for sure.

He stood in the shadows away from the riverside walkway and watched as she left the restaurant, a Styrofoam box and paper-wrapped bottle in her hands. The high, arched lights along the riverbank showed a decidedly determined expression on her face.

The same determination was evident in her brisk stride. She was putting distance between her and the latest place where her tormentor had appeared.

It was a pitiful end for an evening that had started out so right. Watching her leave her office, a practice he had started lately, he'd seen her walking instead of taking a taxi as had been her habit since he'd come into her life. Following, he observed her go inside Bistro Tea. Knowing she stopped by BT often, he had purposefully cultivated the proprietors' friendship. So it had seemed perfectly natural to follow her inside.

More good awaited, in the form of two attractive women sitting at one of the tables, one a photographer and the other a librarian from the paper. Sam knew them well. *Join them*, he had thought, *and make her jealous*.

But he had proven pathetic in the make-jealous department. Distant from her for the past week, he hadn't been able to keep up the ruse. And, naturally, being close to her meant he had to paw her. Just as naturally, she had liked it, but only for a while.

So here he was following her in the shadows, making certain she got home all right. Why she didn't take the Corvette to work, he had no idea. While he knew so much about her, there was much he still had to learn.

But how? And how to make her want to know about him?

Sam wasn't much for courting, if that was the right word for what he was doing. It was more than just hitting on her. That was how they'd met.

No, this was definitely courting, something

he knew nothing about. In school, he had been a star athlete, a trophy stud for the cheerleaders and pep squad and any other female who caught his eye. Stud was all he wanted to be. It had gotten him friends, adulation, the promise of great fortune and, of course, a beautiful wife.

Unfortunately, when the knee went, along with his claim to studhood, so had she. After college, after the divorce, he hadn't been interested in capturing any particular woman. Occasional dates and parties were enough.

And then he had walked into the Hilton bar.

That night, everything had been easy. But nothing, with the exception of a half hour in an examining room, had been easy since.

"What do I need to do to win your approval?" he whispered to her back as she hurried to the refuge of her condo.

Go away.

"Nope, not possible. But your receptionist refuses to schedule another appointment, I'm sure by your orders, and you're using an answering machine to screen your calls at home. What's a guy to do?"

Give up. Leave me alone.

"I tried playing hard to get. I didn't call or try to contact you for seven whole days."

You didn't hold back long enough. Next time make it a year.

He doubted his made-up answers were much

different from whatever she might say. As much as she puzzled him, in some ways he understood her very well.

From afar, he watched as she let herself in through the locked gate that led to the condominiums, then firmly secured the deadbolt after her, shutting him out of her life.

The sound echoed through the night like a shot. At that moment he came to a conclusion he didn't like. On his own, he was getting nowhere. He needed help.

It was quite an admission. With the exception of baseball, he had never been one for team sports. Individual effort and achievement were what counted the most. Or so he had believed until he met Charlie. The trouble was it would take a contingent the size fielded by the U.S. Olympics Committee to help him get her in the same room with him, particularly if they were to be alone.

But who to enlist? Roger was out, way out, and so, too, was that friend of hers who had answered her phone. He thought about the various aspects of his life and of hers, the contacts, the pastimes, the pursuits. Mostly he concentrated on her. Somewhere in all that thinking, the answer popped into his head. The idea was crazy. Still, he smiled. Crazy seemed the only way to go.

He would have to make a few phone calls, line up some specific facts, and then he could get to work. Once he had the initial assault planned, the next step was easy. He would call on his Uncle Joe.

"Ain't no way you're gonna get me to live in a place like this."

Sam didn't bother arguing. With Joe in his country cranky mood, arguing would get him nowhere. Instead, he held open the door to the Golden Years Assisted Living Community and gestured for his uncle to enter.

The front entryway was barely long enough to accommodate two small sofas, one on either side of the glass enclosure. At the end was another pair of double doors.

"Look at the bolts on these things," Uncle Joe said, waving to the locks on the doors.

"They're to keep someone from breaking in during the night."

"Can't fool me. They're to keep the inmates from escaping."

By now they had worked their way into the large circular room that obviously served as a meeting area for residents and their guests. Behind the clusters of upholstered chairs and couches was a glass wall looking out on a flower-and-shrubbery-filled atrium that even in winter resembled a tropical forest.

"Humph," Uncle Joe said as he regarded the scene. "Trying to make 'em think they're outside when they ain't anywhere near it. Looks like one of those open pens they got at the zoo. The bears might look free and easy roaming around for folks to gawk at, but with a moat in front of 'em and a rock wall behind, they know they ain't going anywhere."

"People here are free to come and go as they please. I already told you that. Besides, what difference does any of this make to you? Your name isn't going on the waiting list for a room. They wouldn't have an irascible old coot like you if you gave them all the tacos in town."

Sam and his uncle had been bickering like this for the past hour, beginning at the Blake family house and continuing through the twenty-minute ride to Golden Years. At seventy-six, Joseph Donaldson was close to two decades older than his sister Ellen, Sam's mother. Most of the time, with the possible exception of right now, Sam felt closer to him than he did anyone else in the world.

"Welcome to Golden Years, gentlemen," a soft voice said behind him. "How may I be of service?"

Sam turned and smiled at the middle-aged speaker, hoping she hadn't heard Uncle Joe's gripes. She was wearing a blue dress and sturdy shoes, her brown hair was cut short and brushed back, an angel pin adorned her shoulder along with a name tag that identified her as Mrs. Elvira Cochran, and she had *volunteer* written all over her.

Sam quickly went through the introductions.

"It was his idea to come here," his uncle said, poking a thumb in his direction.

"I'm sure it was, Mr. Donaldson," she responded without blinking an eye. "While you're here, you might as well look around at our facilities. We have brochures for you, naturally, but it's always best to see things for yourself. I'm sure you'll agree."

"Only thing I want to see right now is the men's room. Since I hit seventy-five last year, my bladder ain't worth a damn."

The weak bladder was news to Sam. He was also surprised by the number of *ain'ts* his uncle was throwing around; Joe the Accountant was usually downright refined in his speech. He really was in a foul mood. Before he could apologize, however, the unflappable Mrs. Cochran hurried on.

"If you'll go down the hallway," she said, "you'll find it immediately on the right."

Uncle Joe strode off, looking sprightly in spite of his complaints. He was wearing the red suspenders and navy blue shirt his sister and brother-in-law had given him for Christmas. Sam's contribution had been the usual argyle socks and a promissory note for tickets to any play-off games involving the San Antonio Spurs basketball team.

Some years he got away with buying just the socks; with the team's current winning record at .752, this year would probably be more costly. As Uncle Joe, an avid Spurs fan, well knew. Which was why Sam had felt no compunction about asking for his uncle's help courting the woman he had chosen to be his wife. The problem was that the man didn't believe courting was his real purpose.

"No woman's going to get her claws into you," he had said when Sam put the request to him. A widower for ten years, Joe had fended off more than his share of widows. He could live without female companionship, and as far as he could see, so could his nephew.

Sam hadn't told him the identity of the woman he had in mind, nor her occupation. But he had said visiting Golden Years was very important, and he needed his uncle's cooperation to get him in.

Uncle Joe was not impressed.

"I know why we're going to this hellhole," he had said while they were still sitting out front in the car. "You want to put me away. Okay, so I burned out the bottom of the coffeepot the other day, leaving it on too long, but that don't mean I can't take care of myself. Anybody's entitled to one mistake."

"I agree," Sam had said in all sincerity.

"No, you don't. What you're doing is trying to shut me up."

Sometimes the old man was too wily for his own good.

In his uncle's absence, Mrs. Cochran led Sam to her office, which was off the hallway to the left, assuring him as they walked that he shouldn't worry about anything his uncle said. She had heard just about everything.

She was handing him a slick folder filled with four-color brochures when a pretty young woman in her early twenties walked in.

"Mr. Blake, this is Marie Contreras, a member of our staff. Marie, Mr. Blake is here with his uncle to visit Golden Years. This is your first visit, is it not, Mr. Blake? I recognized you from your picture in the paper and, of course, television. I know I haven't seen you here before."

"You're that Sam Blake?" Marie asked.

She opened her brown eyes wide and flipped back her long, black hair. She was wearing a short skirt and snug sweater, and her right ear was studded with four earrings. She made Sam feel as old as Uncle Joe.

He muttered something about being a sportswriter, that was all. He was never comfortable with even his small slice of celebrity-hood.

Uncle Joe returned, took one look at Marie, and smiled. "Hello, there, young lady, my name's Joseph Donaldson, Joe for short. My nephew here dragged—that is, he invited me to look over the facilities you have here. It's for my sister, you understand. She's a great deal older than I and sadly showing signs of a decline."

Sam managed to keep his mouth shut while Uncle Joe, abandoning country cranky, preened. He half expected him to snap his suspenders and click his heels. So he didn't need female companionship, did he? Every man did, if only for a brief time.

Mrs. Cochran excused herself, and Marie, her arm linked with Joe's, took them on the tour.

"What's a pretty young thing like you doing in a place like this?" Sam heard his uncle say as they headed down the nearest hall. He rolled his eyes in disgust, but Marie gave no sign she was taking offense, either for herself or for Golden Years.

"It's part of my graduate studies in social work at Our Lady of the Lake," she said. "I love it here."

"I remember when I was in graduate school," Joe said. "Those were fine times."

Sam kept quiet on the tour of the rooms, the library, the pharmacy, the dining room, and the gift shop. They passed several dozen residents, walking, sitting, reading, or visiting with one another. He guessed the median age at eighty-two.

Most of them gave a friendly nod and greeted Marie by name. It was the ones who weren't so friendly that caught Sam's attention. Despite the pleasantness of their surroundings, they looked separate, not a part of anything, as if they were lost in their own world.

Their loneliness struck him hard. He could see himself growing old like them, with no family close by. No Mom and Dad. No Uncle Joe. No Charlie. Meeting her had been his wake-up call.

When Joe started asking Marie when she got off work, Sam stirred from his reverie. A glance at his watch told him it was time to make his move.

"You have an auditorium here, don't you?" he asked from his position at the rear. "A place where groups of people get together?"

Marie nodded over her shoulder. "We can take a peek inside if you like. There's a meeting there now, but I don't think they'll mind if we're quiet and don't stay long."

"What kind of a meeting?" Sam asked with all the innocence he could muster.

"One of the doctors who treats quite a few of the residents holds a session once a month for whoever wants to attend. Sometimes she has a specialist in to listen to the residents and guests. Today there's a speaker."

"I see," Sam said, though he could have named the doctor and time and date of the sessions for a good part of the year. He even knew the name of today's speaker, a nutritionist from an area health clinic who was presenting evidence concerning the effects of diet on the aging process.

Charlie occasionally dropped by; today she was nowhere near. He had known she wouldn't be, otherwise he would have come at another time.

"Are these sessions open only to residents of Golden Years?" he asked.

"They started out that way, but Dr. Hamilton's programs have proven so popular, we opened them up to the general public. For a small fee, of course, though our residents get in free."

Again, she wasn't telling him anything he didn't know.

Stopping at a closed door, she peered in through the glass panel. "It looks like they're taking a break. We can go in."

The auditorium was one of those all-purpose kinds with a stage at one end, a kitchen at the other, and in between rows of folding chairs. Hanging on the wall extending down from the entry door were obviously amateur paintings, photographs, and message boards. The opposite wall of windows opened onto tree-studded grounds and walkways centering on a vine-covered gazebo.

Sam was impressed. Not so Uncle Joe, who viewed with a frown the two dozen people gathered around the coffee, punch, and cookies laid out on a table under one of the message boards.

"Nothing but old folks," he grumbled.

"Do you think I could steal a cookie and some coffee?" Sam asked.

"Of course," Marie said. "There's always plenty. Since the nutritionist has been speaking, everyone's probably too intimidated to eat very much."

On the contrary, the people were piling their plates high. Sam ventured toward them. Joe and Marie held back.

The women outnumbered the men two to one; they also gave him the most attention when he came up and introduced himself as a visitor.

One gray-haired lady in a black turtleneck sweater and black slacks eyed him more carefully than the rest, although he got a goodly share of smiles and nods. She was tall and trim and had a diamond on her left hand that must have made lifting her cup a formidable chore.

He plunged in, asking questions about the sessions, the topics of discussion, numbers who attended, and finally, the name of the person who had started the group.

"Dr. Charlotte Hamilton," one of the men said. "She's a pip. I didn't think I'd ever get into this group-therapy foolishness, but you know, it's not so foolish if it's done right."

Several others, men and women both, agreed. The woman in black stayed to the side and remained silent, but she was looking at him the way his mother did when she was certain he was up to no good.

"I was hoping I could get my uncle interested in joining," Sam said, gesturing over his shoulder to Uncle Joe. Joe was so engrossed in a story he was telling Marie, he didn't notice.

Still, he served his purpose. He was there.

"Actually, I've met Dr. Hamilton," he added in what had to be the champion of all understatements. "I'm not sure she's open to welcoming new faces. Uncle Joe can be outspoken at times."

Again, he got a wave of endorsements for Charlie, this time concerning her open-mindedness. Clearly, they saw a side of her he didn't see.

The woman in black continued to watch. This time she was joined in her watchfulness by the man who had called Charlie a pip.

The day's speaker, a woman in white who had been at the side consuming a bottle of fruit drink, said it was time to conclude her presentation.

Sam was about to ask if he could talk to them after the nutritionist was done. That was when the woman in black broke her silence.

"I'd like a few minutes of your time," she said. Without a glance at the others or a pause to await his agreement, she struck out for the far door that led to the outside walkways.

When they were well away from the building, she turned to him. "You don't recognize me, do you?"

She was an attractive woman who had to be around seventy: her gray hair was short and neatly coiffed, her skin smooth and almost wrinkle free, but with a papery quality to it that gave away her age.

"Should I recognize you?" he asked.

"My name is Stella Dugan." She hesitated a moment, as if waiting for him to recognize her. "I was at Dr. Hamilton's office the day you were there."

Sam closed his eyes for a moment and saw her in another time and another place.

"You were one of the heads that popped out."

"I was." She nodded toward the windows. "So was Walter Farrow. His vision's not too good. He didn't recognize you right away, though I believe he was beginning to grow suspicious."

"I can explain—"

"Don't bother. I'm not a fool. And don't think I'm here to chastise you, young man. I've seen and heard too much in my seventy years to pass judgment on the activities of consenting adults." Something dark fluttered in her eyes for a moment. "As long as both are unattached and no one is harmed."

"Charlie felt harmed."

"By what she said or what she had done? I assume at some point the two of you have done something together."

Sam stared at her, nonplussed. To admit anything, even if the examining room were not mentioned, would be like a betrayal of Charlie's privacy. On the other hand, Charlie had pretty much already messed herself up on the privacy front.

"Never mind," Stella Dugan said. "If I want to know the answer, Dr. Hamilton is the one I should ask."

The idea of Stella Dugan asking Charlie about her sex life was not one he could contemplate long.

"She thinks she's been harmed."

"Did you hurt her in any way?"

"I can honestly say no."

Stella Dugan looked him over with all the care Uncle Joe had given to Marie.

"No, I don't believe you did. No wonder she yelled out the way she did, standing out in the hallway where everyone could hear."

"Did you hear my proposal of marriage? It came just before the yell."

"My eyesight's fine, but unfortunately my hearing isn't what it used to be, Sam. The main thing I heard was Dr. Hamilton's talk about sex."

Ms. Dugan might not be embarrassed, but he was.

144

"The thing is—" he began, not quite knowing where he was going. But Stella cut him off.

"Goodness knows I enjoyed it in my day," she said, "and of course I thought . . . but none of that. We're talking about Charlotte Hamilton. I wasn't aware of any such inclination on her part. Good for her. She's been far too lonely for far too long."

Sam grinned. He couldn't help it.

"Ms. Dugan—"

"Mrs. Dugan. I'm a widow, as are most of the women here."

"Mrs. Dugan, you are the answer to my prayers."

"You have strange prayers, young man."

"I'm here seeking help. Charlie doesn't want to see me again."

He got another once-over. "I can't imagine why not. Are you incompatible in some way? Sexually, I mean. That's what is important here, I assume."

"We're very compatible," Sam said, thinking he should be uncomfortable with the question, but finding himself liking Stella Dugan very much. "Charlie and I are about as compatible as a man and woman can get. The thing is, I want more. I meant it when I asked her to marry me. You heard her say what she wants."

"Have you known her long?"

"A month. But each time I'm with her I know more certainly that we belong together. Until

Charlie, I had been feeling restless. Something was not right in my life. I don't feel that way anymore. Except when she's rejecting me, which is getting to be a serious problem."

Stella Dugan studied a flock of grackles that had landed in the brown grass to peck around for bugs.

"This is a most unusual situation," she said. "In my life I have met people from all sorts of backgrounds, not a few of them criminal. I've seen some unusual things in that time, but nothing like this."

"Crazy, isn't it? I know you and her other patients mean more to her than just about anything in the world. If you could help me convince her she needs to take me seriously—"

"That's why you're here?"

"I found out about the meeting. And I knew she wouldn't be attending. Her receptionist won't make me another appointment, but she did let me know Charlie—Dr. Hamilton—would be seeing patients all afternoon."

"And your uncle?"

"He was a way to get me inside Golden Years without arousing suspicion. I wasn't sure I would be welcome."

"Maybe you are and maybe you aren't. You're asking us to convince her you're serious. That's something you'll have to do." She tapped a manicured forefinger against her pursed lips. "But perhaps there is something we can do to get you two together. Something to put her in a more favorable frame of mind."

Sam's hopes rose, only to be dashed right away.

"If you pass muster, of course," Stella Dugan added. "We can't turn our Dr. Hamilton over to just anyone."

"I wouldn't want you to," Sam said, wondering what kind of test he would have to pass.

"An interrogation will do for a start. We should begin right away."

"Interrogation?"

A smile crinkled the corners of Stella Dugan's eyes. It was not a comforting sight.

"Most definitely. Tell you what, Samuel. This is Friday. You show up here Sunday afternoon. Say around 3:00 P.M. We'll meet in the gazebo."

"We?"

"There will be others. This isn't a decision I can make on my own. The gentleman who came in with you—"

"Uncle Joe."

"Right, your uncle. Bring him, too. One of the curses of growing old is boredom. That's why I've joined this psychotherapy group. What you're offering is far better than recipes and suggestions for exercise. Uncle Joe might provide his share of diversion. It's time we had some fresh blood around here."

Chapter Ten

"The only reason I'm here is because of that little Marie," Uncle Joe said as he and Sam walked through the parking lot at Golden Years on Sunday. "She said for me to drop by anytime I wanted. She let me know without any doubt she would be working today. If I fail to show, she'll be very disappointed."

Joe adjusted his red suspenders. Today he was wearing them with a black shirt and black trousers, and Sam thought he looked like a disreputable gambler. Worse, he smelled like the inside of a bottle of Old Spice. Not that Sam had anything against the smell. It was just best in small doses.

It was a good thing they were meeting outside. His uncle needed to be kept in the fresh air.

Stella Dugan met them at the front door. Again she was wearing a black sweater and trousers, and the diamond on her ring finger sparkled in the afternoon sunlight.

"You're late," she said.

The reason was Uncle Joe, who had taken an extra-long time to get ready. Sam hoped tardiness was not a mark against him.

She took a long look at Joe, who was busy looking around at the half-empty room behind her. When Sam introduced his uncle, she sniffed a couple of times and wrinkled her nose.

"Let's stay outside," she said. With a wave of her hand she led them along a sidewalk that ended at the back of the building and then onto one of the footpaths leading to the vine-covered gazebo.

Walter Farrow was seated on one of the benches, along with another man and two women. Walter was spiffily dressed in gray trousers, a navy sport coat, and striped red tie; the man beside him, shorter by six inches and heavier by twenty pounds, looked scruffy by comparison in his faded jeans, plaid shirt, and worn cardigan sweater.

On the telephone earlier Stella had filled him in on the inquisition board he would face. At eighty-five Walter was the oldest of the group.

Fifty years ago he had begun a county-wide ambulance service, sold it for great profit, and lived high for a while. His wife currently resided in the Alzheimer's wing of Golden Years. Walter's home was in one of the low-lying apartments scattered on the landscaped grounds behind the main building.

The man beside him had to be Morris Weiss, an eighty-three-year-old widower and retired plumber whose only son communicated with him through e-mail though he, his wife, and two teenage daughters lived in San Antonio.

Morris claimed to like it that way—"I don't have to be bothered with a bunch of fussiness"—but Stella doubted he spoke the truth. Like Walter, he lived in one of the apartments. Unlike Walter, he looked his years, all signs of robust youth a long, long time in the past.

The women seated across from neat Walter and scruffy Morris were an equal contrast, the thinner of the two clad in a purple warm-up suit and cross-trainers, the plumper woman in a flowered dress and matching jacket.

Purple suit he pegged as Ada Profitt, seventy-eight, widow and former biology teacher, an "eccentric," as Stella put it without going into details, except to mention Ada always wore brightly colored warm-ups and athletic shoes, even to church.

That left flowered dress, sixty-eight-year-old

spinster Irene O'Neill, who was determinedly generous with the goodies her nieces and nephews frequently brought to the community. Both Ada and Irene lived in apartments on one of the upper floors at Golden Years.

As different as the committee appeared, all had two things in common: gray hair and attentive eyes directed toward Sam. He had chosen a brown leather bomber jacket, white shirt, and dress slacks for the occasion and had polished his shoes twice. The women looked more approving than the men, but it was probably too early to call for a vote of confidence. First he ought to at least introduce himself.

Ada cut him off. "Is this the one Dr. Hamilton wants for sex?" She shook her head. "There's no accounting for taste."

So much for thinking her look was approving. Before he could think of a response, which considering her criticism might have taken a week or two, Irene came to his defense.

"Now, Ada, we shouldn't embarrass the young man. Besides," she added with a giggle, lashes fluttering, "I think the doctor's taste is perfectly fine."

"Didn't I warn you to expect anything?" Stella said to him.

For the moment Uncle Joe stopped casting glances at the main building of Golden Years.

"What's this talk about sex?" he asked. "What kind of meeting did you bring me to?"

"I already told you," Sam said. "I'm after a wife."

"Humph," Ada said. "That's what they all say. Once they get what they want, then it's good-bye, don't call me, I'll call you."

"Now, now," Walter said, "let's not be hasty in our judgment. Not all men are like that." He straightened his tie. "Besides, we're here to gather facts before we make any decisions. There's a chance the man might be perfectly suited for Dr. Hamilton."

"Don't try to reason with Ada," Morris said with a click of his dentures. "She won't listen to reason."

Sam was beginning to think he had made a terrible mistake. There was no way these people could agree on anything, and what he was asking was hardly just anything, not when it concerned the rest of his life. He was considering grabbing Joe's arm and beating a fast retreat when Stella spoke up.

"Is there anyone present who doesn't want to help Dr. Hamilton? If so, speak up now and leave so the rest of us can get to today's business."

She spoke with a firmness that verified her self-appointed position as chairman of the board. Since Friday, Sam had recalled that her late husband served several decades as a district judge, making her something of a public figure, too. He also vaguely remembered a scandal involving the judge, but Stella's past wasn't his business and he hadn't bothered to research it in the paper's library.

All eyes remained trained on Sam but no one spoke, and Sam decided it was time to make his initial pitch.

"I'm Sam Blake," he said, feeling as if he had stepped into a pool of quicksand. "I write a sports column for the *San Antonio Tribune*—"

Morris interrupted. "Been meaning to e-mail you about that column last Sunday on the Super Bowl. You picked the wrong team to win. Seems to me you got a habit of stuff like that. And while I'm thinking of it, why didn't you cover the game? Just about everybody else down there at the paper did."

The truth was Sam hadn't wanted to go to the Super Bowl. He'd covered six of them, and that was enough for him. There were only so many times you could ask multimillionaire jocks just how big the game was to them. If only once one had stated, "In the overall scheme of things, I'd rate it right below the day I got my college degree," he might have continued with the interviews.

This was not the time, however, to explain his attitude.

"Fix your dentures, Morris," Ada said, "and keep to the subject."

With a grumble, Morris settled back on the bench and Stella nodded for Sam to continue.

"This is my uncle, Joseph Donaldson," he said. "Uncle Joe's supposed to be a character witness so you'll know I'm serious about Charlie. About Dr. Hamilton, that is."

"You call her Charlie?" Irene said. "How sweet."

"It was the way she introduced herself when we first met," Sam said.

"Where was that?" Walter asked.

Heedless of the danger, Sam plunged ahead with the truth. "In a bar."

"Told you he was up to no good," Ada said. "I'm not often wrong when it comes to men. My late husband—that is, my supposed-to-be-late husband—"

"Ada," Stella said in a tone that made her sound more like a retired teacher than the woman she addressed, "follow your own advice and keep to the subject. Besides, there's nothing necessarily wrong about meeting someone in a bar." She looked at Sam. "You didn't pick her up or anything, did you? Or try to. Dr. Hamilton would not be party to any such foolishness."

"There's not much telling what she would do," Walter said. "Remember what she said about sex. I was right there not ten feet away when she said it. Everything was really quiet, too. I heard it loud and clear."

"You told us," Ada said. "Fifty times."

"There's that sex word again," Uncle Joe said.

"Oh, dear," said Irene.

Sam felt the quicksand creeping up to his waist. "I'm sure you know Charlie has just ended her marriage," he said, then hurried on before anyone could interrupt. "She isn't eager to jump into another relationship."

"It sounded to me like that was exactly what she wanted," Walter said.

"I had just proposed marriage," Sam said, trying to look innocent, sincere, and worthy. "She chose a unique way to turn me down."

"You don't want sex with her?" Morris asked.

"I want to talk to her. I want to take her out to dinner. I want to let her get to know me and then decide how she feels."

"And then you'll have sex."

Sam waited for someone to interrupt, but they chose that moment to let him speak.

Again, he opted for the truth. "As often as she wants." Ada grimaced, Irene giggled, and the men nodded. Stella was the only one who did not react.

"The way Stella explained it," Walter said, "she won't talk to you. Why? You must not be as harmless as you look."

"He doesn't look harmless to me," Ada said.

"Hush," Morris said. "Let the man answer."

"She's afraid of starting another relationship so soon after the divorce," Sam said. "She swears she's no good at relationships."

The last worried him a little. Charlie had said

that to only him, and the revelation seemed like breaking a confidence. But the reason he was here was to get help in changing her mind about both him and herself; he wouldn't do much good by holding back information.

"Dr. Hamilton is wonderful with relationships," Stella said. She looked around at her compatriots. "Remember, Ada, how she sat up with you before the bypass surgery to let you know you were going to be all right? And Irene, when your niece was hurt in that accident, she checked on her condition so you would know doctors were treating the girl right and not lying to you about how she was doing."

"She's done good deeds for us all, and that's the truth," Morris said.

"True," Walter said. "The first time my wife didn't recognize me, what with the dementia and all, Dr. Hamilton was right there to explain things, how Rose hadn't stopped loving me, not in her heart. It was the mind that was at fault in keeping her from showing it. She helped me get through Christmas, I don't mind telling you."

They all dropped into a reverie that Sam was hesitant to break. Not so Uncle Joe.

"I haven't met the woman," he said, "but it sounds to me like she's a saint. So what's wrong with my nephew here? If she's so good and smart, why doesn't she see he's prime husband material?"

"Because she's been hurt," Stella said.

She spoke as if she had dragged the comment out of some place deep inside her, a tender place that had been wounded and was still raw. Here was a new side to Stella, who up until now had been very cool and in control.

It was then Sam remembered the scandal involving her late husband, the judge. He had suffered a fatal heart attack while in the bed of a young woman on the district attorney's staff. The newspaper had downplayed the incident, but the television news shows, finding themselves in the middle of ratings week, played the incident big.

Stella Dugan had not only been hurt, she had been publicly humiliated. He remembered that last Friday she had spoken favorably about having sex. The judge must have been a fool.

"I don't want to hurt Charlie," Sam said, and he was speaking only to Stella. "I want her to be a part of my life."

They looked at each other for a long while. Stella spoke first.

"Our doctor is a strong woman, Sam, but she's also very vulnerable."

He got the feeling she was also describing herself.

"Her strength and vulnerability are what I fell in love with." Plus a few more attributes that were best left private. He wasn't a complete blabbermouth.

"You have admitted you've hardly been with her. How do you know it's love?"

"I've never felt like this before. I want to be with her all the time. I want to make her laugh. I want to protect her from all harm. Right now she thinks the only thing she needs protection from is me. At least that's what her logical mind is telling her. Please help convince her she's wrong."

"How old are you?" Walter asked.

"Thirty-eight."

"Isn't that a little old to be looking around for a wife? Doesn't that make you what they call a confirmed bachelor? Leastwise, they used to."

"Some people still do. I was married once before, right out of college, but it didn't work. We postponed starting a family, and then she left me for another man. I just sort of gave up on the institution. But lately, I don't know, I've been feeling kind of restless, like something was missing in my life."

He saw no need to go into his desire to quit the newspaper and write a book. People who did things like that were sometimes viewed as unstable.

"When I saw Charlie, I knew what that something was. Deep in her heart she feels the same. I'm sure of it, though you'd never get her to admit it. At least, I can't get her to admit it. So that's why I'm here, talking to the people she feels closest to in the world."

Sam was speaking with all the sincerity he could muster. Thus far no one had laughed or sneered, not even Ada Profitt. The quicksand was holding steady at his waist, giving him cause for optimism. Things might yet work out the way he wanted.

And then Uncle Joe spoke.

"Humph, Sammy," he said. "I've never heard you grovel before, and I'll be damned if I like it. These folks are too picky, if you ask me. Let's get out of here. Go look for that little Marie Contreras. She must be wondering if I'm going to show."

Joe's words destroyed the sense of fellowship and understanding as effectively as if he'd thrown a firecracker into the gazebo.

"What business do you have with Marie?" Stella asked.

"That's none of your concern," Joe growled.

A feline smile crept onto the woman's face. "Your business is just what I thought."

"What do you mean by that?" Joe asked.

"What I meant is none of your concern."

"It is if you're saying it to me."

"Isn't Marie a little young for you?" Stella asked.

Joe's face turned a shade of red Sam hadn't seen since he choked on a turkey bone at Thanksgiving. "Young for what?" he boomed. "For talking sense and being civil? She ain't too young for that. With the way you're yakking at my nephew, seems to me a little sense and civility would be things all of you would want to copy."

Country cranky had returned, all for the benefit of a woman his uncle should have preferred over Miss Contreras. But not Joe. Dissatisfied with tossing a firecracker, he was now pitching sticks of dynamite. The men stood, the women gasped, and Irene said, "Oh, my," her hands fluttering.

Sam threw his hands up in disgust.

"Uncle, you are not earning your keep this afternoon. Ladies and gentlemen, I'm sorry if I have taken up your time."

He had started back down the path, Uncle Joe close on his heels, when Stella spoke up.

"Wait there a minute, Sam," she said. "Don't let your uncle ruin everything."

While Joe was striding off down the path, muttering about bossy women who didn't recognize quality when they saw it, the group in the gazebo were whispering among themselves. Sam held himself very still. He could imagine a hundred eyes peering out of the windows of the main building and from the apartments that fronted on the expanse of lawn and walking paths.

At last Stella motioned for him to return to the gazebo.

"We've decided to help you," she said. "But

only because we think you might bring some joy into the doctor's life."

"Joy's one way of putting it," Ada said.

Morris's dentures clicked. "It's a great way of putting it. I'm not so old I can't remember joy."

"Was Joy your wife's name?" Irene asked.

The question stopped everyone for a couple of seconds. Ada seemed the first one ready to respond, but Stella spoke faster.

"Before the holidays, Dr. Hamilton used to drop by Golden Years on Sunday afternoons."

"She's not been getting out much on Sundays, except when she's got hospital visits," Sam said.

"Sometimes it's late when she gets here. Many of us don't get to bed as early as we used to. If we see her, we'll get started right away."

He felt a rising panic. "I didn't know about the late visits. I don't want her to see us together."

"Why not?" Walter said. "You want our help but you don't want her to know you asked for it?"

"She might misunderstand. She already thinks I'm coming on too strong." Immediately he regretted the words, even if they were the truth. "That is, she's so caught up in what she thinks she wants, she can't let herself consider the possibilities of a different kind of life. And then when I—"

Stella waved him to silence. "Give it up, Samuel. We understand. She's afraid of taking a big step right now."

Sam nodded at her in gratitude.

Walter's brow wrinkled, and his full gray eyebrows met over his nose. "Let me get this straight. We're to compliment you like all get-out but she's supposed to think we did it all on our own, without ever having talked to you. Are you asking us to lie?"

"You don't have to compliment me. That's not what I want."

"Good," Ada said.

Sam ignored her. "I was thinking more along the lines of getting her to realize that a lonely life is not for her, not with all the love she has to share. She's closer to her patients than to anyone else, except for a female friend who seems to be a real ball-buster."

Damn. There he went again. If he didn't shut up, he would blow the whole thing yet.

"You'll have to excuse me," he said. "Charlie has me turned so many ways I don't know what I'm saying."

"I know Louise Post," Stella said. "I considered using her for some legal work, then decided otherwise. Ball-buster is as good a description of the woman as any."

Stella looked the gazebo gathering over, then shifted her attention back to Sam.

"What you need are some devious minds

thinking about your problem." She glanced in the direction that Uncle Joe had taken on his fast retreat, then back to him. "Believe me, Samuel, there's no one more devious in all the world than a group of old folks with a formidable and somewhat scandalous goal."

Her words bore a dismissive tone. With a nod and a thank you, Sam departed, refusing to consider what details they would come up with in their newly agreed upon joint venture. Now was the time for trust, in them and in his decision to ask for their help.

He found Uncle Joe in the Golden Years lobby talking to Marie Contreras, snapping his suspenders and looking for all the world like an old man with a formidable and scandalous goal.

A couple of children were chasing one another in the atrium, and a middle aged couple were seated at the side with an elderly woman, the latter gripping the handle of her walker as if she wanted to escape.

In another chair, one of the residents, a man, dozed over the Sunday paper, and in the background someone was playing the piano.

Except for the snap of Joe's suspenders, all looked peaceful, a typical afternoon at Golden Years. Still, he was struck by a sense of loneliness, of isolation from the real world that hung over some of the residents. More than ever, he realized he needed Charlie.

He heard the door open behind him and turned to see the object of his affections walking inside. His heart caught in his throat. She was wearing gray slacks, a navy blazer, and a red silk blouse. Her short brown hair fell in gentle waves around her face and he thought she looked smashing. He also felt more than a little powerful, as if by thinking of her, he had conjured her up.

And he didn't mind in the least that she had discovered his presence. He welcomed it. He rejoiced in it. Uncle Joe, his ostensible reason for being at Golden Years, was right at his side, and there wasn't a member of the get-Charlie-for-Sam committee in sight.

He could lie all he wanted about the purpose of his presence and she wouldn't suspect a thing.

She didn't see him until she was three feet away from where he stood. The reaction came fast: Her tawny skin whitened, her pale blue eyes widened, and her startled gasp of "Sam!" woke the man dozing over the paper.

It was not the all-out happy greeting he would have preferred. Obviously, her heart was not caught in her throat.

"Good afternoon, Charlie," he said, unable to keep from smiling.

"Is this the woman who's got you all stirred up?" Uncle Joe asked. "I've a good mind to tell her right here and now what a mistake she's making." He took a deep breath, and Sam knew he was ready to continue.

"If you don't hush, Uncle, I will strangle you with those red suspenders." He didn't try to speak softly, and he certainly didn't use caution before putting his thoughts into words.

Joe understood. Charlie didn't. Her eyes shifted warmly to his uncle for a minute, then returned to him, definitely narrowed.

Sam wanted to throw her over his shoulder and run with her to the parking lot, duck behind one of the towering pecan trees that bordered the asphalt, and kiss her for the rest of the afternoon. Satisfying as that would be, the scorn eventually aroused in her heart would be far more damaging than his only other alternative: a strategic retreat.

Even he knew this was not the time to pursue his courting of her, not even an opportunity for polite conversation, whatever that might prove to be between them. Their usual habit when they got together was to get down to basics.

With a smile, Sam thanked Miss Contreras for talking to Joe again, letting everyone within listening distance know the two men were there to look over the place, nodded politely to the woman of his dreams, and dragged his protesting uncle through the double doors and out into the January sunshine. Already the waning day had begun to slip into twilight gray.

He was in the process of unlocking his car when he heard Charlie call his name. This was a new experience, her calling him, her wanting him not to leave.

It was what he'd been hoping for when he'd been so cool inside Golden Years, but where Charlie was concerned, hoping didn't always get him where he wanted to be.

"Uncle Joe," he said, "please get in the car. I won't be long." Which could very well be a lie. He hoped it was.

He turned without waiting for his uncle to comply and was rewarded with the sound of the car door opening and then closing. He fairly leaped to the sidewalk where Charlie was waiting.

Maybe staying away from her had been a smart move. Maybe all on her own she had decided she missed him and needed him and was ready to welcome him into her life.

With more spring in his step than he'd exhibited since the age of sixteen, he closed the distance between them fast. Smiling down at her, fisting his hands to keep from grabbing on to whatever body part he could reach first, he said: "You called?"

Chapter Eleven

With Sam standing close enough for her to undress him and putting out enough sparks to start a 747, Charlotte recognized her mistakes right away.

She should never have followed him outside, not with him looking the way he did in his leather jacket and white shirt, his skin tan, his body lean and fit.

Worse, she should not have called out to him, knowing even as she did so he would respond in that *where shall we go for a quickie* way he had. Even though she knew a quickie was his least dangerous goal.

He definitely put the thought in her mind. Not surprisingly, when he started toward her,

her mind had immediately turned to what offices inside Golden Years would be unoccupied on this Sunday afternoon.

Worst of all, she should not, most definitely not, be staring at his lips and remembering the way he kissed and wondering if she shouldn't test her memory to make sure it was working right concerning the kissing before she picked out one of the rooms.

She tried to compensate for all those mistakes by scowling and snapping, "What are you doing here?"

Sam's smile died and his big brown eyes narrowed.

"I was hoping you'd do better than that, Charlie. Especially after all we've meant to each other." He paused a moment. "And all we're going to mean."

She took a fortifying breath of cool air. The next big mistake would be to let him go on the offensive.

"You haven't answered me. Did you come here expecting to see me?"

"I had no idea you'd be here," he said with a shrug. "I came here with my uncle to look the place over."

His voice dripped with offended innocence, but Charlotte knew him far too well to fall for such a ploy. Besides, she clearly remembered the sharp way he had talked to his uncle, threatening to strangle him with his suspenders, practically dragging him outside when she walked in. Too often she had seen the uncaring way people treated their older relatives, as if along with losing their teeth they had sacrificed their dignity and their sense of self.

She hadn't expected such behavior from Sam, and it bothered her more than she would have believed. Looking past him, she saw the uncle sitting inside the car in the nearest parking space, window rolled down, staring at his nephew and at her.

How had he described her? Oh, yes, she was the woman who had Sam "all stirred up." That was the point at which the strangling had been threatened.

Which brought up another concern.

"How many people have you told about us?" she asked.

"I didn't know there was an *us*." Again, he was all innocence.

"You know what I mean."

"Remind me. What could I have told Uncle Joe?"

Before she could respond, he leaned close, very close, and she stared, mesmerized, as his mouth stopped a whisper away from her cheek.

"I didn't mention the small brown birthmark at the base of your spine," he said, so low even she could barely hear, yet loud enough to buckle her knees. "I didn't say a word about how you like me to lick the spot, or about how—"

Several more things buckled. Covering her ears, she took a step away. "How dare you say such things?"

"About as easily as I dared do them. And I didn't do anything without invitation. But I'm willing to forego mentioning them again, if that's what you want. You pick the topic, Charlie. All I want to do is talk."

This was not turning out at all the way she had thought it would when she'd followed him outside. Or maybe the trouble was she hadn't thought, she'd just followed, as if he had her on an invisible leash. The breeze whipped her hair, and a strand caught between her lips. She watched him watch as she pulled it free.

"The problem with us," he said, "is that we've got a couple of yesterdays that won't let go of today. I've already reached the inevitable conclusion that we were meant for each other. I'm betting my future that eventually you'll feel the same."

Charlotte closed her eyes, but that was the coward's way of dealing with him. Besides, the image of him in her mind was as unsettling as the reality of his presence.

"We have no future together. We've scarcely had a past. Okay, maybe that's not entirely accurate, but you have to admit it was brief.

We have to be the most unlikely couple in the world. You're Redeye, Roger's fishing buddy. I'm his bitchy ex-wife. We have nothing in common—"

"I bought a Bach CD," he said. "I've even listened to it a couple of times. I have to admit the music's growing on me."

She sighed in exasperation. "You know what I mean. We have nothing really substantial in common on which to build any kind of relationship."

"Other than the fact that you've got me thinking about places we can travel and how our schedules fit and whether we'll use my towels or yours. I have a feeling yours are in better condition." He grinned. "Everything else about you is."

"Your problem is you've got too vivid an imagination."

"I've also got a good memory. Forget the towels. I'll think of something we've already shared. It's what you're thinking of, too."

"You're talking about sex."

"The word crossed my mind."

He was right. It had crossed hers, too—every time she looked at him. "There has to be more to a long-term relationship than just sex. And no matter what you say, it's all we've got."

"It's not a bad place to start," he said.

"And a better place to stop. I won't be around for the long-term. I've already told you that."

He stared at her so long and with such solemnity that she began to feel she was winning the argument. Then his eyes glittered as his gaze slipped down past her throat and back again to her face.

"Are you wearing the red bra?"

"That's none of your business."

"It was a month ago. Are you?"

"No. I packed it away."

"Along with the matching panties."

"My panties are none of your concern."

"They were—"

"I know, they were a month ago. But not now, Sam. You've got to understand the way things are."

"I could say the same thing to you. Tell the truth, Charlie. If you could have me do anything in the world right now—anything, no matter how down and dirty—what would it be?"

As if compelled, her mind raced through the possibilities. Images of long, strong limbs in twisted sheets skittered across her mind, and of hands and lips in unexpected places. Taking a deep breath, she managed one word: "Vaporize."

"Is that some new position we didn't try?" he asked.

"It's the only defense I have against you. I want you turned to mist and blown away by the air. Materialize in Dallas. I'm sure you'll find a woman there who will be delighted to marry you. You're not without charm."

Her voice quavered on the last word. Using *charm* to describe Sam was like using *tall* to describe the World Trade Center.

"You won't get rid of me with compliments," he said.

"So what would it take?" she heard herself say.

"Today I'll settle for this."

His words were the only warning he gave her as he pulled her into his arms and slanted his lips against hers. Struggling lasted a nanosecond. He tasted good enough for the world to do the vaporizing, and she was aware of only the two of them. She leaned into his warmth and gave in to his insistence, which was a great deal easier even than breathing, particularly right now, what with air being in suddenly short supply. When he touched her, she was like butter on a griddle, melting and sizzling and ready to burn.

How could she react otherwise? He had great lips and he knew just what to do with them. And his tongue was just as good. Pitiful creature that she was, she sucked him inside her and rejoiced in the low moan that sounded in his throat.

She wanted sex, all right. Man, did she ever.

Her hands pressed against the front of his shirt, hungry to feel the heat and the shape of him. Hungry hands, a ridiculous concept but accurate enough to meet any scientific test. Foolish hands, too, that wanted to rip the clothes from his body and examine him in ways she had never learned in medical school.

She was busy kissing and pressing herself against him when a shocked, "Well, I never," came from close behind her. The words would not have registered with her except that Sam eased back from the kiss and gradually put a few inadequate inches between them, but not until after he had smoothed her hair and straightened the lapels of her blazer.

The breeze died. Everything died, everything, that is, except the words hovering in the air. And her awareness of the returning world.

Unfortunately, she recognized the speaker. Or thought she did. She had to be wrong. Some things just could not be. Gritting her teeth behind a very fake smile, she forced herself to turn around. Worst fears confirmed: Her ex-mother-in-law stood on the sidewalk not twenty feet away.

Felicity Ryan was the most inappropriately named person Charlotte had ever met. Wife of Edgar Ryan, a stiff-backed successful banker, and mother of one self-centered son. At fifty-nine she was sleekly turned out: shoulder-length bleached-blond hair, sharp features, and a tall, trim figure that sported designer clothes with all the warmth and humility of a runway model. She probably thought of herself as a gazelle. To her former daughter-in-law, she came closer to a barracuda.

Which should no longer be any of Charlotte's concern except that she suddenly remembered socialite Felicity, member of a dozen art and charity boards, had taken on Golden Years Assisted Living Community as her latest project. Fortunately, in their separate capacities, their paths had never crossed. Until today.

"Mrs. Ryan," Charlotte said, struggling in vain to think of something else to say, other than the obvious. Eventually she gave up. "What a surprise."

"I've no doubt it is."

Her accompanying sniff reminded Charlotte of Roger. Allergies must run in the family, along with critical attitudes and a sarcastic tongue.

Felicity Ryan's thick-lashed green eyes flicked to Sam, but there was no recognition in the harsh study she gave him. Roger did like to compartmentalize his life, the best example being how he had kept his wife and female friends apart. He must never have introduced his mother to his fishing buddy, Redeye. It was the lone detail in the scene for which Charlotte could be grateful.

"The thing is," Felicity Ryan added, "I am not the least surprised. I told Roger you were not the stick in the mud you seemed. You must have been seeing men on the side." This time the look she gave Sam was not entirely harsh. "But I never expected a man like this."

It was the closest Felicity had ever come to complimenting her daughter-in-law. She had been pleased by the marriage—because of the prestige she believed a physician in the family brought—but very much displeased when she found out that Charlotte actually worked at her profession.

And she had been furious when Charlotte had kept her professional name.

Roger's divorce had been the first on either side of the family. All of the fault had been dropped at Charlotte's feet, for which she couldn't entirely condemn Felicity. Ignorant of how to treat his wife, her ex-husband had been brilliant at playing the loving son.

None of these family particulars offered any help for Charlotte now. What the scene needed was a little dignity. It was also time for Sam to share the blame.

She took a deep breath. "Mrs. Ryan, forgive me for the lapse of decorum. And let me introduce—"

Before she could get out the name, a fourth party joined the group.

"You gonna be all day?" Sam's uncle snapped as he glared angrily at his nephew. "I could be inside talking with Marie instead of watching you trying to crawl all over your woman."

So much for dignity and decorum.

"See here—" Felicity began.

"I'm not his woman," Charlotte said.

"Uncle Joe, get back in the car," Sam said.

They all spoke in unison, no one listening to anyone else.

Charlotte touched the sleeve of Sam's jacket. Beneath her fingers, the leather felt smooth and warm, almost like Sam's skin.

"Please leave," she said. "I'll be all right."

He looked at her warmly. "I'll call."

"No." The word came out practically as a shout and got everyone's attention. "No," she said, more softly. "I told you I would be all right."

He grinned. "You're more than all right." He didn't say it softly at all.

For a moment, no one spoke, as if they were all considering the meaning of his remark. With a nod toward Felicity Ryan, he took his uncle by the arm and guided him, under protest, to the car. Weak woman that she was, Charlotte watched him walk away, thinking, despite all common sense, how good he looked in khakis. He looked good out of them, too.

As if the world could read her thoughts, she grew flushed. A glance at Felicity revealed that the socialite do-gooder was watching Sam, too. For just an instant, Charlotte felt a ripple of pride that such a man wanted her.

Of course he was more than a little

deranged. Otherwise he wouldn't be after her the way he was.

She stared after him until his '86 Toyota was chugging out of the parking lot and into the flow of traffic on the busy street. Looking back toward Felicity, she glanced at the row of windows that opened onto the Golden Years library. Onlookers were pressed against the panes. She recognized several of them, patients who were members of her counseling group— Stella Dugan, Walter Farrow, Ada Profitt. Even Morris Weiss and Irene O'Neill were there.

She couldn't remember a session being called today, but she knew that several of her patients got together on Sunday afternoons to fill some lonely time. It was why she had stopped by today, why she frequently stopped by. Her friend Louise had flown to Houston for Monday morning negotiations on a very important case—all Louise's cases fell into that category—and Charlotte hadn't felt like being alone.

Alone meant thinking too much. Alone meant dreading the phone would ring and dreading it wouldn't. Alone meant thinking of Sam. So she had escaped her apartment.

Some escape.

"Charlotte," Felicity said, smoothing the jacket of her St. John's suit. "As a member of the Golden Years board of directors, I have to say your behavior here this afternoon was most inappropriate."

"I am well aware of how it must have looked," Charlotte answered, hating the fact that she felt required to defend herself. "It was not planned."

"It was an impetuous act, is that what you're saying? It does not mitigate the impropriety. If I hear of a repeat, then the matter will have to be taken up with others on the board."

"With what purpose in mind?"

"That would be up to the board."

Normally slow to anger, Charlotte felt her temperature rise. But Felicity had already turned on her Bruno Magli heels and was making tracks for the Golden Years door. What she planned to do inside, Charlotte couldn't imagine. Bringing warmth and succor to the residents was not even a remote possibility.

Charlotte had little time to speculate or even decide whether to go or stay. Stella Dugan, followed closely by Walter Farrow and the other psychotherapy-group members, was bearing down on her with what looked strangely like an evangelical zeal in her eye.

"Dr. Hamilton," Stella said, "wasn't that the handsome man who visited you in your office recently?"

"I'm sure it was," Walter Farrow said. "Not likely to forget something like that."

Unfortunately for Charlotte's peace of mind, the others looked as if they knew exactly what Stella and Walter were talking about.

"We wouldn't bring it up," Stella said, "but everyone saw him kiss you. Most of us were wondering how you let him get away."

Chapter Twelve

With her faithful station wagon parked right beside her, its engine still warm after the fast ride home from Golden Years, Charlotte scrunched down in the nestling driver's seat of the Corvette and drummed her fingers against the steering wheel in irritation. She would have punched in some Bach on the CD player, but Sam said he had begun listening to her favorite composer and the music would just remind her more of him.

Not that her mind wasn't already filled with images of the man—when she wasn't remembering the barrage of comments laid on her by Stella Dugan and her band of merry meddlers. Not only had they demanded to know more about the stranger they had seen kissing her, they extolled the manly virtues that had been most observable.

"He's a pip, I can tell," Walter declared. "Knew it as soon as I saw him in your office."

"He knows how to kiss," Ada said. "And you know, Dr. Hamilton, how I hate to pass out compliments."

"Looks like a with-it guy," Morris added.

With-it guy? Where had the retired plumber picked up a phrase like that?

The most surprising comment had come from sweet, naive Irene O'Neill:

"I might have gotten married if a man had ever kissed me like that. Goodness, I'm not sure I would have bothered with a ceremony."

Even Stella, normally the most imperturbable of women, had stared at Irene in surprise.

Mostly their comments hovered around the abrupt manner of his departure and queries about whether Charlotte felt disappointed after he left. After all, she had seemed willing enough for a physical relationship when he had shown up at her office, though other than Walter's initial statement about him, they hinted at the scene in only the most circumspect of terms.

Not that her relationships were any of their business, they had hastened to add, almost in a chorus. But she had helped them, and they wanted to help her. If she hadn't known how preposterous the idea was, she might have thought the five were on a crusade to mate her with Sam.

They probably were simply trying to mate her, period, the way they had earlier hinted she needed to get a divorce. How they found out the particulars of her private life, she didn't know. It was probably through one of the nurses at the office.

Lost in the background of the afternoon was the presence of the very disapproving Felicity Ryan. Not that the woman could cause any real harm to Charlotte's standing at Golden Years or with her patients, but she could make things uncomfortable.

In fact, she would probably very much enjoy doing just that.

With her parents and then her guardian grandparents gone much of her growing-up years, Charlotte had gotten used to being alone. Her marriage had done little to alter the condition. So why did she feel lonely now?

Voices echoed in the Central City Condominiums garage, and she saw Justin and Denise Naylor, the architect and teacher couple from 4A, walking behind the Corvette. On impulse, she decided to join them. Normally intense and concentrated, they looked fairly contented today. She knew they must view her as an eccentric—and why not? She was a woman living alone in a two-story condo with an undriven Corvette in the garage. It was time to strike a blow for normalcy, lest she become as eccentric as they thought.

Catching her heel on the floor mat, she stumbled awkwardly from the low-slung sports car and said, "Hello," brightly, as they passed.

"Out for a drive?" Justin Naylor said. His wife elbowed him in the ribs.

"Not yet. I'm so comfortable with the station wagon, I haven't yet worked up the nerve."

Justin stared with obvious envy at the arctic-white 'Vette. His wife looked past it to the station wagon. "I can understand," she said. "Some cars have a comfortable feel to them that doesn't wear out. Cars like that are meant for families."

There was yearning in her voice that went beyond any admiration she might have for a ten-year-old automobile. Denise Naylor, a high school English teacher at an inner-city school, wanted children of her own.

Justin Naylor yearned for a sports car.

Or maybe, if they were having trouble conceiving, he was using a car as a substitute for a son or daughter. The doctor and the counselor in Charlotte made her want to help them. But if she brought up anything serious like the major disappointments and compensations of their lives, they would not only look at her as eccentric, they would probably never speak to her again.

So Charlotte fell in beside them and tried to think of something inane to say. She had never been good at casual conversation. Except once. In a Hilton bar the day of her divorce. Then she had stumbled all over herself getting in all the things she wanted to talk about.

But there she went, thinking of Sam again. She gave up on being inane.

"What kind of architect are you, Mr. Naylor?" she asked. "I've wondered. Do you design houses? Office buildings? If I'm not being too personal."

"Not at all," he responded, "and please call me Justin. You would never guess my specialty."

"Not houses. Not offices, obviously. Skyscrapers? Parks?"

He shook his head, then looked around him.

She followed his gaze. "Pipes? There certainly are a lot of them in the ceiling. I never noticed them before."

"They're hideous," he said. "I design parking garages and parking lots. Public and private."

"I take it you didn't design this one."

"Good God, no. I cringe every time I walk through here."

"Is there much demand for someone like you?" she asked.

"Not as much as there should be," Denise said with more than a little acerbity. "And virtually none locally. Think of the garages where you have parked. Have you ever been in one that doesn't feel like a prison for cars?"

Charlotte had never given garages any thought at all, but she knew a passionate crusader when she heard one. Who was she to discourage anyone?

"You're absolutely right," she said, and listened to a wife's defense of her husband's calling as they walked up the stairs.

Inside her own condo, the fervent few minutes of human contact left her feeling more alone than ever. Changing into jeans and a baggy sweater, she sprinkled a half cup of wheat germ over a half pint of strawberry yogurt and settled in front of the upstairs television to watch *60 Minutes*, but it proved to be a repeat of one she had already seen. Out on the downstairs balcony, she heard the blonde from the apartment below talking to a man with a very low-pitched voice. Occasionally one of them laughed. She went back inside in time to hear the phone ring.

It was probably Louise calling from her Houston hotel room. Louise would assure her she was right to concentrate on her work, right to remain single, right to keep her life free of men. She had been doing a lot of that kind of talk lately. Needing to hear once again all Louise had to say, she answered the phone right away.

"I just wanted to make sure you made it home all right after your encounter with Roger's mother."

Sam. Of course.

She sat heavily in the chair by the telephone. "What are you doing calling me?"

"I told you. I recognized her from once when I dropped Roger off at her house after a fishing trip. I was looking pretty grungy at the time and smelled like a striped bass so she pretty much concentrated on staying downwind and staring the other way."

She tried to picture him grungy: shirt tail out, sleeves rolled to his elbows, faded jeans, stubbled chin. It all went together just right. He had probably smelled good, too, wearing eau de fish. Felicity was too much of a snob for her own good.

"It wasn't gentlemanly of me to run," he added, "but I figured hanging around would just remind her of what we'd been doing. Kissing, that is."

Sam's rambling served one worthy purpose. It gave her time to forget grunge and regain her cool.

"Felicity is no longer a concern of mine," she said.

"She obviously disagrees. Should I have stayed to defend you? I could have told her we were engaged and so kissing was all right."

"We're not engaged. And the kissing was not all right."

"Did I do it wrong? Maybe we need to practice more."

She closed her eyes and pictured him across the miles. She never knew where he was calling from. She didn't even know where he lived.

But she knew how he kissed, and how he had lit a fire inside her.

"We don't need practice."

"Dang it," he said with a smile in his voice. "I keep getting need and want mixed up. Sometimes, where you're concerned, they seem like the same thing."

"You have a way with words, Sam," she said. *And a way with lips.* "You ought to be a writer."

"And you ought to be a doctor. You do examinations very well."

There he went, being sexy again. And here she was, getting warm.

"So why did you really call? You probably circled around and followed me. You know I'm here and perfectly all right. Did you want some kind of examination over the phone?"

"Why, Dr. Hamilton, are you suggesting phone sex?"

"Of course not," she snapped, and meant it. The thought had never occurred to her—at least not seriously. It was an idea so foreign to her nature, she couldn't help shuddering. But that didn't mean she wasn't intrigued. No, she was titillated, she who had never used any form of the word *titillation* in her life.

The trouble was not her interest in the prospect of phone sex. The problem lay in the fact she had not the least idea how to go about it, medical journals as a rule giving short shrift to the activity. Especially those devoted to the practice of geriatrics.

In lieu of education, she could use fortification. It would probably be a little obvious if she excused herself a minute to whip up a pitcher of margaritas. Even if she did, she wouldn't know what ingredients to use, the precise recipe for margaritas being as unknown to her as talking dirty over the phone.

During her minute of contemplation, neither she nor Sam said anything, but she could hear him breathing. It was enough to increase her heart rate an alarming degree.

"Charlie."

"What, Sam?" She tried to keep the anticipation out of her voice.

"No deal."

She would have liked to pretend she didn't understand. She would also have preferred keeping her disappointment to herself, but the whispered "Oh" that came from her lips was a dead giveaway.

189

She worked up to a brighter note. "Well, of course it's no deal. It was a dumb idea. You're the one that suggested it. I didn't."

"Yes, you did."

No, I didn't sounded stupid as a rejoinder. Downright sophomoric. She was a physician, for crying out loud. She had graduated in the top ten percent of her class.

"I need to tape record our conversations," she said.

"To play when I'm not around?"

"To prove you say what you say."

"Don't you want to know why I said no?" he asked. "You could get that on tape, too."

"I know why. You realized I wouldn't go along with it."

"Nice try. Actually, talking about it would be too cheap a thrill. I want the real thing."

They both fell silent. She figured they were thinking along similar lines, about the thing they had shared a couple of times. It couldn't get any more real than that. Psychologists claimed the most important sex organ was the mind. At the moment her organ was working just fine.

The silence was broken by laughter in the background, and a woman's voice. Definitely a woman's voice. The moment between them was gone.

"Where are you?" she asked. If he didn't bother being subtle, why should she?

"At my parents' house. When I'm not out of town covering something, we get together on Sunday nights for games."

"Wrestling? Touch football?"

"Scrabble. Trivial Pursuit. Sometimes chess. We're a very competitive family. My dad is an elementary school principal, but he used to coach high school baseball."

"You told me. When you were giving me your credentials. Your mom works for the electric company, and your uncle figures taxes for friends."

She was embarrassing herself, remembering so much, letting him know she did, but once she got started with the recollection, she hadn't been able to stop. He didn't say a word, but she could hear him breathing and knew he hadn't gone anywhere.

Even the sound of his breathing sent a thrill through her, maybe because it sounded so manly. Manly breathing? She was truly a pitiful case.

"They must have felt very bad when you got hurt," she said, concentrating on the family. "Especially your dad, the coach."

"You remember a lot about me, Charlie," he said in a voice that had grown thicker, lower. And, unfortunately for her, more manly. "I like the part about the hurt."

Her hand tightened on the receiver as she pictured the way he must look right now,

191

halfway between the poster-perfect of this afternoon and grunge. She wanted to respond in kind, to speak thick and low and, real thing or not, for one wild moment give the dirty talk a try. But suddenly a thought struck.

"You called from your parents' home to talk about sex?"

It was more than adequate to shatter the mood that kept settling on her.

"Deny it all you want, you're the one who brought it up, I didn't. You're the one who always brings it up. That's why I keep calling. You give me hope."

"You're impossible."

"Quite the contrary. I'm very possible."

The voice of Sam's Uncle Joe suddenly barked out in the background, "You talking to that woman?"

He went on to mutter something else, but Sam had obviously clamped his hand over the receiver and the words came across the phone line muffled.

After a moment, Sam was back. "Sorry for the interruption. Uncle Joe can't understand why you're turning me down. Would you like to tell him?"

"Telling you did little good. Why should I believe anyone in your family would listen?"

"My mother's having a hard time handling it."

"You told your mother, too?"

"Uncle Joe blabbed. She wants grandchildren here in town. With my sister living in California, her two boys aren't very accessible."

His mother's hopes were not news—she remembered it was why he received Obsession for Christmas. Still, at the mention of children, she caught herself leaning into the phone, as if it offered a warmth she could get nowhere else.

She stopped herself. Neither Sam nor his uncle had the right to raise his mother's expectations.

"I have no intention of having children for your mother."

"I told her we weren't to the point of talking family just yet."

"We're not to any point—we don't have a point—we're not even having sex anymore."

"I've noticed."

Charlotte got up to pace, but for some reason she couldn't begin to understand, she felt incapable of hanging up.

"I've got an idea," he said.

"I'm sure you do."

"I'm flying out to Hawaii this week for the Pro Bowl. Take a few days off," he said, sounding uncharacteristically hesitant. "Come with me, why don't you? I've got a hotel room overlooking Waikiki Beach. Think of mai tais and piña coladas and, for old times' sake, margaritas served in a little cabana for just the two of us. We could lie in the sun—"

I'm on my way.

"The sun's bad for you," she snapped, fighting her own inclinations. It was the strongest argument she could think of against the fantasy picture he spun.

"Then we'll rub lotion all over each other. Lots of lotion. Lots of all over."

Charlotte closed her eyes and pictured Sam in one of those jock-type bathing suits, his sandy hair bleached even blonder by the sun, his lean brown body stretched out on a pristine white towel close by her side. She felt his hands rubbing her back, her arms, her—

"No," she practically shouted. "I can't."

"You can."

"I won't. I have responsibilities. I'm needed here."

"You'll be needed in Hawaii, too. Believe me, baby, you'll be needed more than you know."

He spoke softly, provocatively, the way only he could. No one had ever, not ever, called her a pet name. She'd been Charlotte since as long as she could remember, then Dr. Hamilton. The only appellation Roger the Rat had added was bitch. Now she was Charlie. And baby. Sam saw her so differently from the way anyone ever had. Differently from the way she saw herself. Ultimately, for all the passions and yearnings he stirred inside her, he also made her afraid. For one insane moment, she wanted to fly away with him more than she wanted to breathe.

But sanity returned before she once again made a fool of herself.

"I can't do it," she said. Something in her voice must have convinced him of her sincerity for he gave her no argument.

"Have a good trip," she said. Terror, along with a profound sense of loss, gave her the courage to hang up. The phone did not ring again, no matter how long and hard she stared at it.

She sat back down in the chair, realizing for the first time that night had fallen and she was in the dark. Pulling her knees to her chin, she sat in the gathering chill. For a reason she couldn't begin to understand, thoughts of Sam, of beaches, of her Corvette in the garage, kept skittering through her mind.

After a long, long while, she got up and went to bed.

Chapter Thirteen

"We're failures."

Stella Dugan stared at the small group gathered in her living room. They were a pitiful bunch. No one, not even Ada Profitt, would return her stare.

"We've got close to four centuries of living in this room and not one new idea has been made that might accomplish our goal."

Still no response. Exasperated, Stella looked around the austere apartment that had been her home since widowhood. White walls, brown carpet, beige and black upholstered sofa and chairs, oak tables, and little in the way of decoration—all was plain and simple, the way she wanted it. But right now she regretted there was nothing to catch her eye, nothing to give her comfort in this moment of gloom.

Worse, her harangue wasn't working. Insults clearly weren't getting her anywhere. They ought to be collecting money for a wedding gift instead of collecting guilt.

What would her late husband have done? Before his unfortunate and definitely untimely demise—which she tried never to dwell on—he had been a very persuasive speaker. Six times he had been elected to the bench. Then had come the seizure during one of his trysts and the resultant notoriety. Had his heart been half as strong as his libido, he would probably have talked his way out of his unfortunate habit of bedding vigorous women a third his age.

The son of a bitch.

But Stella could not allow herself even a moment of bitterness. She must concentrate on the judge's style, not his lack of substance. How had he, time after time, talked her out of filing for divorce? By convincing her she had more to lose by leaving than she stood to gain, by offering her stature, social standing, luxuries, friends. In short, he had accentuated the positive.

Of course, after his disgraceful death she had lost everything that made her marriage worthwhile; instead she got a big dose of pity that was as unwelcome as it was insincere. Before fading away to their couples-only parties, the so-called friends had let her know they thought her a little stupid for putting up with him so long.

They did not understand the real reason she had stayed. Despite all her rascally husband had done to her, she had loved him very much. And in his own inept way, he had cared for her.

Enough of this line of thinking. It was the looming failure of her current quest that had started her thinking about the failures of the past. Replenishing the men's coffee, Ada's protein-enriched health drink, and Irene's herbal tea, she decided to reverse track, forget the talk of failure, and concentrate on the possibilities for success.

"Walter," she said, addressing the sharply dressed elder statesman of the group—and in this group elder statesman was saying something. "Remind us again what exactly it is we're attempting to do."

Walter cleared his throat. "We're helping a woman who has helped us." He paused a moment. "Helped me, that's certain."

Everyone present knew that he had just come from a visit with his wife, who, after fifty years of marriage, did not know his name. More than once, Charlotte Hamilton had sat with him before, during, and after such visits. All of them understood his pain, but they also knew the dangers of self-pity.

As did the good doctor.

"We're doing more than just trying to help her," Morris Weiss said. "We're trying to keep her from growing old all alone."

Like Walter, Morris had communicated this morning with his closest relative, his son, as always via e-mail. He had printed the posting on the laser printer that was his Christmas gift from a year ago and had passed it around. It read like a résumé for a job, listing the son's recent successes as an electrical engineer, ending with the accomplishments of his two teenage daughters and, on a lesser note, a mention of his stay-at-home wife.

There were no questions concerning his father's well-being, just a brief invitation to answer by hitting *R* for reply. "If you have the time."

The former plumber had waved the missive around as if it were an object to view with pride. But now he was talking about growing old alone. Sitting on the sofa, he looked gray and shrunken, yet somehow fiercely proud.

"Ada," Stella said, "do you have anything to add?" She knew as she asked that Ada always had something to add.

"It's not enough just to get her a husband," Ada said, tapping a white Nike cross-trainer against the brown carpet. "Quality's got to count. Most men don't deserve a woman's trust, much less anything else she's willing to give him."

199

Ada was of the firm opinion her late husband had not been a trustworthy man. She didn't even think of him as late. He had died while visiting a stepson in New York, and when she got a look at the box that was shipped home, she'd declared it was too small to hold such a big man.

"They brought in a ringer on me," she said more than once. "They think I'm a fool." Never did she explain who *they* might be.

As per the late Mr. Profitt's will, the remains in the sealed coffin had been promptly cremated. But Ada knew, truly knew, he was alive and waiting for her to die so he could collect on her teacher's benefits. The premise was so filled with holes, Stella hadn't known where to begin her rebuttal. She also knew Ada wouldn't listen to a thing she said.

"We all agree," Irene said, "that Sam's worthy of her. He's certainly good-looking and when he talks about her, he gets a nice light in his eyes. I don't think he would have come to us if he didn't love her." She smiled sweetly. "And of course there's the sex. That must be good, too."

Before anyone could react, she hurried on as if she hadn't said anything out of the ordinary.

"Did all of you get a piece of the cake my niece brought me this morning? She called it Better than Sex Chocolate or something silly like that. When Sam gets to talking about Dr. Hamilton, I think he would be a lot better than any old cake." Another sweet smile. "Of course you all would know about that a lot more than me."

The others looked from Irene to Stella, who glanced at her crumb-covered plate on the chairside table.

"At least sex doesn't put pounds on your hips," she said.

"I don't know," Morris said, his sallow cheeks taking on a little color. "After I gave up smoking, I always wanted a slice of apple pie afterward. One year there, after the son went away to college, I put on close to twenty pounds."

Stella felt the meeting slipping away from her. *Positive*, she reminded herself, *be positive*.

"So what have we done to give Dr. Hamilton a chance at this metaphorical piece of pie? Sam asked us to be subtle, remember, and not to mention his name."

After a moment of silence, Walter took the floor.

"I've talked to her about how much I treasured the early years of marriage, about how this time of life is hurtful but that the hurt is bearable because of the memories. I said it's people without memories who are really bad off."

"Good point," Stella said.

"You didn't used to talk that way," Ada said to Walter. "At Christmas you were an old grump. Except when the doc was holding your hand."

"That's because I wasn't looking at things right. Thinking about our cause has made me do some assessing of my own. If I'm going to make a good case for marriage, I'd better believe everything I say."

"Morris," Stella asked, "what about you?"

Morris Weiss bit down on his dentures to tighten them.

"When I was in her office for a checkup," he said, "we talked about computers. I told her they were a little like pipes. I was a plumber, remember."

"We remember," Ada said. "Not likely we would forget the way you complain about your knees."

"Well, knees are the first to go. All that bending and peering under sinks wears 'em out."

"How are computers like pipes?" Irene asked. "I don't know much about either one, but they don't seem at all the same to me."

"You got to hook both of 'em up with the right connections, make sure the sewage don't get mixed up with the drinking water, stuff like that. We talked awhile, and I was telling her life was kinda like that, too. A person needed connections for the good stuff like drinking water—"

"And a place for the sewage to drain, too," Ada said. "Which it seems to me, is what you're piping in here right now."

"Ada, if that husband of yours really is hiding out, I don't blame him one bit." Morris rubbed at his head. "You can be one ornery woman."

"Is something wrong?" Irene asked.

"Just a headache," Morris said. "It comes and goes."

"Exercise, that's what you need," Ada said with a frown that crinkled the nut-brown skin around her eyes. In her electric-blue jogging suit and cross-trainers, she looked ready to take to the track.

"Samuel is back from Hawaii, is he not?" Walter asked.

Morris humphed. "Pro Bowl was a week ago. Of course he's back. Which you would know if you read the sports page. He wrote two columns about the game, which I thought was one more than it deserved. It was on TV, too. Wasn't on C-Span, though, so I guess you wouldn't have caught it."

"Spectator sports—" Ada began.

Stella caught the blank look that settled in Irene's eye when Ada started on one of her diatribes.

"Ladies and gentlemen," she said, "the important thing here is that Sam is back in town. Why did you want to know, Walter?"

"It was something I read about in the paper. The Living Today section. He's already told us seeing our physician friend alone is next to impossible. So what if he sees her in public?"

"You're talking about the town-hall meeting, aren't you?" Stella asked. "The one down at City Hall next Tuesday."

"Right, in City Council chambers. It's open to the public."

Ada, Irene, and Morris looked back and forth between Stella and Walter without a sign they understood what was going on.

"Charlotte Hamilton is the speaker," Stella explained. "She's talking about the Facets of Well-being for the Senior Citizen. Or something like that."

"Bad title," said Ada. "Senior citizen, indeed. So who's a junior citizen?"

Stella let the complaint go. "I went to one of the meetings. There are lots of questions from the audience."

"You want us to go and ask questions?" Irene said. "Oh, dear, I'm not very good at speaking in public."

"She doesn't mean you," Ada said. "She doesn't mean any of us."

Irene's brow wrinkled and she smoothed the skirt of her flowered polyester dress across her lap. "Then who—" Another pause. "Oh, she means Sam."

"It was Walter's idea, not mine," Stella said.

"I went to one of those town-hall meetings," Walter said. "It was about water, you know, not having enough and what to do about it. That's a controversial subject. It got a little violent at

204

times, what with the builders and the Sierra Club taking opposing views."

"Same thing wouldn't apply to next Tuesday's meeting," Ada said. "There's nothing controversial about our well-being. We're for it."

"Anything can be controversial," Morris said. "I guess it depends on who's asking what, and how it's asked."

They all sat in silence for a couple of minutes. Stella waited for someone to come up with a suggestion. She hoped it would be someone thinking along the same lines as she.

Walter spoke first. "The doctor won't dodge anything she's asked."

"As long as it's on the subject," Ada said. "We've got to stick to the subject."

Walter met Stella's eye. "I can think of a question or two to put to her. By Sam, of course. Coward that I am, I don't plan to be anywhere near the place."

"Nor I," Stella said. "We'll feed Sam the questions before he goes, some things that will get her thinking about him and what she's missing by keeping to herself. He'll give us a report when it's done."

Briefly, she gave the others a rundown of what she was considering. Occasionally she yielded the floor to Walter. Gradually the others joined in, all but Irene, who still managed to get in the last word: "Now that that's settled, let's have another piece of cake. Then you can vote if it really is better than sex." She fluttered her wrinkled, ringless hands, then settled them back in her lap. "To be fair, I'll have to abstain."

Having stayed late at the office with a last-minute appointment, Charlotte arrived at the town-hall meeting shortly before it was time to take her turn at the podium. The evening's first speaker, the nutritionist she had gotten to speak to her own therapy group, was already on the dais, well under way with what was scheduled to be a short introduction and presentation of food facts.

The chamber was about half filled, as she had expected. What she had to say was decidedly dull to most people, though to her it was as important as anything they could hear. If they were lucky, they would all get old. If they were smart and showed common sense and, again, if they were lucky, the process need not be excruciating.

Louise Post met her at the door. Charlotte wasn't surprised to find her there. Her attorney friend had been hovering a great deal lately, sensing something was going on in her life, trying to find out what it was.

"I was afraid something had happened to you," Louise said, falling into step beside her as she walked down the side aisle toward the front of the chamber. "I called your office, but all I could get out of Gloria was that you were unavailable."

The nurse did not care much for Louise, thought she was too bossy, too manipulative, two traits Gloria herself exhibited whenever Charlotte let her.

"I saw Roger this afternoon," Louise whispered as they walked. "He had Redeye with him."

Charlotte stopped and dropped into the nearest chair. Louise sat beside her.

"Where?" she asked, clutching her combination briefcase and purse against her chest.

The question came out more loudly than she had intended, and several people turned to admonish her with a glance.

"Eating a late lunch on the River Walk," Louise said in a whisper. "Laughing and drinking a couple of beers."

Immediately Charlotte saw the scene in her mind: a couple of guys sitting at a sidewalk restaurant, in shirtsleeves or maybe an open-necked sweater, longnecks on the table along with a plate of nachos, watching the women stroll by. Given the way these particular men looked, more than a few of the women would be watching right back.

She remembered the way Sam had settled himself on the stool beside her at the hotel bar. In striking up a conversation with her, a stranger, he had been smooth, comfortable, very much at ease. Who was to say he hadn't done the same thing before that evening, and afterward, too? Just because he had denied it was his practice did not mean he spoke the truth. And just because since then he had come on strong with a very serious approach did not mean he had changed his ways.

Both before and after their marriage, Roger pursued other women, and Sam was Roger's friend.

Right now the positive second opinion he had given her about herself seemed a long time ago. She felt a heaviness inside her, as if something were pushing against her heart, and for a moment she didn't know what to say or what to think. Except that only a short while ago Sam was yukking it up with Roger the Rat, probably planning another fishing trip, talking about women, having a good time.

Sam was free to do anything he wanted. She had no reason in the world to feel betrayed. It was an admonition she repeated several times. She knew she was right. So why had her eyes begun to burn?

"Are you all right?" Louise asked.

"Just catching my breath, that's all. It's been a long day." And then, somehow, without too much blinking, she managed to add, "I didn't realize you knew Redeye."

"I'm guessing that's who it was. I heard you

mention him so many times, I got a mental picture of what he looked like."

"So what did he look like?" she asked, trying to sound casual, to ignore the buzzing in her head.

"He's not nearly so handsome as Roger. Not that I find your ex all that attractive, you understand. The scumbag. This man wasn't so tall or dark."

She was ready to go on, but more glances came their way, and they fell silent. Charlotte disagreed with the *not nearly so handsome* tag Louise had laid on Sam. At first she had thought the same thing, but time and experience had changed her mind. Roger might be the better dresser, taller, his razor-cut hair falling more neatly into place. But in every other way Sam's natural magnetism had her ex-husband beat six ways from Sunday.

He looked especially better out of his clothes.

Struggling to erase a few details from her mind, she tried to concentrate on what she planned to say tonight, pulling out her speech and looking it over, making a mental note of what she wanted to stress.

But she kept thinking of Sam sitting around with Roger, drinking and laughing and talking about women. She was a woman. They could have been laughing and talking about her.

The idea wasn't impossible. Since returning from Hawaii, he had called her only once, and then to tell her with more fervor than eloquence that he had missed her and to let her know that if she had any sense, she should have missed him.

Unfortunately she *had* missed him, very much, even though their relationship had settled into a few provocative phone calls. She still wanted sex. She wanted it very much. It was a confession she would take to her grave.

Vaguely, she heard her name being called. Gathering her briefcase and notes, she made her way to the podium, her concentration fully on what she had to say about the necessity of preparing for the passing of years. She made her points quickly, the importance of good health care for all, the quirks that came with age, the need for patience, the possibilities of joy, the favorable odds on leading a full, active life.

Then she opened the session to questions.

Too late she recognized the man who had walked into the back of the chamber, his hand already raised. Her heart bounced from her toes to her throat.

Sam. Redeye. The rascal who had been breaking bread and sharing laughs with Roger the Rat was here. Had he come directly from the River Walk restaurant to City Hall? Had he read about the town-hall meeting in the paper and decided to attend on a whim?

Rage filled her, the kind that burned fast and

settled into cold, angry ash. Unfortunately the ash was not all that settled inside her. He was wearing the leather bomber jacket again, this time with a blue chambray shirt, and looking like a million dollars. Whatever evil lurked in his heart and soul, he came packaged very well. She was weak enough to notice and fool enough to enjoy the sight.

He walked down the aisle, hand waving high, making himself the most visible member of the audience, giving her no choice but to call on him first.

Chapter Fourteen

God, she looked good. Even better than he remembered, better than any woman had ever looked in all the history of the world. For a man normally given to understatement, Sam didn't think that was going too far.

Dr. Charlotte Hamilton, geriatrics physician and world-class tease, did for a lemon-yellow pantsuit and silk blouse what melody did for music, what hot fudge did for vanilla ice cream, what blue did for sky. And the best thing about her beauty was she didn't know how good she looked.

Right now, she seemed unaware of everything except his presence. It was clear he didn't look as good to her as she did to him. From the back of the room, where he had been standing throughout her presentation, he could see the tightness around her mouth as she stared at him, the surprise in her wide blue eyes. And something else that looked surprisingly like fury. Obviously she did not like the fact that he had strolled into the light and raised his hand, before witnesses, where she could not order him away.

He almost felt sorry for her. Almost. If she had once agreed to meet with him in private, he wouldn't be here tonight.

Arm still waving, he took an aisle seat where he could keep his unobstructed view. A few other hands went up, but then one or two members of the audience saw him, started whispering, probably recognizing him from his picture in the paper or last night's appearance on TV; others turned in his direction, and the hands went down. Only his remained raised high.

"You have a question?" she asked. "Since you just walked in, you may be in the wrong place. This is a discussion on the well-being of senior citizens."

She spoke coolly, setting the tone, pretending they had never met. So be it.

Besides, she wasn't fooling him. He could hear the underlying tension in her voice and, still, the curious anger. He could understand irritation or even embarrassment. But what had he done to make her mad? Stay away? In his wildest dreams, he didn't imagine his absence deeply bothered her, not in the way her absence bothered him.

He nodded in his most benign manner. "I'm right where I want to be, Dr. Hamilton. I've been here for a while and heard you mention the importance of keeping physically fit."

It would be best, he had already decided, to start innocently and build.

"Do you refer to diet? Rest? Exercise?" she asked, as if she were speaking to a child. "You must understand there are many facets to being fit."

The condescending tone of her voice made him anticipate all the more what was to come. Dr. Hamilton was about to get what she deserved, or at least the part he could deliver in public.

"Exercise," he said. "Definitely exercise."

Her eyes narrowed. Something in his voice must have stirred a new element in her, this one less fury and closer to fear, as if she had an inkling of the immediate future.

"What I had to say wasn't a startling revelation," she said. Her hands gripped the edges of the podium. White knuckles right and left.

With a brave, determined smile, she hurried on. "The key with people over sixty, seventy, even well into their nineties is the kind of exercise, the regularity and pattern of it. For those who have led a sedentary life, physical activity should be approached cautiously. Did you have anyone particular in mind?"

"Oh, yes. Someone very close to me."

Me. If she pressed him, he would refer to Uncle Joe. But Charlie would know who he really meant.

"Then perhaps you could make your question less general," she said a little too sweetly.

Naughty, naughty, Charlie, let's not show our pique in public.

"I'll try to be more specific. In particular, I was thinking of sex."

That brought more than a rustle of whispers. Titters, one laugh, a couple of exclamations that sounded not in the least appreciative of the topic. Mostly he got stares, from him to her and back to him, and then absolute silence as the audience waited to hear her response.

The woman staring at him from behind the podium was not the coward who hid behind a menu at Bistro Tea, nor was she the friendly temptress from the hotel bar. This woman was calm on the surface, seething inside.

"It is all right if I bring up the subject, isn't it?" he asked.

A woman at the side of the room stood up, ready to speak.

"I'll handle this, Louise," Charlie said.

Louise the Ballbuster, Charlie's attorney friend. She was shorter than Sam had pictured, with a bigger bosom and a smaller waist. But the determined look in her green eyes and the fiery red hair were just what he'd expected.

Charlie turned back to him. "Of course the subject of sex is all right. We're adults here and this is an open forum. If, of course, you're serious about helping a friend. Or a relative, whichever. If, however, you've been down on the river drinking and decided to make a joke of this meeting, you would be entirely out of line."

That brought gasps and a wave of murmurs, but she gave no sign she noticed. After the first flurry, no one in the room stirred. Not a chair creaked.

Where in the hell had Charlie gotten the idea of drinking? And on the river, yet. Was she thinking of the night they'd met? But that didn't make sense. She was the one who had been scarfing down the margaritas. The only thing he knew for sure was that she was agitated in a way he hadn't seen before. And he had seen her agitated in a number of different ways.

"I assure you, Dr. Hamilton, that I'm as serious now as I have ever been in my life. And sober. I'm not much for drinking. As those who have been with me on the river already know."

Doubt clouded her eyes, but only for a minute.

"Be that as it may, again I have to ask you to be more specific," she said. "In what way were you thinking of sex?"

"In favor. Definitely in favor."

That was a titter across the room. The sportswriter and the doctor were putting on a show.

"For those who have aged, you mean," Charlie said. "Matured, I ought to say. When one ages, one definitely ought to mature."

It was a clever riposte. She thought he was acting childishly. She could be right. He was taking a boyish pleasure in the dialogue. Except for her comment about the river and drinking. He still couldn't figure that one out.

"I'm asking on behalf of a relative," he said, sending up a wish that Uncle Joe would forgive him, though he would never be identified by name. "After many years of abstention"—Charlie definitely smirked—"he has developed a powerful interest in a woman. But he's hesitant to even consider a relationship with her." That brought a raising of brows. "And she shows the same hesitation, having been, I understand, in the same situation."

"Someone in your family is afraid of sex?" she asked. Openly incredulous. He gave her another positive mark.

"He needs encouragement. I was hoping you could give it to him."

"There are therapists—"

"I just need a few words from a specialist like you. I assume the topic of sex falls within your area of expertise."

"*You* need a few words? Come, come, sir, you underestimate yourself."

Come, come? Was she putting him on?

He kept his demeanor as serious as hers. "I need the words to pass on to him. I've been doing some reading." Actually, Stella and Company had been doing the reading and passing the information on to him. "About fear of failure, on both the woman and the man's part. Frequency of intercourse seems to ease the problem."

Charlie stared at him, the consummate professional. "Nothing succeeds like success, is that what you mean?"

"I'd call it the pickles out of a jar theory. The first ones are the most difficult, but after a few the rest come easily."

"Practice makes perfect," a man in the audience added, and someone else said something about eating just one potato chip. With one glance, Charlie quelled them both.

"We all seem to agree on the premise," she said. "So what is the problem? You still haven't made that clear."

"It's been a long time since he felt this way. Actually, never. He's never wanted anything with such total conviction, but he needs some kind of jump start. Not because his battery's dead. He's just not generating enough spark."

"Has he tried self-manipulation?" Charlie was cool. She asked the question unabashed.

He matched her cool for cool with a simple, "No."

"You know for sure."

"I know for sure."

"You must be very close."

"Very close. And I didn't mean he wasn't feeling a spark. It's just not strong enough to jump-start her."

As they spoke, Sam felt the rest of the room receding. He was alone with Charlie, telling her the things he wanted her to hear. And she was alone with him.

"Perhaps he's chosen the wrong woman," she said, just loud enough for the words to reach him.

"He's chosen the only woman he wants. And he knows she wants him, too. I guess what I'm after, Dr. Hamilton, is for you to say that sex is natural at any age, that in the absence of physical impairment, abstention is unnatural, that two people who genuinely care for each other can work out whatever troubles lie between them. After the sex, or before, whichever seems right, should come commitment. The commitment is as important as the sex."

"As long as the caring is genuine."

She was doubting him? How could she? Since they'd met, he had bared just about everything, including his heart and soul.

"The caring is very genuine. It's as genuine as caring can get."

"And both want a commitment of some kind."

"He believes they do. At least, he believes both of them eventually can. He's already sure of himself."

She took a deep breath. Her eyes never left his.

"In that case, what you say is right. Physical love as a manifestation of emotional caring is right and natural. As long as both parties are responsible adults." Sam was about to smile, but Charlie was not done. "If, however, the man you speak of lies or pretends to be other than what he is, he is deserving of being rebuffed. Or worse."

As she looked down at him from high on the dais, Sam thought of the vulnerability and strength that had drawn him to her right from the beginning. He forgot his list of questions, the listeners, and thought only of her. He didn't want to badger her; he preferred a caress. If words were the only way he could touch her, it was time to speak.

"He cares for her in ways he did not know existed. She's opened up paths of grandeur and joy that aren't on any map. She's brought light to all the dark corners of his world."

He didn't know where the images came from. He hadn't thought them out. Where Charlie was concerned, not only did she surprise him, he regularly surprised himself.

Tonight, he was surprising her, too. Her arms fell to her sides, and she stared at him for a long, still moment, her eyes taking on shades of puzzlement. At last she looked shaken, truly shaken, and very unsure of herself. She had repeatedly insulted him and questioned his purpose, yet his heart went out to her. He wanted to dash down the aisle, leap hero-like up on the dais, and console her with a deep and thorough kiss.

"And the woman?" she asked at last. "What if she doesn't care?"

"She has to. If she doesn't, there is no justice in the world."

"You speak in broad, dramatic terms, sir. You ought to be a writer."

"He is," someone said, and someone else applauded.

The interruption was shattering. Charlie shook herself and glanced around the room, as if only just now aware she and Sam were not alone. He had almost gotten to her, but too soon he saw her slipping away.

She stared at him for a moment longer than was necessary, and then looked away. "It's time we got on to another question. We've spent quite enough time on sex."

And love, too, he wanted to add. They had also talked about love.

But he kept quiet. He had covered enough sporting events to know when the game was over. He waited a few minutes, then got up to leave, sparing a glance at Louise Post, who was studying him as only a lawyer can study a potential witness. Or maybe she viewed him as the defendant in the dock.

This evening had not gone at all as he'd envisioned. Stella and Company would also have been surprised. When they had discussed the questions, the purpose had been to reintroduce himself to her, to remind her of what they had shared, to make her want him as he wanted her.

Hell, he was supposed to arouse her, then leave, calling later, setting up a date. He had aroused her, all right, but sex was only a part. She acted as if he had somehow hurt her, which was the last thing in the world he wanted to do.

In public, without any planning, he had said things he did not know were in his heart. But he had not lied. Not once had he lied.

Charlie was not so sure.

Outside, the arrival of a blue norther had turned the air bitterly cold. He zipped his jacket, worrying for a moment about Charlie in her lightweight wool suit. But there was nothing she would let him do about it.

If she went to a cold and lonely bed, that was her choice. After tonight, surely even she knew the kind of warmth he offered, the heat he was willing to share.

"So that's the guy," Louise said as she drove Charlotte home.

The meeting had broken up soon after Sam left, but her friend had held off until the car ride to raise the topic that had clearly been on her mind.

"You recognized him." Charlotte could barely get the words out.

"Oh, yes. There's no doubt."

Here was the verification she dreaded. Only an hour before publicly teasing and taunting and practically making love to her with words, Sam Blake, also known as Redeye, had been with Roger in a place and manner he had publicly denied.

Louise had seen him. When it came to judging men, Louise was rarely wrong.

"So what's with you two? He sounded serious."

"There's nothing with us," Charlotte said.

"Don't tell that to the people back at the meeting. They wouldn't believe you."

"You sound as if you want there to be something between us."

"You know that's not true. He didn't look like the kind of guy who would let you live your life the way you want to."

She didn't have to think that one over. "No, I don't think he is."

"A woman has to take care of herself," Louise said. "You found that out with the Rat."

"Oh, I did."

"So tell me, what's with you and this guy?"

"I told you, nothing." Louise's silence shouted her disbelief. "Nothing personal, I mean. Whatever he made it sound like tonight, he was talking about his uncle. I saw them at Golden Years one Sunday afternoon. I didn't like the way he talked to the man, and I guess my attitude carried over to this afternoon."

She wasn't lying. She simply wasn't telling the complete truth.

Louise braked at the curb in front of Central City Condominiums. "So who is he?"

A steady pounding started behind Charlotte's eyes, and she rubbed her temples for relief.

"Redeye, of course. You said you recognized him."

"Wait just a minute here. You thought he was the one down on the river with Roger?"

The pounding became so fierce, Charlotte could barely think.

"Of course. Isn't that what you just said?"

"Not at all. The guy on the river didn't look nearly so good. This one's the man on the phone. One night when I was at your apartment, not long after the divorce. He called, remember? He claimed to be your patient. I'm not likely to forget that voice." Louise studied her long and hard. "What made you think he was Redeye? I still don't understand."

224

Neither did Charlotte, but in ways she couldn't begin to explain. She collapsed against the seat. All she knew was that Sam hadn't been with Roger. He hadn't been drinking and laughing and ogling women before coming to see her. And just maybe he hadn't been lying when he talked about caring being mixed up with physical love.

But all this thinking and reasoning didn't make Louise go away. She truly did owe her friend an explanation. What she couldn't give her was the truth. At least not all of it.

"He was Redeye, all right. After the divorce I remembered his real name. And then I found out he writes a column for the paper. It's in the sports section. I think he's pretty well known around town."

"I don't read sports. He's not known to me."

Charlotte reached for the door handle. But her friend was not done.

"So why didn't you tell me you had Redeye pegged?"

"You know why. I think of Roger and everything about him as rarely as possible."

She fell silent, slipping into the contemplative shell that her friend sometimes recognized and honored. Tonight she needed the shell more than ever. Dealing with Louise the Interrogator after all that had happened this evening was too much. The biggest too much of all was her total recall of everything Sam had said.

She opened up paths of grandeur and joy. . . . She's brought light to all the dark corners of his world.

Sam's words wrapped around her the way his arms had done. *Grandeur and joy.* No woman could bring such things to a man, and no man could bring such things to her. This man wanted things from her she could not give. *Commitment* was the word he had used. Remembering the way he had said it, she shivered and hugged herself.

"Cold?" Louise asked.

Charlotte nodded. In truth, she shivered from fear.

Sam couldn't possibly care for her the way he let on. If he did, when he got to know her, when the years passed and she disappointed him, the warmth of his caring would inevitably turn cold.

"Something's out of whack here."

Charlotte felt the shell crack. When Louise got hold of a bone of contention, lawyer-like she chewed it to bits. And tonight, she had a very big bone.

"You know for sure he's Redeye. From remembering his name and from the paper. Since when did you get interested in sports?"

"One of my patients, a retired plumber, is very much interested. The subject comes up from time to time." She sighed. "Believe me, I know for sure who he is."

"And he shows up tonight."

"Don't forget he's got an uncle."

"So have I. His sex life is something I absolutely don't want to think anything about."

"Men are different."

"They sure are. Do you think the Rat put him up to it? You know, getting him here to harass you like that."

"At first I did. Remember, I thought you saw them together. But I don't think so now."

What a web of truth and lies she was weaving. And she wasn't satisfying Louise one bit.

"Look," she said, "let's talk about this later. It's been a long day and a long night. I have to be at the hospital early. Thanks for the ride."

She was out of the car and in the CCC entryway before her friend could protest. Bypassing the lure of the garage and the protective atmosphere of the Corvette, she hurried up the stairs. In the sanctity of her own place, she considered calling Sam and trying to explain why she had been upset tonight. He had left his number on her answering machine more than once, and for reasons she did not understand, she had memorized it right away.

But anything she might say would only confuse them both. And she might encourage him.

He cares for her in ways he did not know existed.

The burn returned to the back of her eyes. If there was one thing Sam needed less than he needed a dose of confidence, it was encouragement.

Chapter Fifteen

The flowers began arriving the next day at the office. Huge baskets of them, tropical blossoms she had never before seen, and delicate bouquets of daisies, elegant vases filled with long-stemmed roses, even an old-fashioned gardenia corsage.

The first one to arrive bore a card from Sam: *Whatever I've done to hurt you, I apologize.*

The rest carried only his name.

"Sam Blake," Gloria said as she watched Charlotte look over the array that filled her office.

Charlotte nodded. There was nothing she could say.

"I guess he's wasting his time and money," the nurse added.

If he's after more than just sex.

Charlotte could hear Gloria thinking the words.

He's not getting even that, she shouted back, but only in her mind. No way was she going to fuel the woman's already revved up speculation. It was difficult enough to maintain a professional atmosphere in the hothouse her office had become.

Gloria's fellow nurse Claire stuck her head in the door. "Another just arrived."

The young aide, Barbara Anne, drifted by the door. "How romantic," she said with a sigh. Confined to handling records and insurance claims all day, the girl clearly hungered for romance.

"There's nothing romantic about it," Charlotte declared to a skeptical audience. "He is obviously trying to embarrass me into calling him."

"I'll call him if you don't," Gloria said.

"You're married with a grandchild on the way," Claire said.

"I'm not looking for a permanent relationship," Gloria said. "I'm like the doc."

Obviously the sex declaration was on everyone's mind. If she told them she truly did not want sex with Sam anymore, they wouldn't believe her. Remembering the way he had looked as he walked down the aisle last night, she knew for sure it was a lie.

The next day and the day after that were the same. Bouquets and innuendo in the office and, out there somewhere in the wicked world, Sam waiting for her response. When she had distributed the flowers to all the nearby offices that would take them, she called a delivery service and sent them to the biggest charity hospital in town.

The flowers that came to her condo went to nursing homes. At Golden Years, Stella intercepted one particularly spectacular display of passion flowers and sent them back with a note saying Dr. Hamilton surely hadn't meant to be ungrateful to her gentleman admirer.

Oh yes, she had.

Friday evening, as Charlotte was leaving through her private door at the back of the office, she was met by one of her fellow physicians in the building. Dr. Jeremy Chapman was known as the resident lothario. Married and divorced three times, father of five, he usually directed his attention to the young, attractive women—nurses, patients, physicians—who gave him the eye.

There were enough around to satisfy even his appetites. Charlotte had never given him the time of day.

Dr. Chapman was short and peppy and looked more than a little like Mel Gibson. Or so

Charlotte had been told. She had never seen one of the actor's movies, but Barbara Anne swore it was true.

Whatever charm Dr. Chapman bore was now directed at her. At this late hour the hallway was deserted and the lights were dim.

"Dr. Hamilton," he said as she was turning the key in the lock, "how fortunate to run into you."

She jumped and turned around. "You startled me," she said.

"Did you think it was another flower delivery? You've stirred up passions in someone's heart, that's obvious. I must say I'm surprised."

It was not the most complimentary comment she had ever heard. The trouble was she agreed.

He stood close, studying her carefully, as if she were a specimen under a microscope.

"By God, I understand it now. You're lovely. I never really looked before."

"Look, Dr. Chapman, it's been a long day—"

"I was thinking the very same thing. Why not let me buy you a drink? Dinner, too, if you would allow. We've never really gotten to know each other. I think it's time, don't you?"

"I'm really very tired."

"We could compare practices."

Since she specialized in geriatrics and he was a pediatrician, she really couldn't see they would have much to talk about.

"I'm sure the evening would be most interest-ing—"

He reached out to tuck a strand of hair behind her ear. "Most interesting."

"But not tonight," she said, completely unmoved.

"You have other plans."

"Yes." A hot bath and early bed.

"He's a very lucky man."

He leaned toward her. Since he wasn't much taller than she, that put his mouth far too close to hers. He had recently used a mouthwash. Clearly he had expected more than just physi-cian talk.

With a dexterity that came from her regular walks, she eased around him and hurried down the hall, sparing only a "Good night" thrown over her shoulder as she headed for the River Walk. Stopping by Bistro Tea for a take-out dinner, she did not fear Sam would show up. She had started reading his column—only to keep up with his whereabouts for self-defense—and learned he was in Houston this weekend for a celebrity golf tournament.

Thank goodness she wouldn't be bombarded with flowers for a while.

She was wrong. Saturday brought a hanging basket of impatiens—*For the balcony, Juliet* the card read. At least he hadn't signed it *Romeo*.

Her neighbors Cerise and Fernando Lambert strolled out their door just as the deliveryman was leaving. Cerise's artistic eye brightened at the floral display.

"What lovely shades of pink," she said. "I must try to capture them on canvas."

Charlotte almost offered the basket to her, but something held her back. Juliet would never have passed on such a beautiful offering from her Romeo, even though the comparison was as ludicrous as it was embarrassing.

"You can visit them anytime you want," she said instead.

"From an admirer?" Cerise Lambert asked.

"A grateful patient," Charlotte lied.

"How is the Corvette?" Fernando Lambert asked.

"Great mileage," she said.

"Ah, you've driven it."

"I didn't say that. But in all the months I've owned it, I haven't had to fill up yet."

He laughed. He always laughed when she made light of her peculiarity about the car. She knew that she ought to sell it, that starting the engine and letting it idle was doing the motor little good. But somehow she couldn't bring herself to part with her free-at-last purchase. Perhaps because she hadn't yet learned to feel free.

Let him laugh. He would laugh a great deal more if he knew what else was going on in her life.

Bidding them good-bye, she closed the door

and with more than a little difficulty lugged the massive basket out to the balcony, suspending it from a hook the previous owner of the condo had left behind. The impatiens were indeed a gorgeous shade of pink. Whatever his faults, Sam had great taste.

Over the next two days she donned sweats and met with her therapy group to get ready for the Senior Olympics, which would be coming up in a couple of months. They met at the downtown Y. Only Ada demonstrated much enthusiasm in the more difficult challenges like basketball, swimming, and track and field. Irene leaned more toward bridge. The others declared they had not yet made up their minds.

Not being one for exercise, Louise kept her distance. Her favorite pastime other than checking on her friend was to watch the soaps. She even recorded them when she was in court. This weekend she was catching up with the tapes.

For a woman who claimed not to have the least interest in men, she strangely preferred the shows with the hunkiest guys and the most airtime devoted to bedroom scenes. Charlotte had tried to view one once. Even as a physician, she had been shocked.

Since Tuesday night, the brief telephone conversations between the two women had been blessedly free of any mention of men. Charlotte figured Louise was concentrating on the hunks. She also knew the lull in the Redeye interrogation was only temporary.

Monday morning found her back at the hospital. The first family waiting room she came to was filled with bouquets. A floor nurse passed as she was staring at the display.

"The card said something about cutting out the middle man and delivering them directly to the hospital. But your name was on them. We put them in here until you could tell us what to do."

"Any patient who doesn't have flowers gets one," Charlotte said. She spoke each word grimly. Enough was enough.

Checking with her office, she found no awaiting emergencies and managed to reschedule the afternoon patients for another day. Then it was off to the *San Antonio Tribune* sports department and a confrontation that was long overdue.

The receptionist in the lobby told her Sam's private office was in the far corner of the sports department on the third floor. After Charlotte emerged from the elevator, several pairs of interested eyes followed her as she wended her way to her destination. One of the men—a reporter?—asked her if she needed help.

"No, thanks," she said and kept on wending.

She had no trouble picking out the right door. Sam's name was painted on the glass, followed by the word *Columnist*. She went in without knocking—he never gave her warning when he was about to appear—and found him sitting at his desk, shirtsleeves rolled to his elbows as he stared at the screen of a computer.

His big brown eyes slowly shifted to her.

"I've been waiting for you," he said. "I figured sooner or later you would show up."

Sam was talking cool, talking collected, when he really wanted to leap Tarzan-like over the desk and claim his reluctant Jane. Instead, he leaned back in the chair and waited for her to speak.

She closed the door firmly behind her.

"Stop it," she said.

He didn't pretend incomprehension.

"You mean the flowers, of course. I have. I'm just about tapped out."

"Good. I mean, I'm sorry you spent so much money, but you have to admit it was your choice."

"Flowers are a time-honored tradition when a man is wooing a woman. And when he wants to apologize."

"Sometimes the best apology is not to say or do anything. Respectful silence in the face of animosity is a time-honored tradition, too."

He leaned back in his chair and looked at her straight on. She was wearing the lemon-colored pantsuit again, but instead of a silk blouse she had some kind of soft blue knit top underneath. Her short brown hair was brushed until it caught the reflection from the fluorescent lights. A small gold stud glittered in each earlobe. Except for a pale pink polish on her nails, her hands were empty of adornment. On her left wrist was the watch that could be read across the room.

As always, Jane/Juliet looked very good. Just staring at her gave Tarzan/Romeo an erection, as effectively as if she had walked around the desk and put her hand between his legs. If she truly wanted to discourage him, she would be better off moving to Mars.

Sam cleared his throat and shifted in the chair. "Is that what you feel toward me? Animosity?"

"On occasion."

He took encouragement. "And the other times?"

"Indifference."

"I don't believe you."

"You're not trying hard enough."

"You have no idea how hard I am."

She took a second to respond.

"I'm a doctor, remember? I get all the little sex cracks you make."

"I promise I'm not going to say a thing about cracks. Not even about sex. I don't care why you're here. I'm just so damned glad to see you, I could polevault over this computer and give you a big, sloppy kiss."

"You're a liar. I think there was something about sex in all of that."

"So I'm not perfect."

"But you are. That's the problem."

For a change, he was the one to pause. Something was going on here he didn't completely understand.

"I'm perfect?" He tried not to smile. "And it's a problem?"

"Of course it is. You look the way men ought to look: solid and strong without being over-muscled. You don't preen, but you could. You dress casually, but I doubt you would look out of place anywhere. You're pleasant, friendly, smart, and with the exception of your uncle, you generally treat others with kindness and consideration. Everyone but me, that is."

She threw a lot at him. He went from preening to slumping to being more than a little annoyed.

"What do you mean about my uncle being an exception?"

"I heard the way you talked to him at Golden Years. You bossed him around."

"He expects it."

"That doesn't mean he likes it."

She didn't understand the relationship between Joe and him, and he wasn't about to explain it now. He didn't completely understand it himself, except that they were adversarial and devoted at the same time. It was the kind of relationship he might someday have with her. Sort of. Especially the devoted part.

"And what about you?" he asked. "When have I ever been anything but kind and considerate?"

"Every time we're together. Every time you call."

"I'm a real beast, all right."

"Of course you're not. You're perfect, remember?" She sank into the chair on the opposite side of his desk and dropped her purse on the floor. "What you are is very, very inconvenient."

Sam had been insulted before, lots of times, by both women and men. Never had the insult come so mildly wrapped and yet so strong.

"I'm an inconvenience."

"Yes. I told you I'm not good at long-term relationships. I just got out of one, only, of course, it didn't turn out to be very long-term. But it was supposed to be. And here you are badgering me to be someone I can't. To do something I will never do."

"Which is?"

"Commit myself. Be silly-willy crazy. Fall in love. I don't think I know what that is, not the kind you mean."

The telephone jangled. Sam punched in the speaker phone. "I don't want to be disturbed. Hold my calls."

"Forget the love and commitment for a

minute," he said, "and tell me something. What was going on the other night? Why were you so upset? I'll admit, I wanted you at least stirred up by the time I left, but all I did was walk in and you were already mad."

For the first time since striding through his door, she didn't look so sure of herself.

"I owe you an apology. Louise told me something I misinterpreted."

"Louise is not my friend. I'm not sure she's yours."

"Don't be ridiculous. She made a mistake. She saw Roger down at one of the River Walk restaurants having a few beers and apparently a pretty good time with someone she assumed was Redeye. The description she gave me sounded like you—"

"Virile, handsome, charming—"

"Not quite so tall or dark as Roger, not so good-looking."

"I'm sorry I asked."

"It was her description, not mine."

"You still thought it was me." Suddenly what she had been saying kicked in. "And you figured I was partying with the Rat. Looking for women. Laughing about you."

She nodded, but she didn't look very happy doing it. Tough. He wasn't very happy listening to what she had to say.

"You didn't trust me," he said.

241

"I didn't trust myself. I thought whatever infatuation or interest you had in me hadn't lasted long."

"So I'm fickle and inconvenient, not to mention short and pale, but otherwise perfect, right?"

"You make me sound ridiculous."

"No more than you are, Charlie. No more than you are. I'll tell you which of us is an inconvenience. You. That night at the bar I was feeling restless, thinking it was time to quit the paper and start working on my book. I had the overall plot already in my head, the theme, the purpose, right down to and including the characters. Now I don't remember what the damned thing's about."

"And you're blaming me."

"Damned right."

"You certainly are damning a lot."

"You ain't heard nothing yet."

"You're giving me up."

Was that regret in her voice? Probably not, just speculation and a little surprise.

"No way, Charlie. Quit fighting your feelings. Go out with me."

"To a hotel."

It was possible that here she sounded a little hopeful.

"Nope." This was not an easy thing to say, especially since he was remembering red lace panties and a red lace bra.

She closed her eyes. "You can't mean a date. You're not asking me to dinner and the movies again, are you?"

"The Texas Bach Choir is performing Sunday afternoon. Don't look surprised. I read it in the paper. We could go there."

"And Eric Clapton's coming for a concert at the Alamodome."

"You'll go with me to hear Clapton?"

"No. I'm not going with you anywhere. You can't be serious about forming a permanent relationship with me. You don't know me well enough. And don't smirk like that. You understand what I mean. If you knew the real me, you'd be pitching me out the door."

"So who is the real you?"

She sat at the edge of her chair, hands on his desk, eyes directed at him, letting him know she meant business.

"I'm going to tell you something I've never told anyone. My father was a wildlife photographer. When I was eight, he and my mother were killed in a plane crash in the Serengeti Plain."

She was trying to be matter-of-fact, but he could see the pain in her eyes. He wanted to go around the desk and comfort her with a hug, no kisses, just gentle holding. Right now, that would be a mistake. Brittle as she was, she might very easily break.

"That must have been tough," he said, using the tone she had set.

She shrugged. "They weren't around much anyway."

He pictured her as a child, skinny legs and arms, dark hair in pigtails, and a brave, lost light in her pale blue eyes. At school, when the other parents showed up for Open House, she would have stood at the side and held herself rigid, the way she still did when she felt someone getting too close.

Not in a physical sense, but on an emotional level. The level that really mattered where a man and a woman were concerned.

"They sent pictures," she added. "Lots of pictures. I got them before they appeared in *National Geographic*. Autographed, too."

Sam hated her parents. But he kept quiet. She wasn't done, and this was her time to talk, to make her point, as if anything she said about her past could change his mind about her.

"My mother's parents raised me, but they were adventurers, too. Pre-Columbian and Mexican Indian art was their speciality. I used to go with them into Mexico, but eventually they had to put me in a boarding school."

"And they died, too."

"They were on a hiking trip down into Copper Canyon. It's south of Chihuahua—"

"I know where it is. I've been there."

"They were gathering artifacts from the Tarahumara Indians. It was a freak accident. I was just starting my premed studies."

She was still talking bravely, trying to make a point. And he was still fighting the urge to hold her in his arms. If she wanted matter-of-fact, that was exactly what she would get.

"You've got an interesting past, Charlie, but I don't see how it affects us."

"I never knew a stable home. I don't know what one is like. With Roger, I wanted children, but I don't want them anymore. Too often I've seen how people who haven't been nurtured properly don't know how to provide love. You told me your mother wants grandchildren here in town. She won't get them from me."

Her voice quavered. At the end, getting out of the past and dwelling on what was to be, she was close to breaking down. He let her sit back and compose herself. If she wanted to convince him she was cold and unloving, she was going about it in all the wrong ways.

He reached out and touched her hand, which still rested on the desk. At first she tried to pull away; then she changed her mind and held on to him tight. He could feel the heat passing from skin to skin.

At last she looked up, and there was a strange light in her eyes. He would have called it lust, but that was wishful thinking. Neither could he call it love.

Freeing herself from his hold, she stood and eased out of her jacket. He was base enough to notice how the knit top clung in all the right places. And he was also base enough to get an erection again.

"So you see, Sam, why I can't date you. But that doesn't mean we can't have sex again."

Chapter Sixteen

"You've got a weird sense of humor, Charlie. Who do you think you're fooling?"

Sam sounded sure of himself, but he wasn't looking that way, not with the tightness around his eyes and the set of his mouth. In the few months she had known him, she had gotten to know his mouth very well.

She liked him uneasy. As he would phrase the situation, it put them on a level playing field.

The trouble was he was more than simply uneasy. He was thinking her weird, which was a much kinder assessment than she was bestowing on herself.

"You won't take me to a hotel, where we

could behave like any two normal modern
adults, have another round or two of whatever
this is between us, and get it out of the way. So
I'm looking for another place."

"When did you come up with this idea?"

"Just now. Well, maybe not exactly now. It's
crossed my mind once or twice." *Or fifty times
since you walked into City Hall.* "We used my
office for sex. Why can't we use yours?"

"I can think of a hundred reasons. The windows, for one thing. If there's one thing you're
not into, Doc, it's voyeurism."

"That's a tough one, all right. But you've also
got shades for those windows."

"Did you case the joint as you came in?"

"Of course. With you, Sam, protecting myself
is getting to be a habit."

"If you're here to protect yourself, you're
going about it in a strange way."

"I'm not too sure why I'm here. I thought it
was to complain about the flowers, the questions the other night, the whole scene. Now I'm
thinking something else."

She was talking bravely. If he only knew how
she was trembling inside. But she was also
eaten up with wanting him. There were so
many things in life she couldn't have. But right
now she could have sex with Sam.

She put her shaking hands to work pulling
the shades into place and turning the lock on
the door.

"People will hear," he said.

"Wimp. You sound like me. You've got a back corner office. There's not much traffic around. Besides, they're all working furiously. Which is exactly what we're about to do."

She could see another protest coming. Lifting her purse from the floor, she dug inside for the package of condoms she had brought.

"It's a three-pack," she said, dropping them on the desk in front of him. "I figure today we'll need only one."

Actually, she had started taking the Pill, only because her periods tended to be irregular, she told herself, but she'd been on them only a few weeks and knew they hadn't taken effect just yet.

"You bought these?"

"They came into the office as a sample. Along with the literature on Viagra. I put them in my purse a long time ago."

"Just in case."

"Sort of a reminder. I never planned to use them."

"But you changed your mind."

"I changed my mind."

She waited for the next argument. Instead, Sam sat back in his chair. "Okay, what's next? In your office, I was already naked when you came in."

She could see he was taunting her, thinking she wouldn't go any further. For all that he thought he knew about her, he really didn't know her very well.

Right now she didn't know herself, but that was another matter altogether. The one thing she knew above all else was that right now, this instant, without delay, she was going to have sex with Sam. She wanted him so much she felt her lungs squeezing closed and her heart pounding in her throat. One time, she told herself, one more time. Sex was truly all she was after, and if he could only see the truth, it was the same with him.

In one quick motion she grabbed the bottom of her sweater and pulled it over her head, shaking her short bob back in place. She was wearing a low-cut blue lace bra to match the knit. Her taut, dark nipples showed through. She didn't think Sam was noticing her too-long neck.

He probably wouldn't notice her oversized bottom, either, at least in a critical way, but she didn't want to test him too much.

"It's awfully bright in here," she said. "Is there a way to dim the lights?"

"We can turn them off and use just the screensaver on the computer."

"Which is?"

His lips twitched. "Bouncing balls."

"How appropriate," she said.

She turned from him long enough to find the switch. The resulting dimness was perfect.

Right now everything was perfect. If she didn't overanalyze exactly what she was doing.

In the glow from the computer, she unsnapped her bra and tossed it aside. She wasn't large, but still, her moves caused some bouncing that wasn't limited to the screen.

Sam was sitting very still behind his desk, and she could see his eyes. The tightness was still there, but something had been added—disbelief, maybe, and interest. Definitely interest. Along with her very basic lust, it made her feel not so much like a fool.

Propping one foot on the desk, proud of her suppleness since she wasn't exactly a child, she eased out of her shoe, then did the same with the other foot. Okay, she was showing off. If he had given any sign he thought her stupid or silly, she would have run from the room, not caring how undressed she was.

But he gave no such sign. Instead, he continued to sit very still, watching very closely, and he didn't seem to be breathing any more than she. But he pulsed. She could sense his rhythm. It matched her own.

Now for the trousers. She tried to put herself in a state of suspended awareness, at least of time and place. The two of them were back at the Hilton, where he was giving her the second opinion she had needed so much. Pretending wasn't very difficult when she had Sam close by, with his special warm way of urging her on.

Unfastening the waistband of her trousers, she eased down the zipper. The sound bounced off the walls.

"It's awfully quiet in here," she said, suddenly feeling the need to whisper.

"You said no one could hear us."

"I've changed my mind."

"I thought you would."

She lifted her chin in defiance. "But only about the noise. I'm not backing down on anything else."

He let out a long, slow breath. "You're calling the shots for now."

He reached over to snap on a radio at the side of his desk. A commercial for car wax boomed into the room. Adjusting the volume, he switched from radio to tape player and Eric Clapton filled the air. The beat of the music was pronounced. It was also perfect for what they were about to do.

When her trousers dropped to the floor, she began to wish very, very much for a sample paper gown to accompany the condoms. Or maybe her lab coat. Sam had seemed to like it before.

Slowly she came around the desk, and Sam swiveled to face her. But he didn't stand. He just sat there, continuing to watch, his eyes very much on the blue panties that matched her discarded bra. She wondered if he understood how difficult he was making this for her.

Probably. He wanted to make sure she was sure.

"I thought I'd leave the thigh-highs to you," she said.

"Don't do this, Charlie. I'm telling you, don't do this."

He didn't say it firmly, but still, he said it.

"That's my line, not yours," she said, trying to sound flippant, hoping he didn't hear the tremor in her voice.

Bending, letting her breasts fall free, she rolled the stockings down slowly, one after the other, and dropped them on the floor. She was burning, throbbing, embarrassing herself but wanting him so much she could not stop. Surely he knew what this was costing her. He was cruel not to help.

But he didn't mean for her to quit. He couldn't, not with the way he had wanted her before. Pursuing her had become a habit, his purpose, his goal. Whatever lofty name he put on it, she knew what he wanted: He wanted sex.

For her, he remained her second opinion, the man who told her she was very much desired. He wouldn't desert her now. Not the Sam who had picked her up in a bar.

She stood in front of him, naked except for the damp strip of blue lace that went by the name of panties.

"You'll have to do the rest, Sam. I don't think I can stand very much longer."

She shivered, and he pulled her down on his lap, letting her straddle him, the fabric of his pants rough against her inner thighs. Then he kissed her. Lightly. No tongue, just lips, and those delicately applied before he broke away. Her body tensed. Eyes closed, head bent, she kept her back straight, offering herself, ready to curl against him and enjoy what they had enjoyed before.

And then leave. Quickly. And hope she never saw him again.

She could feel him tremble, and she waited for his erotic assault.

What she got was a whispered, "No."

It took a moment for the word to register. Slowly she lifted her head and stared at him, their faces level, their eyes locked.

Apparently he wanted another approach. She began to unbutton his shirt, letting her fingers brush against his warm flesh. He caught her wrists and stopped her. Again he said, "No."

The room began to whirl around her. "What do you mean, no? I don't understand."

"No means no. Isn't that what women always say?"

Charlotte's brain refused to function in any kind of orderly way. Pulling free, she dropped her hand to his lap. When she brushed her fingers across his erection, he moaned.

But when she tried to hold him more completely, he again caught her by the wrist.

"No, Charlie. Not today. And not like this."

He should have slapped her. It would have been a kinder if not gentler way to turn her to stone. Tossing back her hair, she stared at him in disbelief.

"You don't want it when it's not your idea?"

"I didn't mean I don't want you. What I said was not like this."

Wrapping his arms around her, he held her against him. Gently. Very gently, as if he feared anything else might cause her to break.

"I'm sorry."

His voice was ragged. She scarcely recognized it as coming from him.

"Sorry?" she managed, thinking she must have misunderstood. Holding herself stiff, her hands hanging limp at her sides, she wondered what had happened to desire. Could it be the small, hard knot she felt in the pit of her stomach? Or maybe it was the burning at the back of her eyes.

The burning was getting to be a habit she could never like.

He eased her away from him and met her gaze straight on. Was that pity she saw in his expression? It certainly wasn't the tightness she had seen before, the involvement, the encouragement she needed above all else.

"I'm very, very sorry," he said. "You'll never know how much. But right now I have to stick with what I know is best for us both."

To his own ears, he sounded like a prick. He was hurting her, the woman he most wanted to protect. And he wasn't doing himself a hell of a lot of good. She had no idea how much he wanted to make love to her.

But something told him that if he was ever to win her, truly win her, she could not have her way with him today.

Have her way with him was a peculiarly old-fashioned phrase for what had to be a very modern situation. But old-fashioned was how he felt.

And horny. Definitely horny. If she didn't get off him fast, whatever instinct was talking to him wouldn't stand a chance against the will of the woman in his arms.

He had to give Charlie credit. Once she decided to get off him, she did it fast. Wrapping her arms across her breasts, she stared down at him in what could only be described as total disbelief. And anger. Oh yes, he had definitely riled her again. He wondered if she was hurting as much as he was. And he didn't mean just emotionally. He meant physically. He had never felt so much pain in his life.

"You're crazy," she hissed.

"Most likely. I'll probably be even harsher on myself after you leave."

He watched as the anger turned to hurt and embarrassment, and then to something even worse, total humiliation. Damn, he hadn't planned on anything but anger. If she broke into tears, he would toss aside all his high-minded ideas, lay her back on the desk, and make love to her for the next week.

Three condoms? They wouldn't begin to be enough.

But Charlotte didn't cry. He wondered if she ever did.

Instead, she slapped him. Hard. She was slender, but she was strong. He felt his neck snap.

The slap made him feel better, being a fragment of what he deserved, and he thought it brought her a momentary relief. He should have stopped her right away, as soon as she slipped out of her jacket. But he wasn't Superman. He wasn't even Tarzan or Romeo. He was a simple dope who had gotten himself into the strangest situation of all time.

She took a step away from him, and then another, seemingly oblivious to the fact her arms and a patch of blue lace were doing pitifully little to cover her nakedness. He, on the other hand, wasn't oblivious to a single square inch of silken skin.

"Why?" she asked. "Why did you let me go on like this when you had no intention of finishing what I started?"

"I didn't know my intentions when you started. And I didn't know how far you would go."

"I didn't keep any secrets from you. I certainly wasn't subtle." She shook her head. "Forget I asked. Just turn your head so I can get dressed and get out of here."

Turning seemed the least he could do for her. Staring at the back wall of the office, he listened to the rustle of her clothing as Eric Clapton strummed his guitar. Someday, he told himself, they would laugh about this.

Yeah, sure they would.

He turned back as she was pulling the knit top over her head. She grabbed up her jacket as if he were seeing something he shouldn't see. Picking up the condoms, she bounced them in her hand for a moment, then tossed the package at his chest.

"They're yours. I don't have any use for them. Not anymore."

He came around the desk and took her by the shoulders, holding tight, probably hurting her a little, but he didn't know how else to keep her in place. She struggled for a minute, but she didn't put much effort into it. He had worn her out, but not in any way either of them would have preferred.

This is good for you, he could say, giving a little physician-type advice. He doubted she would agree.

So he added a little sugar to help the medicine go down.

"You are the most desirable, most beautiful, most wonderful woman in the world, Charlie." He spoke the truth. He spoke from his heart. "I will never make love to another woman again."

Charlie was unimpressed.

"Then you'd better plan on castration, because you won't make love to me." She looked as though the surgeon in her could wield the knife. Without anesthesia.

"You're right. I should have stopped you. But do you know what looking at you meant to me?"

"Don't try that grandeur and joy garbage again."

"Ah, from the other night. You remembered."

"I'm trying to forget. We might have shared a little joy a few weeks ago, but forget the grandeur. What we had was sex."

"Which is what you wanted."

"And don't want now."

Sam was beginning to get irritated.

"Listen to me, damn it. I'm after a date. A real, old-fashioned date. I don't care where we go. You name it. The sex today would have been great. It would have been fabulous. I feel as raunchy as I ever have in my life. If it's any

259

consolation, I'll be feeling that way for a long time."

"Self-manipulation—"

"Forget it, Doc. I want the real thing. But not here, not like this. You wanted to have sex, get it over with, then get me out of your life. The flowers would be gone. I would be gone. You would have proven something to yourself, but you would have been playing a part, the cool divorcée who wants no part of commitment. All I want is a date."

It was time to shut up, which was what he did. Still holding on to her arms, he felt the tension drain out of her.

"I don't know what to do with you," she said.

She made him sound like a stubborn stain on her rug. He refused to be discouraged.

"Just go out with me."

"You're not at all like any man I've ever met."

"I don't think you meant that as a compliment, but I'm taking it that way."

"You won't listen to me."

"I could say the same."

She looked around the room. "I've never been so embarrassed in my life."

"You've never looked more beautiful. There's not one thing about you that isn't glorious. I can't believe what I was able to do. If you had hit me where you wanted to hit me, I was so hard you would have broken off something very important to me. And I'd like to think still important to you."

Was that a twitch he saw at the corner of her mouth? For the first time in what seemed an hour, he was able to draw a deep breath.

"That's physically impossible," she said. "But I could have hurt you. I could have caused a great deal of pain."

"Want to take a shot? I'm not completely deflated."

"I want to go home and go to bed. Alone. Definitely alone."

"To each his own. I'm taking a cold shower."

With that, Sam shut up and stood there letting her work things out. She didn't take long.

"You won't give up until we go out, will you?"

He nodded, sensing victory was almost his. But he would have preferred she didn't view what she was about to say as defeat.

"All right, one date. You can get to know me, as you put it. I don't think it will take long."

"Two dates. I changed my mind. I want two dates."

"Two." She sighed. "That's it. And you've got the last strip you're getting from me."

Sam smiled. Without saying another word— why take a chance on blowing his hard-won victory?—he smoothed her hair, he straightened her jacket, he snapped on the light. At last he turned the lock and opened the door, escorting her through the office as a dozen pairs of eyes watched each step.

At the entry to the sports department, he shook her hand.

"The last strip?" he said. "We'll see about that, Dr. Hamilton. We will have to wait and see."

He watched as she walked to the elevator. Not once did she look back. She had great carriage. She had great buns. She had great everything. When she was gone, he went back to the seclusion of his office, ignoring the stares of the reporters and editors in the room. With the door closed, he sat behind his desk and stared at the bouncing balls on his computer screen.

He must be loony. He had risked everything. He might lose her yet. And what about her? How would she feel when she got home and began remembering exactly how the afternoon had gone? She would be justified in putting out a contract on him, and he didn't mean anything she could get from Louise Post.

He was just about to close down and leave when the door swung open and Roger Ryan walked inside.

"I could have sworn I saw Charlotte down in the lobby," he said. "What the hell was she doing here?"

Sam leaned back in his chair and groaned. The fates were definitely testing him today.

"How should I know?" he asked. "Maybe she was renewing her subscription. Maybe she was putting in a classified ad." He couldn't keep from adding, "Did she see you?"

Roger shook his head. He looked a little rattled. Dragging a hand across his hair, he mussed the razor-cut locks.

"Did I tell you she's seeing some lowlife?"

"No, you didn't tell me. I haven't seen you but once since the divorce." He hesitated a moment before giving in to weakness. "How do you know?"

"My mother saw him pawing her in front of one of those charity places she hangs around. She was probably seeing him all along. I should have known."

Sam gave up on playing cool. "Is that why you came up here?" he snapped. "To talk about your former wife?"

But Roger wasn't listening. "She was probably screwing him, too. Poor bastard. He must be pretty hard up. Charlotte is about as loving as that desk of yours."

Sam lost it. He stood so fast, his chair slammed against the back wall.

"Out," he said. "Get out of here, Roger, or you're going to find that pretty face of yours sporting a broken nose."

Roger blinked at him. "What got you so riled? Hell, she doesn't mean anything to you."

That was definitely suspicion he heard in Roger's voice. Suspicion and surprise. How had he ever gone fishing with this guy?

He forced himself to calm down. "I still want you out. I'm working. Whether you believe it or not, writing is work."

Roger studied him a minute. The man might be a jerk. But he wasn't stupid. Just self-centered and, probably, more than a little mean. Why had he never seen it before?

"I just thought we could go fishing. It's been a long time. I've missed you, Redeye. Hell of a lot more than I missed her." He caught the look in Sam's eye. "All right, I'm getting out. I guess you're not ready to talk fishing."

"I've given it up."

"You've given up striped bass?"

He made it sound like Sam had given up food.

And then he smiled.

"A woman. Someone's got her hooks into you. Landed the perennial bachelor Sam Blake."

"Out."

Roger stopped at the door. "Give me a call when it's over. Believe me, and I know from experience, there's not a woman in the world that's worth the trouble she causes. A group of 'em, yeah, maybe. But not just one."

Chapter Seventeen

Charlotte spent a major part of Saturday afternoon trying on a dozen outfits, every one of them pretty much like the others, trousers and matching jackets, and all of them reminding her of the scene in Sam's office.

No way did she want to relive that episode, even if only through her clothing. Anyway, this whole episode was crazy. A date. She was thirty-five years old, divorced, a respected physician. If she wanted anything from Sam, she wanted a dalliance. He knew that.

But she was restricted to a date. If she hadn't known he wanted her as much as she wanted him, she would have been hiding out in her Corvette. What she needed was to get him hot and bothered and then tell him no thanks, she'd rather not, fearing he would bring up the *M* word again.

Or maybe it was the *C* word. Marriage or commitment, she couldn't remember which he had used last.

Finally she decided on an above-the-knee fitted skirt and long-sleeved blouse, both in mauve silk. She added a gold leather belt and neutral high heels, which she had purchased for a Bexar County Medical Society banquet she and Roger had attended.

Rather, she had attended. The Rat had bailed out at the last minute. Redeye needed him. Redeye was ill.

She found it more than a little ironic that she was wearing them for a man who had been used as her ex's cover on one of his trysts. Redeye would not have known he was the Rat's excuse.

At least she didn't think he would.

She left the blouse unbuttoned more than decorum dictated but less than was outright vampish. When she leaned forward, the lace bow on her bra peeked out of the opening. Praying she wasn't indulging in overkill, she put a drop of Chanel No. 5 on the bow.

Sam claimed he didn't want sex until the right time came—the right time according to him, that is. Let him say the same tonight. To her eye, she looked good. She thought he might agree.

And if he didn't, she hadn't lost much but a trip to the dry cleaners for the clothes.

The phone rang just as she was finishing getting dressed. She jumped, and her heart pounded. It had to be Sam, newly come to his senses, saying something had come up and they would have to postpone their date, he would call her later, and so forth and so on.

How dare he? If anyone was going to cancel tonight, she would be the one. She hadn't wanted to go in the first place. The last time she saw him, he had embarrassed her beyond belief. Or maybe she had embarrassed herself. She didn't dwell on placing blame.

Arming herself with anger, she jerked the receiver from its cradle and barked an uncivil, "Hello."

"What's wrong? I knew something was wrong. I'll be right over."

Charlotte breathed a sigh of exasperation and, she admitted, of relief.

"Louise," she said, putting a fake lilt in her voice, "I thought you were a salesman who's been calling. Sorry I sounded so abrupt."

"A salesman?" her friend asked, not sounding in the least convinced.

Charlotte thought fast. "Actually he's an investment counselor. He heard about my divorce and wants to take over the maintenance of my savings." The lie was plausible. A month ago she really had received such a call.

Louise still wasn't buying it. "I'm coming over. We can grill chicken. I'll bring the breasts."

She pictured her friend's figure. Sam's influence gave her a cheeky comeback, which she forced herself to swallow. Better a lie than rudeness.

"Thanks for the offer," she said, "but I'm going to bed early." For all Louise knew she spoke the truth. "The answering machine will be taking my calls."

Louise argued awhile—she'd been doing that a great deal lately, checking up on Charlotte with phone calls and visits, certain that something was going on in her friend's life she didn't know about—but eventually she gave up. The moment the receiver hit its cradle, the doorbell rang. The unwanted date had arrived. Despite all her apprehensions, Charlotte smiled. So maybe the date wasn't so unwanted after all.

She kept up the smile until she opened the door and saw Sam standing there staring at her. Her insecurities returned, along with details of the humiliating scene in his office. He didn't say anything, but then, when she got hold of herself, she decided he didn't have to. She could see all the compliments she needed in his eyes.

While he was looking, so was she. Navy blazer, designer jeans, white shirt open at the throat. If he ever made it up to her eyes, he would be seeing the same compliments.

For days she had been wondering how she would react when she faced him again. Now she knew. She gawked. And why not? Here it was Saturday, and she hadn't seen him since Monday. She had a right to look. And, she guessed, so did he. They were quite a pair, the two of them standing and staring.

Cerise and Fernando Lambert chose that moment to leave their apartment and pass by Charlotte's door. Forcing her attention from Sam, she nodded a greeting. She even managed an introduction.

"Sam Blake," Fernando Lambert said. "You're a sports reporter, aren't you?"

"That's right."

"A sports columnist," Charlotte said. It mattered little to her what he did, but she wanted the clarification made for everyone else.

"You must have some pretty wild stories," Lambert said.

Sam shrugged.

"He's going to write a book," Charlotte said, wondering why she had turned into such a chatterbox as far as Sam was concerned.

"Someday," Sam said. "Maybe."

The tone of his voice let everyone know the subject was closed. Charlotte filed away

269

another bit of information about him: His book was off-limits as fodder for casual conversation.

All the while the others were talking, Cerise Lambert was looking Sam over. Probably wanted to get the color of his tanned skin on canvas. Or maybe, like any woman with a brain and good taste, she simply wanted to look.

For some inexplicable reason, Charlotte felt a burst of pride, as if she had put Sam in the sun to tan and then dressed him for display, the way a little girl might handle Barbie's Ken.

When the Lamberts were at last departed, Charlotte asked Sam if he would like to come in for a drink.

"We'll miss the movie," he said. "Dinner, too. In fact, if I go in there, we'll probably miss the next week."

"Liar," she said, then told him to wait while she got her purse and wrap.

Tonight she was the one wearing leather—a neutral jacket to match her purse and shoes. It seemed she could get everything coordinated but her life.

As they walked down to his car, he held her hand. She felt self-conscious at first, as if she were pretending to be a teenager going out on a date. But she didn't pull away, and when he squeezed, she squeezed him right back. No commitment in that.

He held open the door of his metallic blue Toyota for her to slide in.

"An '86," he said. "I plan to drive it until the fenders fall off."

"You sound as if you're apologizing."

"Roger—" Sam glanced at her as he slipped the key into the ignition.

"You can say his name."

"He told me you bought a Corvette."

"Did it bother him?"

"Yep."

"Good."

At least, she thought, the sports car had served a purpose other than being a grand space for meditation.

Sam glanced in the direction of the Central City Condominiums' garage.

"You'd like to see it," she said at last. It was not a question.

"I rode in one once. It was owned by a wide receiver for the Dallas Cowboys. But a Corvette owned by a woman is something else."

"I didn't know it was a sex-connected thing."

He shifted his attention to her. "With you, babe, everything is sex-connected."

Hanging her purse strap over her shoulder, she led the way into the dark, low-ceilinged garage. "We've got a resident here who designs parking garages. He didn't design this one, or else I'd recommend career counseling."

The arctic-white 'Vette was nestled in its resting place beside its battered station wagon brother. Ships might be considered female, but Charlotte knew that cars were definitely male.

She unlocked and opened the driver's side door. "Get in." She didn't have to say it twice.

He smiled as he settled himself inside. "Red leather seats. Wow."

Taking the keys from her, he switched on the ignition and lowered the window, then made a racing sound deep in his throat, in the manner of little boys, and jiggled the wheel. He spent a couple of minutes studying the dashboard, as if he understood what was called by the manufacturer the Corvette Information Center. Maybe he did. Charlotte had read the manual for half an hour before learning how to turn on the tape deck.

"What kind of mileage does it get?"

She'd been afraid he would ask questions like that.

"Good."

"Handle well?"

"Very well. It's done everything I've asked of it."

He glanced up at her. She was leaning against the door. Maybe she ought to jump into the station wagon and flee.

"So why does the mileage gauge read twenty-five?" he asked.

She might as well tell him the truth, especially since she could come up with no lie that sounded plausible. Besides, she wasn't ashamed of her reaction to the car. She just didn't fully understand it.

"Because that's the distance from the dealership to here," she said. "Plus a little roaming around beforehand with the salesman, so I could test it before setting out on my own."

"That's all you've driven it?"

He made it sound as if she had passed up lottery winnings.

"I'll drive it. Eventually."

He leaned back in the driver's seat, his arm resting on the open window, and looked far too probingly up at her. It was a habit he had. She wouldn't get used to it if he stayed around a million years.

"So what do you use it for?" he asked.

Charlotte cleared her throat, but before she could respond, a new voice intruded. "She sits in it."

They both looked at the newcomer, Charlotte's blond bombshell neighbor who never spoke except to whatever man was accompanying her. For a change, she was alone. And she wasn't exactly speaking to Charlotte now. Leaning one shapely hip against the rear fender, she was looking at Sam. He, in return, had twisted in an awkward position to look right back.

"What she needs is a man to drive it," Blondie said. "Something hot like this needs a man's strong hands for control."

273

Just in case he didn't get the message, she gave him a great big smile.

"You would know, of course, about men's hands," Charlotte said.

Both Blondie and Sam stared at her. While she tried to pretend she said things like that every day, in reality she was as shocked as either of them.

Blondie recovered first.

"I'm sure you don't. Strong ones, at least. In your practice, don't you treat old geezers? That's what I heard."

"Geezers?"

Charlotte thought of Stella Dugan's pride and courage and Walter Farrow's compassion for his ailing wife. Her blood boiled.

"Geezers?" she asked again.

Sam came out of the car. "Time for that movie," he said.

She barely had time to raise the window and push the button that locked the doors before he was hustling her away from the scene, leaving Blondie with hands on hips, staring after them from the middle of the garage.

"What a hypocrite," Charlotte said as they approached the Toyota at the curb. She took the passenger seat. "I haven't seen her with a man under sixty-five, and I'll bet she doesn't call them old geezers to their faces."

As quickly as her blood had boiled, it turned

cold. "I almost hit her. Why? I've never done anything like that in my life." She buckled her seat belt. "I seem to be in for personal embarrassment lately. It's got to stop."

Sam started the engine and steered the car into the traffic. "It was the strong hands crack that did it. You didn't like her talking about my hands."

"Why on earth not?"

"You want them for yourself."

She glanced at him out of the corner of her eye. He was innocently staring straight ahead.

"Don't be absurd," she said, when she should have answered *Don't be so right.*

They rode in silence for a couple of blocks. Of course she wanted his hands for herself. She wanted them on her right now. What a mess she was in. He was determined to keep them to himself.

She studied them for a minute as they curved lightly over the top of the wheel. She couldn't see any hair on the backs, but she remembered noticing a little light fuzz when they were in the hotel. It matched the dusting on his arms. His other body hair was dark. Especially . . .

"What movie are we going to go see?" she asked a little too loudly.

"A romantic one. I forget the title, but it was reviewed in the paper as a great date movie."

"No war movies showing? Or one about aliens from the Planet Kojak stealing our oil and gas?"

"Nope. Just love stories, on every screen in town."

He reached for the tape deck. She prepared herself for the sound of a guitar. What she got were two dozen strings and brass playing Bach's "Brandenburg Concerto No. 4."

She refused to satisfy him by looking surprised. But she couldn't help it twenty minutes later when he pulled in front of a two-story limestone house in an old neighborhood on the south side of town.

"They have a movie screen in there?"

"Let me think. Cribbage board, card table, basketball net in the driveway, twenty-four-inch color TV with a five-year-old VCR that Mom can't program yet. But no movie screen."

"Mom?" Charlotte stiffened. "You've brought me here to meet your mom?"

"Dad, too. Uncle Joe you already know."

She tightened her hold on the seat belt that angled across her chest. "I'm not getting out."

"Then they'll come out here. We're a very flexible family, and very stubborn."

She buried her head in her hands. "This isn't fair. What have you told them about me? That I'm going to be the mother of their grandchildren? That I'm the shameless hussy you met in

276

a bar and believe, in a state of delusion, you cannot live without?"

"Not quite so much. Nothing that would compromise you. Nothing that would embarrass you."

He was out of the car and holding open the door for her before she could get in another question.

"They really will come out here," he said. "I promise, we won't stay long. We don't want to miss the start of the movie."

"You haven't said exactly what you told them."

Before he could respond, the front door opened and a round, maternal woman in her late fifties stepped onto the porch.

"Sam, is that you?" a sweet voice trilled.

"She knows it is," he said out of the corner of his mouth. "She could close her eyes and draw what you're wearing, and she's had a stopwatch on how long we've sat out front."

Uh-oh.

She plastered on a smile. Somehow she would get Sam for this. If he ever again came on to her, she just might have the motivation now to turn him down.

A gray-haired man with a developing middle stepped out beside her. Dad. Uncle Joe was probably right behind.

The woman came down the sidewalk to

meet Charlotte, followed closely by her husband. "I'm Ellen Blake," she said, hand extended, "and this is Thomas. That's Joe lurking in the doorway, but I believe you already know him."

"We met at Golden Years," Charlotte said.

Ellen Blake's voice dropped. "Don't mention that place to him. He's convinced Sam's going to lock him away in one of the cells."

"Rooms," Sam said. "And suites. Apartments, too. There are no cells at Golden Years."

"That's what Joe calls them. Anyway, Dr. Hamilton, it's so nice of you to agree to drop by. When Sam said he was dating a doctor, we were quite surprised."

"Why?" Charlotte asked as she walked up the front steps onto the porch. "who does he usually date?"

"I don't know. He keeps them a secret. I've always thought maybe he was ashamed of them, you know, with the way young women can be these days."

Charlotte knew, since she was, if not exactly young, definitely a woman of these days. The kind that got picked up in bars.

"But he's not ashamed of me," she said.

"Oh, no, is he, Tom? You're the first woman he's brought by since . . . well, since that unfortunate person he married. But we won't go into that."

"Do you have time for a drink, Dr. Hamilton?" Thomas Blake asked. "Tea? Coffee? A martini?"

"Please call me Charlotte," she heard herself say. "And nothing to drink, thanks."

"You ought to take the martini," he said. "Ellen's not through pumping you for information. She'll know your blood type before you leave."

"B-positive," Charlotte said, then glanced at Sam, silently asking him if it weren't time to go.

She preceded them into the living room, where Joe was standing, snapping his red suspenders. "If you've come to take me away, forget it. I'm not leaving."

No one seemed to be paying any attention to him, so she followed suit.

Ellen Blake took Charlotte's leather jacket, then gestured for her to sit on the sofa and sat beside her. The men took facing chairs, except for Joe, who continued to stand close to the door, looking out, as if someone would be coming along any minute to drag him away.

Charlotte took a second to study the room. She saw lots of comfortable-looking furniture, canary-yellow walls, matching draperies, and a worn Oriental carpet on the floor. One round table held a gallery of framed family pictures. On another, the card table Sam had mentioned, was a chess set, a game obviously in progress.

She didn't know whether to feel at home or

out of place. The latter, probably, considering the way Ellen Blake was studying her.

"Sam didn't tell us much except that you aren't married," Ellen said. "Have you ever been?"

Sam started to speak, but Charlotte shook him off. "I'm recently divorced."

It was the first time she had actually said the words to someone she'd just met. She expected to feel remorse, embarrassment, regret—something. But she felt nothing, not even relief. She was divorced. It was a fact, like the color of her hair.

"Were there any children?"

"No," Charlotte said. She started to add that as far as she knew she was fertile, if that was a concern, the way she had volunteered her blood type, but that would have sounded rude. Besides, she dealt with blunt-speaking people every day. Sam's mother did not intimidate her.

But she did cause some irritation.

Charlotte smiled at Sam's dad. "You're a school principal. I'm sure that's a difficult job."

"Challenging," he said. "It's a great deal harder than being a coach, which is how I started out." He hesitated a minute. "Did Sam tell you he played ball once? Could have been a professional. Except for the knee injury. Bad one, it was."

She could see he still hurt for his son.

"At least," she said, trying to take an upbeat tone, "it didn't leave a bad scar."

That brought all conversation to a halt. It was winter and there was no way she could have seen their thirty-eight-year-old son in bathing trunks or shorts. Except boxer shorts, of course. Sam really did wear boxers. He looked great in them, too.

Ellen was the first to break the silence. "I've got a collection of Sam's columns and news stories. They go back more than ten years, to when he was covering high school games." She reached for a scrapbook on the coffee table in front of them and flipped it open. "Here is the first one where they used his picture." She stared at it for a long time before passing it on.

Charlotte felt Sam's eyes on her as she looked at the yellowed clipping about a high school football game. Mostly she looked at Sam's picture. His hair was longer, practically covering his ears, his face leaner, his eyes wide and dark. He looked young and handsome, and something turned inside her. Like his mother before her, she found it hard to look away.

When she finally glanced up, she saw Sam staring at her. It was as if he were testing her on something, and she had no idea whether she passed or failed.

She set the scrapbook aside. She felt a tightness in her chest that seemed far too close to panic.

"Don't we have a movie to catch?" she asked.

"Yes, we do," Sam said and stood.

Giving up on courtesy, she beat him to the door, grabbing her coat on the way, and turned to bid his parents a good evening.

"Sam's a good man," said Joe, who had kept apart from the rest. "Don't go treating him wrong."

She turned in surprise toward him. Here was a Joseph Donaldson she hadn't seen before—a concerned uncle who wasn't afraid to speak up for someone he loved. Before she could respond, Sam hustled her out the door.

"Do come back, Charlotte," Ellen called out as they walked down the stairs. "You look like you might be good at Trivial Pursuit."

Charlotte responded with something non-committal. In the car she was not quite so vague.

"Why did you do that, Sam? What are you trying to do to me?"

"Nothing bad, Charlie. They wanted to know what I was doing tonight. I told them. They asked me to bring you by." Resting his arm on the steering wheel, he shifted to face her. "Was it so horrible?"

Remembering the photo in the newspaper clipping, she looked at him in the growing evening dimness, then looked away. Her insides were still turning, but not in panic, not now. She felt as if something strong and solid was giving way. She loved the feeling and hated it at the same time.

"No," she said with a sigh. "It wasn't horrible."

That was the problem, she could have added. It should have been awful, but Ellen and Thomas Blake loved their son very much and were proud of him. They had kept a scrapbook of his writing, for crying out loud. And played Trivial Pursuit, as well as chess. They had provided a loving home for their son, and they knew, better than he, that he needed the same thing when he started his own family.

Needed and deserved.

His uncle knew it, too.

Sam was too perfect. More than ever he made her feel inadequate. She couldn't stand him just then.

He didn't seem to notice. Leaning over the four-on-the-floor gear shift, he managed to put his arms around her.

"They're watching," she said, as if mere words would stop him when he was on a quest.

"Let's give them something to see. It will make Mom's night. And if I do it right, it just might make mine."

He did it right. Of course. His lips slanted across hers, warm and soft, then slanted the other way, and his tongue tickled its way inside her mouth. She moaned. He tickled some more, and then he seemed to swell inside her, making her forget tickling and concentrate on sucking and holding on to him and wishing they were naked and lying in a bed.

Kissing Sam wasn't nearly enough. At least not just on the lips. She wanted to kiss him everywhere, and suck and hold him, too.

He broke the kiss and leaned his forehead against hers. Neither of them spoke for a couple of minutes, focusing instead on drawing ragged breaths. She was holding on to his coat sleeves as if he would bolt from the car if she let go. He was doing a pretty fair job himself of holding on to her.

"What will they think?" she managed when it seemed safe to expend air on words.

"Who?"

"Your parents."

"Oh, them. They'll think we like to touch each other."

"They already figured that one out."

At last they broke their respective holds, and Sam started the car while Charlotte pulled out a mirror to fix her lipstick. She felt like she was sixteen years old.

And as old as the Blakes' limestone house, which she figured was built around the turn of the century.

"What was it really about, Sam? The visit. It wasn't just your mother's idea."

"That part's true. But I thought if you met

them and stayed a few minutes in their house, you would see how such a place could be yours. I don't mean the furniture. I meant a place with a family inside."

She closed her eyes a moment. He tempted her and, worse, he hurt her more than he could ever know, and all in pursuit of a good cause, the way he had in his office when he turned her down. She wished that just once he would be intentionally cruel. Cruelty she knew how to fight.

"You were wrong," she said. "I didn't feel at home. I felt awkward. Out of place. I felt like an importer pretending to be a daughter-in-law candidate when I'm no such thing."

"That's not how they viewed you."

"How in the world can you know that?"

"Mom asked you to play Trivial Pursuit. She doesn't do that with very many people."

"So she can't judge me any better than you can. What does that prove?"

They looked at each other in the darkened car, and Charlotte could imagine the regret in Sam's eyes.

"Okay, I rushed things," he said. "She was ready and you weren't."

She sighed. It was as close as she could get to extracting an admission of wrongdoing from him.

"Wanna grab a bite to eat?" he asked, gunning the engine. "We can go to the late show."

She nodded, not trusting herself to speak. Try as she might, she could not stay angry with him. With good reason. Every time she licked her lips, she tasted him. Every breath she took brought his scent. There was no escaping him, even if she had wanted to. He gave her things to think about.

But she could not allow him to make her dream.

At the Mexican restaurant where he took her, a popular new place near downtown, she picked at her food. She even declined to order a margarita, asking for water instead. Several times she could see him debating whether to ask her what was wrong. But he never did.

What would she have told him? That they didn't belong together on any kind of basis? That he needed to start looking for a real woman to be his real wife? If she had ever for an instant doubted it before, a half hour with the Blakes had convinced her of the truth: She was not the woman for Sam, not for any purpose, not even sex.

He was, of course, the perfect man for her, for the purpose she wanted, but she had already told him that.

Outside, as they stood in the bright neon lights that fell on the foliage bordering the sidewalk, she watched in dismay as Dr. Jeremy Chapman and a very young woman walked by.

The two doctors nodded in greeting, and Sam got a very thorough once-over.

Behind them came Mrs. Elvira Cochran, a volunteer at Golden Years, accompanied by the daughter Charlotte had met a couple of weeks ago. She nodded at the pair, then turned away and could have sworn she saw one of the anesthesiologists from the hospital standing in the restaurant door. Half the medical and caregiving professionals were out for Mexican food tonight. Just as she was noticing them, they were noticing her.

The night could not possibly get any worse. Shutting them all out, she begged off from the movie.

"I must be a big disappointment to you," she said softly, just to him. "Some hot date. One kiss. Not even any groping. You could have at least expected a touch or two."

"You're never a disappointment." He leaned close and brushed his lips against her cheek. "Let's go where we can talk."

My place or yours? She could almost hear him say the words.

What she actually did hear was a loud, "I'll be damned. It's Redeye and my cold, cold ex."

She cringed, Sam muttered "Damn," and they both looked up to see Roger and a statuesque redhead in a tight bodysuit walking their way. Her first thought was that the woman must be chilled without a jacket. She would be coming down with a chest cold.

Considering her chest, the illness could be serious indeed.

Sam put a protective arm around her and they both faced the pair. One couple having a chance meeting with another couple, most of them acquainted, all of them out for a good time on a Saturday night.

That was what she hoped it looked like.

Actually, she could see the anger in the Rat's glittering little eyes.

"I knew my wife was screwing somebody," he said so everyone within fifty yards could hear. "I just didn't know it was my best friend."

Chapter Eighteen

"Cool it, Roger," Sam said.

He was trying to be calm, trying to be civil, when he wanted to yank the jerk's arm from his shoulder and beat him over the head with it.

Roger, of course, had no intention of civility.

"When did you two get together?" he asked. "About the time I moved out, I'll bet. Or earlier. Definitely could have been one of the nights I wasn't home."

Sam leaned close. "Lower your voice or I'll rip out your throat and I promise you will never talk again."

He said it amiably enough, for anyone who

might be looking at his expression, and low enough so that no one could actually hear.

Roger's answer was a smirk. "I knew it. I just knew it."

"Roggie, honey, is something wrong?" It was the redhead speaking. "Do you know these people?"

Roger's companion for the evening had obviously been chosen for attributes other than mental acuity.

Like Roger, Sam used her, but not in the manner his former fishing buddy would ever have chosen. He smiled at her in a polite and respectful way.

"Good evening. I'm Sam and this is Charlotte. And you are—"

"Cut the crap."

Roger really was a bore, Sam decided. And loud. He was always quiet by a fishing stream.

Roger stared at his ex. "You didn't answer me. How long have you known him?"

Charlotte looked from Roger to Sam with a stunned look in her eyes, as if she couldn't believe what was happening, after all that had gone before. Sam had never seen the look before. He would have bitten off Mike Tyson's ear to put a smile of confidence back on her face.

"Careful," Sam warned. There was a threat in his voice. Even the redhead heard it. Roger should also have taken notice.

But of course he didn't.

"You're the one that was pawing her in front of my mother," he said to Sam. "I'll be damned." Another thought occurred, not a particularly brilliant one. "Hey, in your office the other day, you said you hadn't seen her. Buddy, you lied. I'll bet before I got there, you two were getting it on."

What the statement lacked in subtlety, it unfortunately compensated for in accuracy.

"It's been nice meeting you," Sam said to the round-eyed companion. "You, Roggie honey, can go to hell."

Roger took a swing at him. Sam ducked and drove a fist into Roger's gut. Finally the guy shut up. Doubling over, he worked at breathing again. Sam, on the other hand, was feeling fine, better than he'd felt since Charlie's kiss. He felt so good he yearned for the Rat to swing at him again.

The redhead's contribution was a scream, which drew the attention of anyone in the Saturday night crowd who was not already observing the argument.

He looked at Charlie, who was rooted to the sidewalk, her face the color of white neon. Taking her by the arm, he dragged her away from the lights, into the dark street, thinking if she didn't hurry he would sling her over his shoulder and carry her to the car.

Tarzan did such things for his Jane.

Behind them, he could hear some talking, a few exclamations, but nothing specific, nothing resembling *STOP THAT MAN!*, which was all right with him.

Charlie said nothing as he eased her into the car, started the engine, put distance between her and her ex. She didn't speak until he pulled up to the curb in front of CC Condominiums.

"I'm moving to Canada," she muttered to the windshield. "Tomorrow. I wonder how long it will take me to get a license to practice medicine there."

"Don't you think that's a bit drastic?"

"Not in the least. For the first couple of miles I was considering Egypt, but I wouldn't like all those veils."

"I'm not sure all the women in Egypt wear veils."

"I would."

"You're not making sense."

She buried her face in her hands. "I know."

He peeled down a couple of fingers to make sure she wasn't crying. Good. He wasn't sure he could soothe away her tears. Or rather, that she would let him.

Since she seemed incapable of moving on her own, he helped her out and held her arm as he guided her up the stairs to her front door. Fumbling in her purse, he found her keys and followed her inside. She made it to the living room couch before collapsing.

Awkwardly, he eased her out of her jacket and tossed it onto a chair, along with his blazer. She kicked off her shoes and dropped her head back, eyes closed, legs stretched out in front of her. Her short skirt hiked a little higher and pulled tight across her thighs. He shouldn't have noticed, but he did.

"You need a drink," he said. "Don't tell me you don't."

"Sherry," she said. "There's a bottle in the wine rack over the sink."

He brought two glasses, but decided this wasn't the time for a toast. Sitting up, she downed half of hers in one swallow, shuddered, finished it off, then stretched out once again. If the sherry was doing for her what it was doing for him, she was beginning to feel relaxed.

He touched her arm. She felt as unyielding as the floor.

He set his glass aside, along with hers, and kneeled in front of her. She paid no attention.

"What kind of hose are you wearing?" he asked, rolling up his sleeves. The room was getting warm.

"Huh?"

At least he was getting noticed.

"The hose. The kind." He should keep to one-syllable words for a while.

"Panty hose."

"Drat it. You'll have to take them off."

"You're crazy."

"I want to massage your feet. Nothing like a good foot rub to settle a person's nerves. Reflexology, it's sometimes called. Manipulating the reflexes, you understand."

"I know. I'm a doctor."

He kept kneeling. At last she sighed. "Look the other way."

He started to say something about locking the barn door after the horse had been stolen, but he didn't think she would appreciate the comment. So he looked away, then after a minute looked back again when she returned to the couch. The hose formed a soft flesh-toned mound on the table beside her.

Taking up one now-bare foot, he worked his hands against its tautness, using fingers and palms.

She sighed. "That was awful. Not the foot. Not this. Earlier, I mean."

"I know. Roger's a jerk. He should never have talked about you that way. There were people around who recognized you."

"He's a rat. But I wasn't thinking about me. I'll survive. I was thinking about you." His thumbs worked the arch, and she caught her breath before going on. "You're known around town far more than I am. And you hit him. There's bound to be talk. And writing. Yours isn't the only column in town."

"As long as they spell my name right. Besides, he tried to hit me first."

"You did a better job."

"Yeah, I did, didn't I?"

She peered at him through slitted eyes. "You enjoyed it."

He shifted to her other foot. "It had its moments."

"Men."

She fell silent and he kept on rubbing. He didn't know just when the rubbing became caressing, but he began to breathe a little heavier, and after a moment so did she. He shifted to her calf. She parted her legs, just a fraction; if he were hoping to have sex with her tonight, the movement could definitely be taken as an invitation.

But he had promised himself to tease her, to taunt her, to drive her crazy with wanting him, so crazy she would agree to be his wife.

He hadn't taken into account the way she had needed him tonight, the way she needed him now, not just physically, but emotionally as well, to serve as her support and her comfort. Wouldn't he be a bigger prick than he had been in his office if he walked out after making her want him?

If they were not going to have sex tonight, he had better sprint for the door. Immediately.

Instead, he stroked the backs of her knees. She caught her breath and opened her eyes.

"If you start something right now and don't finish it," she whispered, "I'll run out on the balcony and start screaming rape."

"Some Juliet you are."

"I just want a Romeo."

"Casting closed. I'm it."

His fingers worked to the inside of her thighs, where her skin was smooth as velvet and warm as the sun, and he could almost feel the moisture forming, like dew on the petals of a rose. He knew he could push up her skirt, pull down his pants, and take her right here on the couch. But that wasn't the way he wanted it. And it wasn't the way she needed it, not with the way things had gone tonight.

Standing, he took her hands and pulled her to her feet.

"I'm not stripping," she said.

"I know." He ran his hands down the cool silk sleeves of her blouse and felt the warm flesh beneath. "You said you wouldn't, and I believed you."

He lifted her in his arms and felt relief when she didn't fight him. "The bedroom?"

She nodded toward an open door. She had a high, wide bed with a hundred pillows and a comforter made of satin, everything in shades of brown with touches of red. There were a couple of chairs, a carved mahogany armoire the size of Utah, a dresser with a big gilt-framed mirror hanging over it on the off-white wall, and at the far end a wide glass door opening onto the balcony. Windows flanked the door, providing a great view of the river and the city lights beyond.

Romeo never had it so good. Neither, of course, had Tarzan.

He dipped his head to the opening in her blouse. "You smell good."

"It's the perfume."

"You choose good stuff."

"I choose good men."

He lifted his head. "Not all of the time."

The half smile on her face died a quick death. "I was thinking of you. Not . . . anyone else."

"And I reminded you of him. I'm sorry."

"So make me forget him again."

"Can do." At least he hoped he could. He would keep working at it if it took all night.

He set her on her feet and unbuckled her belt, tossed it aside, and pulled her blouse from the waistband of her skirt, made fast work of the buttons, and studied the pink bra she was wearing underneath.

"You have a lot of underwear."

She looked down. "I have to wear something. This is about as little as I can get away with and still have the thing do its job."

"I didn't mean all at once, I meant collectively."

"Not so much. You've seen only three bras."

"But they're different colors. And they match

297

what you're wearing. You dress good from the skin out."

"I didn't before I met you." She looked up at him. "Most men wouldn't notice."

"Most men aren't perfect."

She grimaced, which was not the response he was after.

"You're perfectly slow. If you don't hurry up, I'm going to do something we'll both regret."

"Which is?"

"Go to sleep."

"You know how to hurt a guy."

He sped up, unhooking her skirt, letting it fall to the floor, watching her kick it aside. She was down to bra and panties, both pink, both smaller than the dot in dot com.

She reached back to unhook the bra and tossed it aside.

"I know I swore I wouldn't," she said. "But you motivated me."

"Hot damn."

"Or maybe you just took too long."

"You like it slow. You know you do."

She made a little cat-like sound in her throat that was very satisfying.

He looked at the hard brown tips of her breasts and at the wider circle of slightly paler brown surrounding them, and at the creamy fullness that finished them off. They were not merely nice breasts, they were world class.

Looking, he made a tiger-like growl in his throat that brought a smile to her lips.

"We're animals," he said.

"Yeah." Her eyes burned. "Strip down to your fur."

He showed her he wasn't always slow, getting down to his boxer shorts before she could take a second breath. There they were, panties and boxers, man and woman, hard and full where they ought to be. Mostly she was soft. And incredibly desirable.

Turning away from him, she began to throw the pillows off the bed. One landed against his chest. He picked it up and hit her rear, gently but solidly enough so that she felt it. She looked at him over her shoulder. He wedged the pillow between her legs and brought it up to where it made contact with her underwear. And he pulled it back and forth.

She forgot the pillows. He was getting her where she wanted most to be got. And she wasn't thinking of anything except what he was doing and where he was touching. He almost came just watching the arch of her back and the concentration she gave to what had started out as a game.

Easing the pillow from between her legs, he held himself in its place, his loins against her buttocks, his erection probing the right places, the way a divining rod probed for gold. Heck, maybe it was water. He couldn't think very clearly at the moment, searching as he was for the mother lode.

Hooking the band of his boxers with one thumb, he tugged them to the floor, then eased her panties just low enough to give him the access he needed. He had never taken her from the rear, and he wasn't sure he wanted to right now, but he couldn't find a time when he wanted to pause. She certainly wasn't trying to pull away.

Wrapping his arms around her, he held her close and his thumbs got to work again, this time way down low in the front. Her cat-like mew became a cry, and he knew he had hit pay dirt, which wasn't the best comparison for him to make, Charlie being as hygienically perfect as she was every other way.

Still, she began to grind herself against his thumbs, he did his part for himself from the back, and suddenly he was spewing himself on her, forgetting all the traditional, sweet ways he had planned to make love to her again. She trembled in his arms and he shuddered against her back, the two of them pressed together like they were one body, one heart.

His knees held, even the bad one, and he kept them both upright. At last they straightened. His hands slipped up to cup her breasts, and his thumbs played with the hard tips. He realized he hadn't touched them before, and he hadn't kissed her, either.

Turning her to face him, he made up for the omission. He made up for it several times.

"I told you we were animals," he said. "Was I too fast?"

She shook her head and rested her forehead against his chest.

Taking her hand, he led her toward a closed door he supposed opened onto the bathroom. They ended up standing in a large double closet. She giggled.

"You're supposed to be too carried away with passion to laugh," he said. "You're supposed to save the show of amusement for when I'm gone."

"I'm sorry."

He backed up and tried again, this time meeting with success. The bath could have held a couple of armoires. Instead, it had a sunken Jacuzzi, double sink, shower stall that would accommodate the center and a couple of guards for the Spurs, and lots of cabinets. He couldn't imagine what could be in them. His bathroom had a medicine cabinet and one shelf over the john.

A facecloth hung from a brass rack by the nearest sink. While warm water ran over it, he slipped her stained panties down her legs and tossed them in the sink. At last he kneeled and began to bathe her. She was watching him all the while. He expected her to protest, but she didn't, she simply watched. Even when he got very personal. He was tempted to tease her, to linger for a while. Instead, he played the gentleman, which wasn't exactly accurate considering what he was doing, but what the heck.

"We're animals," he said, "but we're clean ones."

"Yes, we are. Now it's my turn."

He stood and she did for him what he had done for her. Except that she did a more thorough job, running the cloth up and down in a very strategic area. Teasing him, the wench. When she finally stopped, he was ready to go again.

"You're a good doctor," he said. "You understand the human body very well."

"I understand yours."

But she didn't understand his heart. He would have to leave that part of his anatomy for another lesson at another time. Right now he wouldn't be able to concentrate.

Back in the bedroom, this time in the bed, pillows scattered around the room, he took her in his arms and kissed her, from where her hair grew in short wisps at her temples to her ears, her lips, her chin, her throat, and on down to her everything.

And they made love, glorious love, using the condoms that turned up mysteriously in his billfold. He hadn't remembered putting them there. At least his conscious mind wouldn't let him remember since he was not supposed to be loving her like this until their wedding night.

Where Charlie was concerned, he was weak. He was also very strong. They made love three more times, which brought the total to four, which, as he saw it, was damned near miraculous considering he had reached the ripe old age of thirty-eight, and also factoring in how they fooled around a lot in between.

Of course, being a geriatrics doctor, she thought he was a mere youth. When he was with her, she made it so.

Chapter Nineteen

Charlotte had gotten the sex she wanted, and much more. She had gotten it in ways she didn't know existed, and she had gotten it better and longer and sweeter than her imagination could have ever dreamed.

After the fiasco in front of the restaurant, a low point in her life, everything had taken an upward turn. From hell to heaven, there was no other way to put it.

So she was satisfied, right?

Wrong.

Cuddled in Sam's arms in what should have been blissful contentment, she felt lost and, strangely, alone. Something was missing, something left undone, though when she thought

304

over all the activities of the night she wondered what the something could be. She fell asleep in her lover's tender embrace, still wondering.

When she woke up the next morning to a hazy late-winter sky, her puzzlement was gone. She must have been crazy last night to find fault with her situation. Sam was still with her. Life was good.

She took a cat-like stretch, breathed deeply, and thought that she would never need a second opinion about her sexual abilities again. If she ever for one single instant doubted herself, all she had to do was think of last night.

She would also think of it every time she made the bed and plumped the decorative pillows. Decorative baloney, those pillows had a very practical use.

She looked over at Sam, who was lying very close and looking at her.

"You have great eyes," she said. "Very expressive. Right now they look, I don't know, pleased, I guess."

"They ought to."

She stroked his cheek. "You even do stubble right. But I guess you've heard all this before." She hesitated. "On the morning after, I mean."

"I've never slept over before."

"Never?"

"Never."

For some reason she didn't investigate, that made her feel very proud.

"You can spend the day if you like."

She almost said he could hang around, but he might turn that into a joke, and while she loved his jokes, she also wanted him serious, too. About sex. Not about anything else.

But Sam proved stubborn.

Stroking her cheek the way she had stroked him, smoothing her hair behind her ear, he looked at her solemnly.

"No."

He offered no elaboration, but the *no* was clear enough.

"You've got plans?"

"For today? No. For the rest of my life? Definitely yes. More than ever, yes. That's why I'm getting out of here today. I shouldn't have spent the night."

"Isn't that what the woman's supposed to say?"

"Haven't you noticed how we often switch roles?"

She thought of a time or two last night when that had definitely been true. But Sam wasn't talking about anything that had happened in bed—or beside the bed or in the bathroom. He was talking about matters she wished with all her heart he would forget.

Staring up at the ceiling, she felt tears burn in her eyes, at the front where he could see them if he looked close enough. Why she was crying, she had no idea. She had awakened only a few minutes ago with a delicious sense of completion. Now she felt hollow inside, the way she had last night, just because he wouldn't spend the day.

"I'm not going to marry you," she said.

"So you told me."

"If I lied and said I would, would you stay?"

"I'd be calling up a judge I know, getting him to waive the waiting period, and hauling you before him pronto. Then I would stay for as long as you wanted. Longer, probably, but that's another matter."

For just a moment she considered what having him around all the time would be like. The idea was almost too sweet for her to contemplate—Sam across the breakfast table, Sam shaving and hogging the bathroom, Sam going for long walks with her by his side—so she had to think of the downside. It took her a minute. After the honeymoon, she would get wrapped up in her work, he would get wrapped up in his, the world he lived in that she knew nothing about would intrude, hers would, too, and when they were out of bed, they would begin to drift apart.

Their lovemaking would probably turn sour, too, although that part was more difficult to imagine.

The tears dried. "I'm cold," she said, "and selfish. I want things my way, and I truly don't think I would be able to change. I'm finally getting the kind of life I was raised for, one devoted to a cause that doesn't involve the closeness of another human being, one—"

"Bullshit."

She glanced sideways at him. He had propped his head on his hand and was giving her one of the Sam looks that made her forget her name.

Tightening her hold on the cover, she returned to her study of the ceiling. "I'm speaking the truth. You just don't want to hear it."

"Cold, you say. That's not what I hear from everybody else. There was talk at Golden Years about you, about how you visit your patients when they need you, how you counsel them through hard times, about how you care."

"That's different. They're patients."

"I'm not buying it, Charlie. I've seen the laughter and love you keep buried. And I know something else you may not have figured out. I'm the only one that can bring them out. Me. Samuel Blake, star sports columnist and television luminary and, while most people don't realize it, one of the best lays in town. Of course I specialize. You're the only one I practice on."

"So practice now."

"No."

She slammed her fists against the mattress.

"Temper, temper, sweetheart."

She sat up and abandoned trying to cover

herself. Shifting her legs to the side of the bed, she gave him a good look at her backside. Last night it had intrigued him. Right now, stubborn as he was being, she didn't care whether it intrigued him again.

"So leave. I've got some work to do. You think you're the only writer? I've started an article I plan to submit to the *Texas Medical Journal*. Actually, the editor asked me to write it. I've been putting him off."

"I know the feeling."

She glanced over her shoulder at him. The cover was riding low on his abdomen. She shrugged, to show him his naked state was of no concern to her. She especially didn't care about the patterns of body hair above and below his navel. Why she bothered to look, she refused to contemplate.

"We have nothing in common, and you know it. Okay, there's sex. And we're both flexible where music is concerned, at least for the time being. But you know more about a thousand things, about books and movies. You're a film buff. You told me yourself you watched *Rashomon*. Four hours of Japanese dialogue with English subtitles. And then you rented *The Magnificent Seven*. You ought to be writing a movie column as well."

"Yeah, movies. That could be a real problem."

He got out of bed, grabbed up his clothes,

and headed for the bathroom. "If you don't need to come in here, I'm taking a shower. I'll have to think over the *Rashomon* obstacle. It's a tough one."

While he was in the shower, she bathed in the upstairs bath and came down wearing jeans and a sweater. She was in the kitchen checking on the automatic coffeemaker when he came in. The white shirt from yesterday looked a little wrinkled, but the jeans looked fine. Too fine.

At last she made it up to his face. There were two small pieces of toilet paper stuck to his chin.

"How do you shave with that razor?" he asked. "It's downright dangerous."

"It works for me. I'm not very hairy."

He smiled. "I know."

She looked away fast and opened a cabinet next to the stove. "I'll make us breakfast. Waffles okay?"

"I'll skip breakfast. Coffee's fine."

She handed him the cup, and their fingers touched. She knew it wasn't an accident. For a moment she let herself enjoy the little electric tingles that issued from wherever they touched.

The problem was the tingles didn't stay where they started. The simple brush of his fingers against hers sent them shooting everywhere in her body. And her everywhere went on alert.

She turned from him fast. He had already rejected her suggestion they spend the day together. She would not allow herself to beg.

"So when are we going out again?" he asked.

A sip of hot coffee burned her tongue. *Kiss it and make it better.* Would that sound like begging? Probably.

"What are you talking about?" she asked, coolly and, sad to say, dumbly.

"Our date. The second one. You promised, remember?"

She thought about last night, before bed, before the pillow, before the foot massage. Worries that had troubled her as she went to sleep came tumbling back. The uncomfortable meeting with Sam's family had been bad enough; Roger had truly been a nightmare. One of the worst of her life. Just when she thought he couldn't ruin her life any more, he did it again.

Encountering Blondie in the parking garage had been an omen of bad times to come, but she had been too dense to pick up on it. Or too mesmerized by Sam's presence to think beyond the moment. While he was thinking beyond the next few years.

It was his thinking that had her feeling lost and alone, putting ideas into her head that could never be. Why couldn't they have a simple sexual relationship? Why did he have to complicate things so much? Why couldn't he be just a smidgen like Roger the Rat?

The thought stunned her, but it wouldn't go away. Anyway, she knew the answer to all her questions. Things were the way they were because she and Sam were the way they were: a man ready to build a home and a woman who knew a home was not for her.

Opposites attracted; she was smart enough to know they eventually repelled.

She leveled her best no-nonsense look at him.

"Whenever the date is, I don't want any surprises. No visit to your family. And no restaurants. I'll probably never eat out again."

"Okay, we'll go somewhere you've never been before." Sam was looking far too innocent for her to retain her peace of mind. "It's a place neither of us is likely to run into someone we know," he added. "In fact, we most definitely will not. We won't run into anyone."

"A cave."

"A state park. On the Llano River. We'll camp out."

"You're insane. I've never camped out in my life."

"Aren't you the daughter of a wildlife photographer? Weren't your grandparents hiking in the wilderness when they died? Doesn't their blood flow in your veins?"

"And I want to keep it in there, thank you. Besides, camping out is more than just one date. It's at least two. A whole string of them. We'll be together for two whole days."

"Yeah."

He drew the word out, packing it with possibilities. She could feel herself giving in. Then a horrible thought struck, and she eyed him with both suspicion and dismay. "You wouldn't expect me to fish, would you?"

"I was thinking about it. Unless you want to just bait my hooks. You do that very well."

Sam was very good at packing possibilities into very few words. She let her mind wander along paths concerning all the things about him she could bait. But only for a minute. Another horrible thought struck.

"Roger will find us. There will be another fight. What if he gets in a lucky punch? I don't mean to doubt you, Sam, but it could happen."

"We'll go where he never goes. He doesn't like to rough it too much. But I know what a toughie you are, beneath all that softness."

He sat down his cup and stroked the sleeve of her sweater. The tingles started again.

"We'll have a great time," he added, somewhat unnecessarily to her way of thinking.

Sam knew how to fight dirty. Much as she hated to do so, she brushed his hand away.

"So Roger's out as a threat. Or so you say. What about Louise? I'll be gone an entire weekend. I can take a pager for my patients and get someone to take emergency calls, but she will have to be told something."

"She doesn't know about us?"

"She thinks she and I are in some kind of pact to have nothing to do with men. Don't look at me like that. It doesn't mean we have something to do with women. It's our careers that give our life meaning—"

"You sound like a NOW commercial."

"I sound like a woman who wants to take care of herself. NOW has its points."

"There are some things you can't do alone."

She tried very hard not to smile and just about won. He was buttering her up. It was something he did very well. But not today.

"There are some things I can never do. Like fish and camp. You've lost your mind. There is no way I'm going out in the woods with you and . . . and . . . ."

"And what? We won't always have our lines in the water. Besides, you may find yourself having a good time. Come on, Charlie. You promised. You're not a woman to go back on her word."

She thought about it a moment, seriously thought about it. Here was a chance to show him how different they were, to show him the utter foolishness of considering her for his wife. If she had once gone fishing with Roger, the marriage would have ended the first year.

Being dumb, being dense, she couldn't bring herself to end their relationship quite so soon. For a while longer, she needed Sam very much. And she wanted him to need her. She was being selfish. But Sam was so loving, so dear, he made selfishness not such a terrible trait.

So she set her jaw and unflinchingly met his gaze.

"No, definitely not. We'll have our second date, all right, but you'll have to come up with a better idea than that. Earlier in the week you mentioned a Bach concert. That's beginning to sound very, very good."

Chapter Twenty

Sam borrowed his dad's pickup and packed it with a thoroughness that would have done Charlie's meticulous heart good, choosing fishing equipment he knew well, selecting her gear more carefully than he selected his own. They would be staying at one of the waterfront cabins at the park, the one farthest from the main road. For that they needed linens, food, and a grill to cook the fish that he knew they would catch.

With Charlie by his side, they couldn't miss.

But just in case they did, he also threw in a couple of cans of tuna. He wanted to be prepared for every contingency.

He took a great deal more care than he ever

took when he was going with the guys. This was a date, and for a date a man wanted to show off a little. Already he envisioned Charlie as the perfect wife. She would be beyond perfect if she truly loved to fish.

"I'm doing this for one reason and one reason only," she said as he guided her down to his truck.

"I know. Sex."

She stopped in her tracks. "What do you think I am?"

He found silence the best response.

"Okay, so you know what I am. But I wasn't thinking of sex. I'm going to show you once and for all that we don't suit each other."

"What if we do?"

"We won't. We don't."

Again, he didn't respond. As right as Charlie was in many ways, she could also be very wrong.

"Did you have any repercussions from the scene outside the restaurant?" She asked the question as she was buckling herself in the pickup cab. She sounded truly worried about him. He was low-class enough to be glad.

"If you mean did I hear from Roger, no." He started the engine and pulled into the sparse Saturday morning traffic. "Well, not exactly. He left a message on my answering machine, but I let it go."

"Did he threaten to sue?"

"He wanted to know what was going on between us. I figured a wedding announcement in the paper would be answer enough."

"You're very sure of yourself."

"Not really, Charlie, but I have high hopes."

Coming to a red light, he spared her a long glance. She had closed her eyes. Her lashes made nice patterns above the ridge of her cheeks.

He smiled with pure pleasure. "Very high hopes," he said.

She frowned, but it wasn't a let-me-out-of-this-truck kind of frown, so he continued to hope.

"You didn't have any trouble, did you?" he asked. "About the restaurant, I mean. Surely Roger wasn't stupid enough to bother you."

"I didn't hear from him. A pediatrician in my building caught me in the hall and made a couple of off-color suggestions. He was there, of course, Saturday night. And put the worst possible slant on everything."

"Give me his name. I'll beat him up."

That got a slight smile. "I told him you had been giving me boxing lessons and if he didn't leave me alone I'd show him what I had learned."

"You want lessons, you got 'em. In case he takes you up on your offer."

"You're very agreeable."

"Sam the Agreeable Man, that's me."

She laughed. It wasn't a big laugh, but it wasn't a big joke. Still, she laughed. The weekend was starting out great.

"I also heard from Mrs. Cochran at Golden Years. She assured me she was not going to repeat a thing about what she saw and heard. In fact, when she mentioned you and what you did, she sounded very admiring. She thinks you're my knight in shining armor."

Sam let that one go. Any vote of support he got in his quest was nothing to joke about. In fact, he would take Mrs. Cochran a giant box of Godiva chocolates the next time he went to Golden Years.

He owed a great deal more than chocolates to Stella Dugan and her crew. They were the ones who'd sent him to the town-hall meeting and helped things along between him and Charlie. At least, it had put them in communication with each other again.

In return, he had been giving them updates on what was going on. Not details, he wasn't that much of a cad, but they knew she had gone out with him, and that she was going out with him again.

For a woman who claimed to be making it through life alone, Dr. Charlotte Hamilton had a lot of people interested in her well-being. He started to ask what she had told Louise Post about the weekend, then decided he didn't care. For the next two days the world must not intrude. If Charlotte didn't bring up her lawyer friend, neither would he.

The morning drive to the park took a couple of hours on the interstate, right through the Texas Hill Country. Charlie fell silent. It was beautiful country. She stared out the window the whole way. Knowing her as well as he did, understanding her better than she understood herself, he did not believe her silence was because of the passing landscape. With the miles separating her from her condo refuge, she was beginning to feel trapped, beginning to doubt she had made a good choice.

She didn't look trapped; in her jeans and yellow sweatshirt she looked just right. The white sneakers wouldn't stay white very long, but once the love of the outdoors rejuvenated itself in her blood, she wouldn't mind.

The ride through the park was rugged, the shocks on the pickup being a little worn, and became more so when he turned off the main road and took to the trail that led to their secluded cabin. She bounced, along with everything in the back of the truck, but not once did she complain. She was being a trouper. For a while. She wasn't ready to show him she didn't belong away from civilization. She wasn't ready to fail what she considered a test.

But he wasn't testing her. He wanted her to understand herself. And to understand him.

For that, he needed to isolate her beside a stream. He would teach her all that she needed to know about fishing, about camping, and, weak man that he was, about making love on a single camp bunk. He would be learning the love part right along with her, never having done it before.

Right away she started teaching him. Easing out of the car, she started moving slowly, reluctantly, but the cool, dry air and the smell of the outdoors got to her. He could have told her it was the primal scent of freedom, but that might sound like gloating and slow her back down.

Soon she was doing more than her share of the unloading. She caught his smile, which was not supposed to be a smirk but probably was.

"I want to get all this over with," she said. "Anyone can unload a truck."

Not just anyone looked so good doing it, though. Her clothes fit loose enough to allow her to move, yet tight enough to let anyone watching know exactly what was going on beneath them. After a minute of sharing in the work, setting the cooler and boxes on the ground, Sam leaned against the back fender and admired the view.

The muscles in her rear and legs allowed her to bend and lift everything he had unloaded. Until she came to the heavy box of food. Conscience made him take over, but he was motivated to brush his lips across hers as he offered to help.

She dropped the box in his hands, winked, and turned on her heel, disappearing inside the screened-in cabin. The inside canvas shades were rolled to the top and he could see her silhouette as she moved about inside, found a broom, and gave the place a swift sweeping.

She proceeded to make the bunks—both of them—and gather wood for a fire in the stone fireplace that would be their sole source of heat.

Unless one considered the shared warmth of their bodies, which was something he definitely considered. It had been early on in the journey, glancing at her from the corner of his eye, that he gave up on his abstinence plans. She might not be thinking of sex, but he was. It was a good thing he had packed protection. He knew his weaknesses better than he knew his strengths.

A couple of times he caught her looking pensive. He let the look go the first time, but at last he broke down and responded. It was while he was laying out the fishing gear on the grass near the Llano River bank.

"You're doing great," he said as she stared into the brown, flowing water.

"I know. That's the problem. I don't want to. I know I shouldn't be worried. I'll goof up yet.

And the only reason I'm getting any pleasure at all out of this is because it's so different from anything else I do."

"So what's wrong with that?"

She shifted her gaze to him. "Nothing. But I'm sure it won't last." She looked back at the river. "I lied to Louise. I told her there was a seminar I had to attend."

"In a way you are. A seminar on river fishing."

"In Dallas, I told her. I said I was flying there for the weekend with a couple of other physicians. Both female. I don't like to lie."

"So tell her the truth."

"I can hear me now. 'I'm running away to the wilds to have fantastic sex with Redeye and to bait his hooks anytime he asks. I'm also going to goof up terribly at the camping part, but I'll be pretty good at the sex.' "

"Sounds like a plan to me."

"She's my best friend, Sam. She supported me when no one else in the world knew what I was going through with Roger. I owe her more than lies. But if I tell her the truth, she'll never let me forget it."

Here was a dilemma Charlie would have to work out for herself. Her lawyer friend was like family to her, the only family she had, closer, he supposed, even than her patients.

Even at his age, he couldn't imagine lying to his parents. Evading issues, yes, but not outright lying.

On this issue he had no solution for her, not one she was ready to accept.

He changed the subject. "We'll need hip boots. They're still in the back of the pickup, under the tarp. And I didn't hide them, in case that's what you're thinking. I forgot about them until now."

"What do we need them for? Wading through the lies?"

"For the river. This weekend I want you to share everything with me."

"I don't do rivers."

He glanced at the murky Llano. "This one's not exactly white water. You'll do fine."

"No, I won't."

"Okay, you won't. But you'll have to prove it to me."

That got her.

They took a long time helping each other into the boots. He didn't really need any help, but in the putting-on process she put her hands in interesting places and he wasn't about to tell her to stop. He took advantage by returning the favor with his hands.

Everything was going smoothly, including the moment when he pierced a nightcrawler with his hook. They were standing on the dirt bank, the boots pulled over their jeans, both of them wearing khaki hats studded with lures.

His was old and well-worn, but he'd fixed up a new one especially for her. Her hair was twisted up under it, leaving a few dark wisps around her face and some longer strands against the back of her beautifully long and slender neck. Like everything else, she did khaki fishing hats very well.

While he was looking at her neck, she was staring at his hands.

"Give me a worm. I'll do mine," she said, and when he gave her a skeptical laugh, she added, "I'm also a surgeon. When it comes to cutting flesh, you're the amateur."

She had no trouble with the bait. He didn't think she relished the activity as much as she had predicted, but he wasn't about to say anything. She also had no trouble wading a half-dozen feet into the water, although she did sway a couple of times as the flow of the river hit her.

"Careful," he said. "The riverbed's rocky and uneven in places. And the current's stronger than it looks."

"Don't worry," she said. "I brought plenty of ballast with me."

He glanced at her rear.

"Nice ballast," he said.

"Do you really think so?"

She looked serious. How she could doubt her appeal, he had no idea. He had gone over her ballast with hands and lips many times, complimenting her as he went.

"I think so."

He was grateful for the coldness of the water. He'd never had an erection wearing hip boots before, and he thought it might look a little strange, like he was packing an extra fishing rod.

He concentrated on demonstrating the use of his genuine rod and reel. After only a few tries, she took to hers like a born fisherman, a fact he very carefully did not point out. She also displayed the required patience when the fish didn't bite right away. He hauled in a couple, and eventually she reeled in one, rather expertly, having watched the way he had done it.

It was as if all those genes she had inherited from her parents and grandparents were taking control, ruling her DNA. He was having a hard time not saying, "I told you so."

He was humming, she was humming, all was well.

Then the snakes got her.

Standing in the river beside him, under the shade of a giant pecan tree whose trunk was ten feet up the slope behind them, she was practicing fishing patience again, admiring the trees and boulders on the opposite bank of the Llano, when the first reptile swam by.

Eyes wide, Charlotte watched its slithery progress across the river's surface in front of her.

"It's only a water snake," he said by way of

reassurance. "You don't bother him, he won't bother you."

When the snake had gone its way, she let out a long, heavy breath. "What does he consider a bother?"

"Handling him wrong."

"Why would I handle him any way at all?"

She was bravely trying to concentrate once again on her line in the water—quiet, no humming—but she made a tactical mistake. She glanced up. A second snake had draped itself from one of the pecan branches over her head.

She screamed, pitched the rod, and made for dry land. Sam reeled in his bait, grabbed her rod, and followed. When he caught up with her, she was standing in a clearing free of trees and branches. Her hip boots, made for a larger body, swallowed her legs, making her look lost, out of place. And she was quiet. Very quiet.

She was also hugging herself and watching his approach with narrow, accusing eyes. They peered out from under the brim of the hat with a glare that would have sent a lesser man running. She wasn't lost. She was furious.

But Sam was made of stern stuff. He kept on walking toward her, his boots making a squishing sound with each step.

"You didn't tell me about snakes," she said.

"I don't see them all the time."

"Once in a lifetime is enough."

"They don't bite."

"Not unless they're bothered. Isn't that what you claimed? Don't come any closer, Sam. You could say the same about me. And I'm bothered right now. A whole heck of a lot. I knew I didn't belong."

"So you'll bite me? That's not much of a threat."

The tight lines of fear and anger around her mouth softened. Not much, but it was a start.

"If you would enjoy the biting," she said, "I won't do it. I'm not ready to forgive you. Not in the least."

"What will make you ready? How about I clean the fish and fry them, put some roasting potatoes in the coals, fix a salad? Knowing you're a doctor, understanding you'd want a balanced diet, I brought along mixed greens. Special treat, just for you. Along with a bottle of wine that's chilling in the cooler. And the bread. French sourdough. I picked up a fresh loaf on my way to get you."

Her shoulders relaxed a fraction. "You forgot dessert."

"I thought you could provide that. Of course, if you're not ready to forgive me, we may have to go bed hungry for sweets."

She took off her hat and shook her hair free. His fingers ached to touch her. Just touch her. That was all. She might bite him yet, but it was a danger he was willing to risk.

"Does everything you say have a double meaning?" she asked.

"Not with anyone else. Only with you. Anytime I get too subtle, let me know."

At last she smiled, the kind that got her eyes lost in its crinkles, the smile that had conquered him in the Hilton bar. It continued to have the same effect.

"If you ever get subtle, Sam, I promise to let you know. I still don't belong, and you know it. But I like to pull my own weight. About those fish. Show me how and I'll clean them while you take care of everything else."

If she was sounding a little bossy, he forgave her. Especially after she cleaned and gutted the fish, wielding the knife with skill, turning out a plateful of perfect filets.

They ate on the picnic table he had covered with a plastic cloth and pulled into a clearing, away from any trees with low-hanging limbs. Anyway, the afternoon sun felt good, springlike, though the season was officially still a couple of weeks away.

Charlie didn't pick at her food. By the time they put down their forks, every bite was gone, along with most of the wine. They both cleaned up the dishes and frying pan, and they both moved the mattresses and blankets from the bunks to the floor in front of the fire.

He brought her a bucket of water, then gave her a moment's privacy to get ready for bed. He did the same outdoors, undressing in the truck, putting on a pair of pajamas he had never worn. They were white and covered in hearts, a gift two birthdays ago from his ever-hopeful mom.

He felt a little foolish tiptoeing in them to the cabin door, his bare feet thrust into his old fishing shoes, clothes folded over his arm. He heard a rustle in the bushes but decided it was just the wind, or a creature of the wild. Which was pretty much how he was viewing himself.

Inside, Charlie had turned down the battery-operated lamp and lowered the rolled canvas shades, leaving no more than a foot of screened window uncovered at the bottom to let in the fresh air.

She was lying under a light blanket in front of the fire, her hair spread on the pillow, her gaze directed toward the flickering flames. The blanket was pulled to her waist. She didn't have anything on.

Tossing his clothes aside, he watched the play of firelight across her breasts. He groaned. She glanced up at him just as the one big heart across his crotch jumped. She dared to laugh.

"You'll pay for that," he said, kicking off his shoes. "I'll tell my mother."

She propped herself up on her elbows. "No, you won't."

He took in the view she was offering. "Okay,

so I won't. But you will pay. You will definitely pay."

"Tough words, fisherman."

He took off the pajama top and tossed it aside. "You're in big trouble, baby."

"How big?"

He took off the bottoms. She sat up straight and eventually looked him in the eye.

"That's not trouble, Sam." She spoke with a tremor, but he knew she wasn't afraid. "For dessert you've brought me exactly what I want."

Chapter Twenty-one

Sam moved toward the makeshift bed with the grace Charlotte remembered from the first time she saw him. No other man in all the world could sit on a bar stool the way he did. No other man could possibly move so smoothly when he was naked and aroused.

His eyes had turned black as he looked at her. Stripping before he got there had not been a mistake. She started to shake just watching him, thinking with the small part of her brain she had left that there were too many places on him to watch.

Light from the fire glistened against all the places. He was compact and tight, everything proportioned just right—arms, hands, hips, legs, the glorious flat-stomached trunk of his body—except maybe for the arousal. It was all out of proportion—it was Olympic-sized.

Sam went way beyond poster-perfect because he was flesh and blood, hot and tanned and he was coming for her.

She reached for the edge of the blanket to pull it back in welcome. It was the least she could do, considering that what she really wanted to do was tackle him around the ankles and kiss her way up to Olympus.

A noise from outside stopped her, the snapping of a twig, a rustle of leaves.

He caught her apprehension. "It's probably the wind."

"As long as it's not wolves."

"They're long gone from this part of the country. Relax. Even if it's a coyote, he won't bother us."

"Coyotes can be vicious."

"So can I, babe. You hold me off much longer, you'll find out just how vicious."

"That doesn't sound like much of a threat. I thought you were always vicious."

She was talking sassy, but she felt foolish for having reacted to something so natural. For goodness' sake, she was in the wilderness. It was the place for wild things. It was also the place for her. Except for the incident with the snakes, she'd had a wonderful time, a glorious time. She'd had fun.

After all her negative predictions, she would have swallowed her tongue before telling him.

And she had uses for her tongue.

She folded back the blanket so that he could lie beside her, then patted the mattress where she wanted him to be, as if he couldn't figure it out. She was being neat, civilized, when all the while her insides raged with *come on, come on, Sam, do it to me all night long.*

It must be the cabin that was making her crude. She wanted to talk dirty, act dirty, do whatever he wanted. The fire heated her backside, but Sam's skin scorched her front as he lowered himself to lean against her. He bent his head to lick the tips of her breasts. She practically levitated to get closer to his lips.

Instead, she dropped back her head and arched her back. His hand rubbed against her belly, then moved down to stroke the inside of her thighs. Good old Sam. A whole pack of coyotes could have circled them inside the cabin and she wouldn't have noticed. To prove it, she parted her legs, and he made a very satisfying wild sound deep in his throat.

After a moment of his tongue's attention, her arms gave way and she lay back down. The tongue followed, still attached to one eager tip. The hand began to move up, doing the funny little circle things it sometimes did against her skin. Sam had a very expressive palm. Her back curved downward into the mattress, this time to lift her hips. The hand took note and shifted slightly. With a cry of pleasure, she rubbed herself against the palm.

The rubbing felt so good, she almost forgot the way he was working on her breasts, which wasn't fair. She wanted to concentrate on everything at once.

He slowed down, which was a good thing since she was about to climax and it wasn't the way she wanted it. How she had gotten so picky, she didn't know. But he was still making her feel fine, thickening her blood, like a master conductor, directing it to all the right places where she would relish it the most.

Stroking his hair, she trailed a finger around his ear, blowing softly when she wasn't making the cat sounds that embarrassed her but seemed to please him very much. In the firelight, he looked more toasted than ever, solid and strong, muscles and sinews shaping his arms the way a man ought to be shaped. She felt small and soft and very feminine.

She also felt afraid, not of something imagined in the wild, but of something very, very real. The feeling swept over her and almost took control. The pleasures were old; the fear was new. And it startled her, not enough to stop the pulsing and wanting, but still, it startled her.

What was going on here? This was her wild time with her wild man, and she ought to be brave enough to make it through the night. She wanted him enough to go at this for a year. She wanted sex.

Want? Not strong enough. She needed the sex, hard and fast and impersonal, if sex could ever be that way. It had never been impersonal between the two of them. Their bodies were like one body. He touched and thrilled her. She did the same for him.

She was more than afraid. She was terrified, and mindlessly ecstatic at the same time. He was reaching parts of her that had nothing to do with her body, tender places deep inside that she had thought protected from the pleasures and pains of the world. She was also more ready for him than she had ever been.

Lifting his chin, she kissed him, licked him, sucked at his tongue.

"You taste like wine," she said.

She felt his lips smile against hers. "And fish," he said.

"That, too. I like fish. I like wine."

"I like you."

"I like you, too."

He held himself still for a moment, and she was afraid he had misunderstood her. *Like*, she wanted to cry, *I said like*. And it was true. She could not do these things with a man she had no feelings for at all.

She was afraid to think more about her feelings. Fear was taking over the night. She could not allow it. Kicking the blanket aside, letting the fire's warmth and Sam's skin burn her, she trailed her kisses everywhere he would let her. He had thought her agile before; he must be amazed by her performance tonight.

She didn't stop kissing until she had covered everything from his forehead to below his waist. She was concentrating on his navel, carved into his hard abdomen, when he took his turn at lifting her chin.

"I love you," he whispered.

I love you, too.

The words caught in her throat, and for a moment she froze. There it was, the realization that had tormented her since the moment he walked into the room. She had made such a declaration to one other man, several times in the months before she took her doomed marriage vows, and she had sworn never to make it again. But she couldn't control her mind. She couldn't control her heart.

Her spirit soared with love, danced with it, sang its sweet, sweet song. She held so much love inside her, she could scarcely contain it. It bubbled out in a giant smile, which she hid by running her tongue across the taut skin of his loins. This was not a time for smiling. He might think she was laughing at him. Worse, he might guess the truth.

She trembled with the knowledge. She must have loved Sam for a long, long time. Probably since he sat beside her at the bar. She would love him until the end of time.

When he eventually drifted from her, the way everyone did, she would love him still. And she would die.

Only one thing protected her for a while from the pain. Sex. She had known it from the start. He should have listened. He should never have begun to care.

And that was when she shoved herself totally into wildness. Kissing lower on his abdomen, blowing at the tight, dark pubic hairs, she finally took him into her mouth. It was the one thing in their mating that she had never done before. She had come close, but something had held her back—shyness, insecurity, fear she wouldn't do it right. She must be doing okay now. She could feel the rigidity of his body; sliding her hand up his sweat-slick body, she rested a palm over his chest and found his pounding heart.

She didn't even care about whether she was pleasing him. Tasting him this way made her completely his, and him completely hers. For the night.

Wanting him to climax in her mouth, needing this most personal of experiences, she fought when he pulled her away from him and eased her up to look into his eyes. But she didn't fight him long. All that she could ever ask for was in his gaze. She gave the look right back to him, everything but the yearning for permanence. That, she could never give him, as much for his sake as for hers.

He looked ready to make another declaration. He looked as if he wanted a declaration from her. She licked her lips and gave him all that she could.

"You taste good. Better than the fish. You shouldn't have stopped me. I didn't get enough."

He growled and laid her back on the thin mattress, then worked his way down to do for her what she had done for him. He had kissed her like this before, but tonight seemed extra special, electric, the ultimate ecstasy.

But she wanted their bodies to join in the regular way. Having admitted her foolish, private feelings, she needed him to be a part of her, and her to be a part of him. Before she reached her peak, she stopped him.

Again he growled.

"Same to you," she said softly, but she knew he heard.

"I want you inside me," she added. "Please."

It was the one request he couldn't deny. He found protection where he had placed it beneath the mattress. Lying on top of her, he thrust home.

She squeezed her burning eyes closed and let

herself love him, let her heart pound, and all that she had inside her pulsed warm and sweet and complete.

Wrapping her arms and legs around him, she showed him in the only way she could how much he meant to her.

Louise stumbled on the rutted road and righted herself.

"You said they were right down here. Thirty minutes ago, you said it. I don't see them yet."

Roger hushed her. "They'll hear."

"If they're out there. Which I doubt. Charlotte wouldn't do anything like this. Anyway, I don't care anymore. I'm cold, and my feet hurt."

He shook his head in disgust. She was wearing a skirt, heels, and hose. He liked the sweater under her jacket, but nothing else. He should never have brought her along. But when he'd called her this afternoon to find out what she knew about the affairs of his ex-wife, she had insisted on accompanying him.

She made the demand after she had thoroughly cursed him for doubting Charlotte's fidelity. If anyone in the world knew how to castigate a man, it was a lawyer. Especially the female kind.

She reminded him of his mother. Why, he didn't know, except for the bossiness. Against his better judgment, he had agreed.

And here they were stumbling along a narrow, rutted road in the dark on a beautiful Saturday night when he could be snuggling down with any one of several women who were just waiting for him to call. He hadn't gotten in touch with them for a couple of weeks, but he assumed they were waiting. His women usually were.

Instead, he was trudging along a deserted former cattle trail with Louise Post.

"You should have worn sensible shoes," he said. "And pants."

"I can't see," she hissed, ignoring him. "This is like walking through ink."

He snapped the flashlight on and off, giving her a brief glance at the path ahead.

"If I break an ankle, I'll sue."

"Go ahead. And what do you plan to tell the judge about why you're here?"

She had no answer for that one. It was the first time since they had abandoned the Lexus a half mile back on the main road that she had kept quiet for more than five seconds. The woman was a real pain. Worse than Charlotte had ever been.

Which reminded him of why he was here. Charlotte and Redeye. Together by the Llano. Fishing. Impossible.

But probably true.

The investigation had started simply enough with a morning visit to Sam's father, who told him about the loan of his truck for a fishing trip to the Llano River. Tom Blake had assumed Sam's usual fishing partner would be accompanying his son, although he didn't know who he was.

So Redeye had given up fishing, had he? As difficult as it was to believe, Charlotte—cold, citified Charlotte—had to be with him, out here in the wild in a cramped cabin without plumbing or electricity. When he put the suggestion to her redheaded, big-bosomed friend, her reaction had almost verified his suspicion.

"When she stopped answering the phone, I knew something was going on," Louise had said. "I've got to stop her before she does something terribly wrong."

"You don't have to worry about Charlotte," he had said. "She's cold as a fish. If I couldn't warm her up, Redeye is bound to fail."

So the two of them had been caught having dinner together. It was not exactly like finding them in bed. He had thrown around some pretty sharp accusations, but he had been hurt that they could betray him by even knowing each other.

It hadn't been necessary for Sam to resort to violence the way he had. Roger's stomach still hurt from his fist.

Louise took another tumble and yelped; this time she fell against his arm. At least one of her breasts did. He had a thing for big-busted red-heads. In that respect, the lawyer filled the bill.

He would have to quit turning on the light. She needed to stumble a little more.

He helped her to stand upright; helped her by missing most of her body entirely and pushing on her boob. She straightened fast.

"Keep your hands to yourself," she said.

He hushed her again, pointing with the flashlight toward a slit of light he spied through the trees, then toward the dark outline of Tom Blake's pickup. The moon and stars were bright enough for her to see the gesture.

"I told you they were here," he whispered.

Was that a smile of triumph on her face? Was she glad to catch her friend in an indiscretion? It must be the light that gave him that impression. She had claimed to be furious that he would suggest such a thing.

Slowly they crept forward. Were those moans coming from inside the cabin? Did a woman cry out?

Yes, definitely yes. He recognized the sound, if not the woman's voice. Whoever was in the cabin was having a damned good time.

"He's hurting her," Louise said.

"I don't think so."

But he wasn't completely sure. His ex had never cried out like that for him.

They tiptoed forward and crouched beside

each other in the bushes closest to the screen windows. Louise grunted when her knees hit the ground, but she didn't back away.

Another cry.

"He's doing it again," Louise whispered.

"The bastard." And then he added, "The bitch."

"Don't you talk about her like that."

"I'll talk about her any way I like."

The noise inside the cabin ceased. All they could hear was the snap of the wood in the fire and the rustle of wind in the trees.

Whatever the couple was doing in the seconds of silence, it led to some whispers they couldn't make out, then thrashing and moaning and a few more cries that communicated themselves all too well.

"How could she?" Louise sobbed. At least it sounded like a sob. No, it was closer to a whine.

Roger couldn't get too irritated with her. He agreed with everything she said. In all their years of marriage, Charlotte had never gotten so carried away over sex. At least she hadn't with him. But he wasn't about to let Louise Post know.

They edged close to the cabin and raised themselves to where they could see inside. Both stared. Two naked bodies were so entwined on a mattress in front of the fire, it was hard to tell where one body began and the other ended.

One of the bodies rose, and Roger recognized the profile of his buddy Redeye. His former buddy. The woman lying under him had to be his ex-wife.

He ducked back down. He had seen enough. Not so Louise, who continued to peer through the screen. She even started chewing on her lower lip.

He grabbed the collar of her jacket and jerked her down beside him, shook his head violently when she opened her mouth to speak, then slowly began to move crablike back toward the road. He gave her no choice but to follow. He didn't stand completely upright until they were back on the trail.

"I've never seen anything like that," Louise whispered, no longer talking out loud even when she could.

"Not outside a porno movie."

"Or an afternoon soap."

"How could he?" Roger said.

"How could she?" Louise responded.

They stared at each other in the moonlight.

"It's as if they're trying to hurt us," Louise said.

"We need to get back at them," he said.

"Retribution," she said. "I like the idea."

"But how?" Roger asked.

"We'll have to put our heads together."

Or something else.

He linked his arm with hers. "Be careful," he

said as he began the long walk back to the Lexus. "I wouldn't want you to hurt yourself."

"How thoughtful of you. I should have worn more appropriate shoes."

He flicked the flashlight on and off. "I like the way your feet look in those heels. Your legs, too. You're doing fine."

"My hose are ruined."

"You'll have to get out of them soon."

He thought about the scene they had just witnessed, about the nakedness of the pair. His jacket and jeans began to weigh heavily on him.

"I don't think it was their first time," he said.

"I don't either. They looked practiced. You might say even skilled." She hesitated, and he knew she was remembering just what he remembered. "Whatever we decide to do, we'd better do it right away."

"My place or yours?" he asked.

She stumbled and rubbed her breast against his arm, but he wasn't sure whether or not it was by accident.

"It doesn't matter to me," she said with a little laugh. "Wherever it is, we'd better go there tonight."

Chapter Twenty-two

When they woke the next morning, Charlie was different, turning from him when he tried to kiss her, saying something silly about how she wanted to brush her teeth first. She hadn't said that after he spent the night in her apartment. But she was saying it now, holding the blanket up around her neck, staring into the dying coals in the fireplace as if they might tell her something.

Sam wasn't completely stupid as far as she was concerned. After the night they had just spent, something was definitely wrong.

He sat up and watched her profile. A new and better idea came to him. Rather than being wrong, maybe something was closer than ever to being right. It was possible she was ready to make the decision he had been waiting for, and the idea was frightening her. Maybe she was ready to declare herself despite herself. He would take the declaration, any way he could get it.

But no, that would be too easy. Where her moods were concerned, she had conditioned him to look on the downside of matters.

Without saying anything more, they dressed fast, pulling on the same jeans as yesterday, changing tops. Hers was green. She did green very well. He noted the dirty condition of her sneakers and smiled to himself. It was like he had marked her in some way. At least the wilderness had, and he was a part of the wilderness.

While she straightened the cabin, he fried up a pan of bacon and eggs. She should have been starving. She barely touched a bite, but took care to thank him for the effort.

What was going on here? After the wild night, the morning had turned her into Miss Manners. He would have preferred having her rude. At least that would be showing emotion.

He stared at her across the picnic table. "What if I teach you how to fish from the bank? No trees. No danger of snakes."

"No, thanks, but I appreciate your thinking of my safety. And my peace of mind."

"Come on. You don't have to put on the hip

boots again, even if you do look cute as sugar pudding in them."

"Sugar pudding?"

"It was the only thing I could think of on short notice. Actually, you look sexy, but a guy doesn't usually talk to his fishing buddy about looking sexy."

"I assume you never talked to Roger about how he looked in the boots."

"Roger didn't like to wear them. I think he thought they would rub something he didn't want rubbed." He leaned across the table. "You got something you don't want rubbed this morning? Or something you do?"

"Don't be ridiculous." She hopped up from the table and started cleaning up.

It was possible he was being too subtle. That was something he could correct fast.

"What's going on here?" he asked, facing her straight on after they had finished loading the truck with the cookware. "What's wrong?"

She put her arms around his neck, kissed him long and hard, then backed away. "What makes you think anything's wrong?"

She was innocence with a touch of tease, but the kiss came a couple of hours late.

"You're being far too agreeable," he said.

She ran a finger across his lower lip. "You didn't complain last night."

She had him there. In a way. But the kissing and the stroking had been her idea of a distraction, not a come-on suggestion that they go back to the cabin for a quickie. He still knew something was wrong, no matter what she said or did. The trouble was, he couldn't figure what it could be.

She was right in one respect. Last night had been fantastic. It had been the Super Bowl of lovemaking, the World Championship, the Final Four, which was about the number of times they had made love, though he wasn't sure. He had brought a big box of Trojans along, but he wasn't crass enough to count how many were left.

All right, so she had seemed a little frantic much of the time, but he figured that was the influence of the great outdoors.

He gave up on the inquisition. But he didn't stop watching her for clues. She helped him finish loading the truck with all of the efficiency and none of the snap she had given to the unloading. Whenever he smiled at her, she smiled back at him, but her eyes didn't sink into crinkles and her mouth looked a little stiff.

Fake smile. Yet every time he kissed her— and he did it a half dozen more times, just to test her—she kissed him right back. There was nothing fake about her enthusiasm. She seemed almost frantic again.

It was the middle of Sunday afternoon by the time he drove up in front of Central City Condominiums. The ride back into town had been quiet. She seemed to want it that way, and she had earned the right to get what she wanted. For a while. As long as she didn't say something stupid, like they shouldn't see each other again.

He turned off the ignition and started to unbuckle his seat belt.

"I can go up by myself," she said.

"Sure you can. You are woman. You can do anything."

She didn't give him a smile, even the fake one. Usually she was more polite about his corny jokes.

"Maybe we shouldn't see each other for a while."

She stared straight ahead. For a woman who had spent the weekend in the sun, she looked very pale.

"Did you get bit by a bug last night? Maybe aliens came down while I was in the pit toilet and exchanged my Charlie for a look-alike."

She braved one quick look at him, then it was back to studying the hood of the pickup.

"I'm not your Charlie. Why won't you listen to me?" The last was practically a sob.

She was out of the seat belt and out of the cab before he could answer, running through the front door of the complex, letting it slam behind her.

He let out a few curses. He could have followed and tackled her on the entryway rug. He could have stalked her up the stairs and burst through her door the instant she unlocked it. Or he could drive away and never see her again.

But, after he had finished cursing, after he calmed down, he decided to choose none of the above. She was upset after all that super sex, and it was more than just sex, the way she had held herself against him and touched him when she wasn't trying to arouse him, and watched him when she didn't know he knew. She was trying to reach a decision. She needed a little room. A very little room. He would give it to her, though it was the hardest thing she could have asked of him.

He reached a decision, too. While she was thinking, he would check in with Stella Dugan and Company. His teammates. It was way past time for another powwow. As a writer, he knew he shouldn't mix metaphors like that, but as a man in love he didn't give it a second thought.

Stella, Walter, and the rest might help him, and even if they didn't, they would understand his worry. He would even bring Uncle Joe along. He and Stella hadn't hit it off right, but Joe wasn't as much against Charlie as he sometimes pretended. He wanted the best for his nephew. As far as the nephew was concerned, that meant marriage to the best geriatrician in town.

After things worked out the way they had to,

Joe could figure her taxes while she explained his aches and pains.

"How about the shot put?" Uncle Joe swung an arm and almost caught Sam in the head. "I tried it once in high school and wasn't half bad."

"You look like the kind who tried several things in high school," Stella Dugan said. "And were probably half bad."

Sam was sitting between the two, looking over applications and rules for the Senior Olympics, which would be starting in another six weeks. The deadline for entering was coming up and Stella and Company had gathered in the gazebo at Golden Years to decide whether to enter.

Uncle Joe glared across his nephew at the judge's widow. "I come from a very competitive family. We don't set out to do something we don't figure to finish. No matter what it is. And we do it right."

Sam got the idea they weren't talking about the shot put. It was time to distract the pair.

He looked across at Ada Profitt, who was wearing a purple nylon workout suit, matching purple socks, and a new pair of cross-trainers. "I haven't decided yet," she said to his unanswered question. "They haven't got wrestling listed, and that's what I was interested in."

"Do they have wrestling for women?" Irene

O'Neill asked. "I was thinking more along the lines of bridge."

Before Sam could tell her no, women's wrestling wasn't a commonly recognized sport outside of a few sports bars with mud pits, Ada spoke up: "If they don't, they should. A woman who's been wronged can wrestle a bear."

Stella rolled her eyes, and Irene looked perplexed. The men were pretty much ignoring her.

"I'm going for basketball," Walter Farrow said.

"You'll need a team for that," Stella said.

"No, I won't. I mean the around-the-world kind. I'll get thirteen shots from different places on the court. I'm tall and that flare-up of sciatica from last week has settled down. Shouldn't be a problem. Like Joe, I was an athlete in high school. What about you?"

Stella smiled and got a faraway look on her face. "There was only one thing I was ever good at. Dancing. Of course, that was a long time ago."

"They've got ballroom dancing listed," Walter said.

"I know, but I lost my partner a long time ago." She shook herself. "Anyway, it's silly of me to think of entering. I'll help all of you, but I have no intention of putting myself before the public again. And people do come to these events."

"What about you, Morris?" Sam asked. The retired plumber was the only one who had not spoken up. He was sitting next to Walter in his worn sweater and pants and down-at-the-heels loafers, listening and watching, not saying much.

Morris rubbed his head. "I don't know. I might skip the Olympics this year."

"Your son and his family always show up," Stella said, and Sam could hear the unspoken addition, *It's the only time they do.* "Here's the chance for you to show them you're getting along fine."

"This year they'll be in London. Morris Jr. has a chance to go there for his company. They'll be taking the girls out of school early so they can go, too."

No one said anything for a minute, but Irene didn't allow the silence to go on long.

"I've got a box of peanut butter cookies for everyone," she said brightly. "It's back in my room, but I can go get it real fast if anyone's hungry."

She started naming the various kinds of sweets her nieces and nephews had brought her lately, and the others started voting on their favorites, everyone but Morris Weiss. Sam watched him. He didn't seem interested in much of anything, which wasn't the way he had been before. Junior needed a good talking to. There was no reason Morris couldn't go to

London, too. At least he should have been asked.

Sam would have bet his father's pickup the question had never come up.

"There are some doubles events in the brochure," Uncle Joe said. "If you want, I'd be proud to enter as your partner. Forget the shot put. I'd probably throw something out of whack."

Everyone stared at him; no one stared harder than Stella. Sam alone wasn't surprised at his uncle's sensitivity. When he wasn't putting on his country-cranky act, which came when he was feeling put upon, he was quite a guy.

"Thanks, Joe," Morris said. "I'll think about it."

Stella set aside the brochures and entry blanks. "Okay, Sam. Tell us what's going on with you and Dr. Hamilton. We need a progress report."

Joe opened his mouth to speak, but Sam cut him off.

"I don't know what's going on. We went fishing over the weekend and everything seemed fine. Until it was time to leave."

"You took her fishing?" Irene asked.

"Just like a man," Ada said.

"My wife and I used to fish," Walter said.

"I used to take my boy," Morris said. "That was a long time ago."

"The judge couldn't stand the smell in the house," Stella said.

"It wasn't the fishing that was important," Sam said. "Not entirely, though she took to it all right. It was the being together."

"Just like a man," Ada said. "We all know what being together means."

"What does it mean?" Irene asked.

Before anyone could answer—if anyone wanted to—Sam saw Charlie walking down the path toward the gazebo. It was Wednesday afternoon; he hadn't seen or talked to her since Sunday afternoon, and she looked great in the light brown pantsuit she had been wearing the evening they met. He was in khakis. It was déjà vu. Maybe they could start all over again.

"Hello," she said with a sweeping glance when she got close. "What's going on?"

Sam wanted to get up and greet her with a big kiss. Probably not a good idea, since she hadn't bothered to kiss him good-bye.

"We were talking about the Senior Olympics," Stella said.

"You sent the brochures here," Walter said. "We thought it was time we got started on making up our minds."

At last she looked at Sam. Her cool brown eyes might have been looking at the vines on the trellis behind him. But there were dark circles under her eyes. She hadn't been sleeping, any more than he. Her hands also gave her away. She was holding them together in front of her, but she couldn't entirely control the shaking.

"You're here with your uncle," she said.

It wasn't a question. It didn't have to be, with Joe sitting beside him. If she could deal with the obvious, so could he.

"That's right." She didn't respond, so he added, "I thought I would volunteer my help in case anyone needs coaching."

Several pairs of eyes turned to him in surprise. This was the first mention they had heard of his offering help, which was natural since he had only just now thought of it himself.

"You know how to play bridge?" Irene asked.

"He can't play worth a darn," Joe said. "If a bridge coach is needed around here, I'll be it."

Sam stretched out a leg, crossed the other one over his knee, and dropped his arm on the bench behind Stella. Charlie didn't miss a movement. When her eyes finally made their way back to his, they didn't look so cool.

Eat your heart out, baby. I'm all yours if you're brave enough to ask.

Tough thoughts. All he said was, "How have you been?"

"Fine. Just fine."

She looked at Stella. "Are you going to enter this year?"

"I don't know. I was just talking to Sam about it. He's so clever about so many things, I decided to let him help me make a decision."

"I know I'll be wanting his help," Walter said. "Good man, Sam. You can't go wrong depending on him."

Ada nodded, a bit less enthusiastically, while Irene mentioned the peanut butter cookies again.

Morris finally responded with an overenthusiastic, "Good man. The best."

They were laying it on too thick. He was grateful Uncle Joe hadn't decided to help.

He was grateful too soon.

"Not a better man in Texas than Sam Blake. Any fool ought to know that."

"There are fools, and then there are fools."

Charlie spoke softly, looking just at Sam. They looked at each other for a minute. He felt a rising anxiety, mixed with a love so strong it was seeping through his pores. Surely she could see it. Surely everyone in the world knew how he felt.

She broke the stare and looked around the gazebo. "I can see all of you are being taken care of without me. Get back to what you were doing. The only thing I wanted was to know you're all right."

She turned and hurried back up the walk. Sam started to go after her, but Stella clamped a hand on his arm and held him back.

"Let her go. She's got some thinking to do. If you push her now, she might go the wrong way."

"Women!" Uncle Joe said. "I ain't ever gonna understand them."

Sam looked at Stella, then back to Charlie, watching until she disappeared around the corner of Golden Years.

"I know, uncle, I completely agree. But understanding them is not the important part. What a man wants in life is to find one to love and, if he's very, very lucky, to get loved right back."

Chapter Twenty-three

Two days later, Walter came in to the office for one of the regular visits he thought he needed. Gloria went through her usual routine, checking height and weight, blood pressure and temperature, all fine, no signs of potential health problems.

Then Charlotte went in to listen to him talk about his wife, which sometimes took a half hour. Today after five minutes of saying she still didn't recognize him but looked happy enough, he was done.

"I've been training for the Senior Olympics," he announced. "Sam Blake's helping me with my shooting technique. I wouldn't be surprised if I didn't come away with a basketball ribbon this year. First place. Sam is that good."

"I'm sure he is."

She *knew* he was. He was so good, she couldn't sleep, she couldn't eat, she could barely bring herself to concentrate when she was at her office. It was a good thing she had no surgeries scheduled, otherwise she would have had to cancel them or get another doctor to cover for her.

He was driving her crazy. Something had to be done.

After Walter had finished extolling Sam the Man's virtues, he left, and she sat alone in the examining room remembering the cabin, remembering the firelight on his skin, remembering all that she had done to him and he had done to her.

When she'd unexpectedly come upon him in the Golden Years gazebo, she had been torn between throwing herself at him and running away in a crying fit. She buried her face in her hands. Her head throbbed from temple to temple and front to back, but the pain was nothing compared to the ache in her heart.

For so long she had been sure of herself, certain of the way she must live her life, because of all that had gone before her marriage ceremony and what had happened afterward.

Now she wasn't certain of anything. Walter wasn't the only one bringing up Sam's name.

Gloria worked him into the conversation at least once a day, and Claire did the same. The aide, Barbara Anne, went so far as to ask if Sam had a younger brother, and to suggest that if he didn't and Dr. Hamilton was done with him, she might call and ask him out.

For just a minute she hadn't liked Barbara Anne very much.

Over the weekend she tried to get in touch with Louise, but she wasn't answering her phone, and Charlotte spent the time scrubbing her condo from top to bottom, even though she enlisted a maid service.

Monday Stella Dugan called to report who had signed up for what with the Olympics: Walter with around-the-world basketball, which Charlotte already knew, and Ada with the 100- and 200-meter races. Ada had tried to enter the pole-vault competition, but she needed her own pole and since she didn't have one, she had changed her mind.

"You'll never guess what Sam talked Irene into entering."

Charlotte shuddered to think.

"Billiards," Stella said.

"Has she ever played billiards before?" Charlotte asked.

"Not that anyone knows. Sam says she's a natural. He's started taking her to a sports bar in the evening when he gets off work. Irene won't say how she's doing, but she bought a pair of slacks and tennis shoes and is ready an hour before he arrives."

Charlotte felt a pang of jealousy. Over Irene O'Neill, for crying out loud. Not even an hour-long contemplation session in the Corvette could help her get over that.

Even Morris Weiss called to say that Sam was quite a man and any woman who let a hot number like him get away was a fool.

"A hot number?" she asked.

"That's what we used to say when I was young. Maybe folks aren't still saying it."

With Sam, *hot number* was more than accurate, but she didn't tell Morris so.

"How are you feeling?" she asked instead. "My records show you're overdue for a checkup. Why don't I connect you with the receptionist and you can make an appointment."

"I'll do it later. I've entered the Olympics myself. Horseshoes. Haven't played since my wife died, but I used to be good."

"You haven't been getting much exercise, have you? Don't do anything too strenuous."

"I won't. Horseshoes is about as easy as anything. And I promise to call you about that appointment. Soon as the Olympics are over and my son gets back to town."

He hung up before she could ask him what his son had to do with anything. She made a note to call the son and put the question to him, and to ask his help in getting his father in to see her. She wanted to respect Morris's right to privacy and to make decisions on his own, but everyone needed a push in the right direction from time to time.

In the meantime, getting pushes from everyone, she had to deal with how her life was turning out. Every day someone was mentioning Sam, and when he wasn't being mentioned, she was thinking of him on her own. She even began to hate the thought of him. He was hemming her in, without doing much except existing. And everyone who knew them both was trying to manipulate her and get her together with him.

Life was not good. She needed someone to shake her and remind her why she was destined to live alone. She needed Louise.

What was going on with her friend, anyway? She seldom answered the phone, and when she did, she always had some excuse about why she couldn't talk or why the two of them couldn't get together.

On the day after the call from Morris Weiss, still troubled by his refusal to make an appointment, she decided to drop by Louise's apartment and try to catch her in. The apartment complex was a twenty-minute ride from downtown; she made it fast in the station wagon, parked out front, and looked up to the second-story window of Louise's place.

A light was on. Good. She could call her on

the car phone and let her know she was coming up, but she was in a hurry for consolation and woman talk and anyway, what difference could five minutes make?

No one answered her knock. She had a key. What if something was wrong? What if Louise had collapsed from overwork or overexcitement from watching the soaps? What if she needed help? As a physician, Charlotte was honor-bound to go inside and find out.

She let herself in without trying to be quiet and called out, "Louise?"

No response, and she went deeper inside the darkened entryway. The living room lamp was out, but there was light coming from under the bedroom door. Her fears rose. Louise could be passed out in bed, or sick with a fever that left her too weak to call for help.

A weak Louise was a difficult image to summon, but stranger things had happened in Charlotte's medical career.

A cry from behind the bedroom door convinced her something truly was wrong, and she burst into the room without knocking. Roger and Louise, both naked, bolted up in bed.

Louise screamed and grabbed for the cover to hide her breasts.

"Charlotte," Roger said, more calmly. "What the hell are you doing here?"

Good question.

She stared from her ex-husband to her best

friend. Louise's hair was a mass of tangled red curls, her lips were swollen and bruised, and her eyes had that sated look Charlotte had seen in the mirror after she had been with Sam.

Louise also managed to look embarrassed and, gradually, angry.

"He's right," she snapped. "What the hell are you doing here?"

But Charlotte wasn't ready to answer questions, having too many of her own.

"What are you doing in bed with the Rat?"

"You were in bed with Redeye. Don't deny it. I saw you in the woods."

"Who's a rat?" Roger asked.

"You saw me?" Charlotte asked. "You spied on me?"

"So what are you doing to me right now?" Louise asked.

Under the circumstances, *checking on your health* seemed like a pretty inane response. Charlotte retreated and stumbled toward the front door.

"Wait!" Louise shouted.

With a blanket wrapped around her, she ran out and grabbed Charlotte by the arm. Someone slammed the bedroom door closed. Charlotte assumed it was Roger, unless her friend—her former friend?—had more secrets she hadn't disclosed.

Louise snapped on the living room lamp, and the two women stared at each other.

"You were at the cabin," Charlotte finally said.

"Making sure you were all right."

"That's the same reason I'm here."

Charlotte thought her explanation was beyond a doubt on a loftier ethical plane, but Louise the Litigator probably wouldn't agree. Why finding Louise her in bed with Roger seemed like a betrayal, Charlotte didn't know. But it did. And she didn't want to hang around and discuss it.

Pulling free of Louise's hold, she hurried into the hall and closed the door after her. She ran down to her car, raced the motor, and peeled out, making an inordinate amount of noise in the quiet neighborhood. She had never peeled out in her life. It felt good.

What didn't feel good was arriving back home, parking the station wagon beside her unused sports car, and seeing Blondie walk by with a man she recognized. Tall, gray, and handsome, there was no mistaking Edgar Ryan, Roger's stiff-necked banker father, whose neck was anything but stiff as he bent it to kiss his girlfriend.

Charlotte ducked down in the seat. She'd had all the confrontations she needed for one day. Was there no honor left in the world? Was no one true to marriage vows?

She stayed scooched down, even after it was safe for her to sit up. Edgar Ryan's philandering helped explain his son a little better. Roger was following in the footsteps of dear old dad. And Felicity Ryan knew it. It was something Charlotte knew without understanding how. No wonder Felicity spent so much time at her charities. It gave her dignity and helped to pass the time.

Worse than she hated seeing Edgar, she hated entering her empty condo alone. The sensation was a new experience. Shadows played on the white walls. The Mexican artworks that she treasured, many of them celebrating death, leered down at her everywhere she looked. Going out to the balcony, she sat to watch the passing riverboat lights and to hear the laughter coming from the walk along the river.

This was no way to live. She didn't want to be judging others. She didn't want to always be questioning whether she should have taken a chance with Sam. Or whether she should have allowed him to take a chance with her.

She was in no state of mind to make a decision about their respective futures. But she wanted him. She wanted him tonight.

The doorbell rang. Her heart did a half-dozen turns. It couldn't be. But it was. When she threw open the door, Sam was standing in the hallway about to ring again. He had on jeans and a sweater, and he was wearing a belligerent look in his eye.

She was in no mood to fight. She wanted to get him out of his clothes.

He opened his mouth to speak. She grabbed his sleeve and jerked him inside, locked and bolted the door, lest Louise pay her back with an unannounced visit, and threw herself against him.

"If you say one word or ask one question or give me any argument about anything, I'll pitch you off the balcony. Understood?"

He nodded.

There was one more thing she needed to do. Brushing her cheek against his, she pushed away and hurried into the bedroom. One phone call later, she turned off the ringer and pitched her pager aside.

"All emergencies covered. Except one. Make love to me, Sam. Don't ask why. Just do it. And do it and do it again."

He had the pillows tossed and the two of them undressed before she could draw more than a couple of breaths. He tumbled her back on the covers. The satin quilt was cold against her back, but Sam was hot and he made her forget the cold.

He made her forget it for a long, long time. Hours, years, a lifetime later she lay in his arms beneath the covers and admitted to herself that she had been wrong and he had been right. They belonged together—as husband

and wife—till death did them part. This time the vow could be kept.

Okay, so he hadn't asked her to marry him in days, but surely he hadn't changed his mind.

Maybe she was too easy.

Her heart stopped at the thought. But easy was what he liked. Or so he'd once told her. He had said it jokingly, knowing that in all her life she had never behaved the way she did with him.

"Sam," she whispered against his chest.

"Am I supposed to talk now?"

"You can listen. About us—"

She felt him tense. She smiled. Boy, was he in for a surprise.

What they needed was a sip of wine to celebrate the occasion. Or maybe she needed it. This was a momentous thing she was about to do, changing everything she believed about herself and what she was capable of.

She eased away from him and slipped from the bed, put on her robe, and said, "I'll be right back."

Her eye fell to the blinking light on the answering machine. Sometime during the night someone had called. It was probably Louise. If so, Sam ought to hear what she had to say. When Louise was done apologizing or making excuses or saying whatever she had to say, Charlotte could tell her lifetime lover about the scene she had burst in on. He would be righteously indignant that they had been spied on, and then, along with her, he would laugh.

And then she would say she very much wanted to be married again. Roger was a rat, but this time she was choosing Sam the Man.

She reached for the machine.

"Don't," he said.

"It's all right. I know who it is."

But she was wrong. Stella Dugan's voice cut into the room, ominously tremulous, as if she were trying to retain her stoic control.

"I've got bad news, Dr. Hamilton. Call me when you get in. No matter what time it is."

Charlotte fumbled looking up the number and had to punch it in twice. Sam tried to help, but she waved him away. Stella answered on the first ring, and Charlotte listened with the heaviest of hearts to what the woman had to say. By the time she hung up the phone, both she and Stella were crying.

Sam took her hand, but she pulled free to wipe away the tears.

"Morris Weiss died this evening."

Saying the words turned her cold inside and weak, but she forced herself to keep standing and go on.

"He suffered a massive heart attack in his living room. The emergency attendants said he had apparently tried to call me, but when someone else took my call, he dialed 911."

Her throat tightened and she had to keep brushing away the tears. She was a physician, a geriatrician who was used to death. Morris Weiss was eighty-three years old. Still, she cried.

"While I was here with you, he was trying to call. I should have been there for him. It's my fault. When he needed me most, I let him down."

Chapter Twenty-four

The day of the funeral Charlotte rescheduled her afternoon appointments, leaving only her receptionist in the office to take calls and refer emergencies elsewhere. A downtown funeral home handled the services; burial was beside the late Mrs. Weiss in an old southside cemetery that still had tombstones marked with carved angels and long messages of love from the bereaved.

Morris's marker was a simple brass plate to match the one for his wife. Charlotte thought it appropriate for a man who had led a simple life. Morris Weiss, Jr. and his family were there, along with Gloria and Claire, three vanloads of residents from Golden Years, and a half-dozen men and women who had known him when he still worked as a plumber.

Sam was there, too, by her side through the brief ceremonies at the funeral home and cemetery. Nearby were his Uncle Joe, Stella, and the small band of her patients who over the past few months had become fast friends. Joe and Stella seemed particularly friendly, a fact that would have gotten her attention any other time, but not today.

The son demonstrated all the grief appropriate to the occasion. But then, so did Ada Profitt, who snapped as they were leaving the cemetery, "Guilt, that's what all those tears are. He should have been around more when his father was alive."

No one disagreed.

Charlotte was still feeling her own guilt. She couldn't have saved him. The heart attack was fatal; after the Emergency Medical Service attendants got to him, using all their skills and equipment, he slipped into unconsciousness and never again woke.

But she could have talked to him over the telephone. She could have given him words of peace.

All the while she was brooding, Sam was reading her mind.

"You're not at fault, Charlie," he said when they got back to her apartment. "You're a doctor. You're not God."

"You're right," she said and meant it. But she couldn't keep from thinking of her parents and her grandparents, who had died far away, out of reach of her care and consolation. Somehow their deaths were mixed with Morris's. The losses gave her a sense of failure she couldn't shake.

"Let me get you some sherry," he said as they walked into the living room.

"No, I'm fine. Really. I just need to lie down awhile." She smiled. "Give me a few days. The weekend's coming up. I'll call you Monday."

He looked at her long and hard, unfairly, she thought, when she was already down.

"No, you won't."

"I will. I'll probably have a full schedule of patients, so it may be late. It might be Tuesday, but I'll definitely call."

She meant it.

He took her in his arms and held her gently, but he didn't try to kiss her. He just held her. And then he let her go.

"Morris was a great guy," he said. "He followed sports, kept up with the Internet, and in his own way enjoyed life. We're going to miss him on our Senior Olympics team. That's how Stella and the rest look at it—our team. He was looking forward to the horseshoe competition. We're calling it the Morris Weiss Memorial Horseshoe Pitch. Unofficially, of course, but it might catch on."

"Doesn't that sound a little disrespectful coming so soon after he died?"

"Morris would have loved it. He's probably watching and loving it as we speak."

Sam started to say more but backed off. At the door he stroked her cheek and tucked her hair behind her ear.

"Remember how you were feeling just before the phone rang. In case you've forgotten, we'd just had great sex. Typical for us, of course. You were getting up to do something or to say something. I call that unfinished business, Charlie. We've got a lot of it between us. I love you. That's the one thing that's not going to change."

He left, and she whispered *I love you* to the closed door. Her head started hurting again. She never had headaches, but she'd had some doozies over the past few days.

Once she got over this depression she had fallen into, they would go away. And she would definitely tell him how she felt. She was stupid, she was weak, she was cowardly, but she would tell him, she would.

That didn't mean she could marry him. Sam was one of the special people in the world. He deserved more than a stupid, weak, cowardly wife. She would also tell him that, too.

She didn't get the chance right away. Throughout the weekend and the following week she was kept busy with her patients, both at the office and the hospitals where several of them were either recuperating from or awaiting surgery. She made sure she was always there for them.

Louise called a couple of times with half-hearted apologies, and Charlotte assured her that there were no hard feelings, that she understood a woman's needing a man. She certainly had demonstrated her need out in the woods, and the calls ended with them both in an amicable if not effusively friendly mood.

But Sam didn't call, and Charlotte found herself postponing calling him. She knew it wasn't his fault she hadn't answered Morris's page. The decision to switch her calls to someone else had been hers. At least she knew that intellectually. Emotionally, she was a mess. She was in no condition to make decisions that would affect the rest of her life. And his.

Friday evening he showed up at her door, just as she was arriving home late with a box of takeout from Bistro Tea. He was wearing jeans and an old University of Texas sweatshirt, his eyes and cheeks sunken, his lips set tight and flat.

He looked beautiful. He gave her the first lift she'd had for a week. It was as if sunshine and beautiful music had come in with him. She wanted to pitch the food over her shoulder, throw herself in his arms, cover his face with kisses, and tell him she had never been so glad to be with someone in all of her life.

He gave her no chance.

Striding inside, he backed her into the kitchen.

"I don't want you to say a word. Not a word. I have been patient, but I'm done. There is nothing more I can do to convince you how I feel or how you ought to feel if you had any sense. But you don't. You prefer to mope and wallow in guilt and inadequacy and a lot of other stupid things I can only guess at."

"But—"

"I'm not done. You rattle around in a big, fancy, empty condominium and you keep an undriven Corvette in your garage, and you talk about living a life alone. If that's what you really want, so be it. You love me. I know it and so do you. But do you love me enough to allow me into your life? That, I don't know."

"If you would—"

"I'm still not done. Roger called and told me about him and Louise. They're more than seeing each other. They're thinking about moving in together. He's not such a bad guy. Not great, but not terrible."

"He had other women," Charlotte managed to work in.

"Yeah, he did. I don't think he did at first, and there was never anyone serious. You were right about one thing. You've been too involved with your own interests to work at a true union with anyone. A lot of women have successful careers and happy marriages. It's a matter of balance. But that's something you will have to figure out for yourself."

He was making her angry. Here he was throwing ultimatums and judgments at her, and all she wanted to do was throw herself in his arms.

But he wasn't making her love him any less. She liked a man who could stand up for what he believed, for what he wanted. And she was gloriously, deliriously happy that he still wanted her.

She also agreed with everything he said, except the part about Roger.

"I'm going away."

That spoiled the happiness.

"What do you mean, going away?"

"My folks have a place up on Canyon Lake. I won't lie to you. There are probably snakes around, but that's not a big problem. I've bought it from them. I've also taken a leave of absence from the paper. It's time I started that book that's been rambling around in my brain."

He took a piece of paper from his jeans pocket and thrust it into her hand. "Here are the directions on how to get there. And the phone number. I'm still easy, Charlie. All you have to do is keep your word and call. But I've got to say, as unsure as I am about this novel-writing business, about whether it will work out for me or not, I'm far more unsure of you."

Without touching her again, he left. Closing her eyes, she pictured the way he had stood in front of her, laying down the facts as he saw them, telling her the way things were and the way he wanted them to be. It was Sam in his tyrant mode. But she still saw the puppy warmth in his eyes.

She very, very, very definitely loved him. She also had to give him credit: He knew how to make a dramatic exit. She stared at the paper in her hand and for the first time since they drove away from the Llano River, she smiled. She was far more interested in dramatic entrances. She had one in mind that would satisfy both of them just fine.

He was unsure of her, was he? That was one ailment this doctor knew how to fix.

Suddenly she was ravenous. She sat down to make a list of things she had to do, and while she was writing ate every bite of food from Bistro Tea, digging so hard she swallowed a piece of the Styrofoam box.

Sam spent Friday evening and Saturday morning moving into the lake house, installing his computer and printer, unpacking clothes and food, sweeping out a few cobwebs, and opening windows to let in the cool hill country breeze.

The two-bedroom, two-bath house was built on the side of a hill overlooking the lake. An open deck covered the back second story outside the master bedroom, providing a perfect view of the lake and surrounding hills. A small road led down to a boat dock and short pier. If he stayed, he would get a fishing boat. If Charlie showed up, he would make it a sailboat. There was nothing like skimming over the water with sails billowing in the wind.

If Charlie showed up. He had taken a gamble throwing the gauntlet at her the way he had. But it was a gamble he had to take.

He knew the gamble had paid off the instant he heard the deep, powerful engine of a car in the circular gravel drive at the front of the house. Standing in the kitchen, fixing a pot of coffee, he grinned. That was no station wagon he heard drive up.

He went out to look at the arctic-white Corvette sitting in the driveway. The weather was balmy and the top was down. The red leather seats glistened in the bright sunlight.

Charlie had her hair twisted under a Texas A&M cap. She was wearing a T-shirt and walking shorts, with a sweater tossed on the seat beside her.

When she got out, she gave him a saucy twist of her hips. "Now you know my secret."

"Yeah, you went to A&M."

"For my undergraduate degree." She reached inside the car for the sweater and tossed it over her shoulder. "We'll have to decide which of the schools our children will go to, UT and A&M being arch rivals and all."

She had put him through hell, and here she was talking about their children, like the future was already set because she said it was.

Maybe it was time he wasn't so easy.

"Children?" he said.

"I thought you wanted them. Of course, if you don't—"

He shrugged. "That's pretty serious talk for someone who just arrived. I was just putting on some coffee. How about a cup?"

She glanced toward the trunk of the car. "I brought a suitcase—"

"You can get it later. If you decide to stay."

He avoided looking her in the eye. It was hard not being easy. But he was tough.

His toughness lasted while they went inside and he got down the cups. It lasted while he set them on the Formica-topped table and got out a box of chocolate chip cookies his mother had packed for the trip. When he was sixty years old, Ellen Blake would still be packing cookies for her son.

Sam had a feeling Charlie would be that kind of mom.

But he was still trying to hold on to the

toughness. It even lasted while she sidled up to him, rubbing herself against his arm, saying how delicious the cookies looked, warm and chewy and sweet.

"What's a nice guy like you doing in a place like this?" she asked.

That was when he lost it.

"Screwing the woman who's going to be my wife."

Her pale blue eyes turned six shades darker. "You didn't talk like that before."

Facing her, he rested his hands against her glorious neck. "That night I was on my best behavior. Now I'm letting you know the real me."

"I know the real you. I love the real you."

He let out a long, slow breath. "It took you a long time to say it."

She gave him her crinkle-eyed smile. "You know how Aggies are."

He ran a thumb up behind her ear and started playing. "How much do you love me?" he asked.

"An oceanful, a skyful. My love reaches to the ends of the universe and back again." She stared at his lips. "You're the writer. I'm just a doctor. That's the best I can do."

"That's all? The universe?"

"How about this? I've scheduled a long-over-due vacation. Beginning now. Three col-leagues, three highly respected and competent and wonderfully cooperative geriatricians, are taking my calls. For three heavenly weeks. One a week. If need be, I'll schedule a fourth, but honestly I'd rather not."

"Now you're getting somewhere."

She rested her hands against his shirt. If she wasn't feeling a wildly beating heart and a pair of lungs pumping with air, she ought to take her stethoscope with her wherever she went.

"At the end of that time," she said with a very promising glint in her eyes, "we can shift to the condo. I've got an office complete with everything you could possibly need to write. And I'll give you all the privacy you want. If you don't want any, you'll get that, too."

"Your place, eh?"

"My towels are better. You said so, yourself. Of course, if you object—"

"I didn't say I objected. But aren't you forgetting something? I asked you to marry me. The answer I got, as best I can recall, was that all you wanted was sex."

"Can't I have them both?"

"Oh yeah."

That was when he kissed her. He also carried her up the stairs, swung her past the open windows overlooking the deck and the lake and the hills, so she could get a glimpse of the view, then rested her on the bed and began to take off her clothes.

Sam was back to being easy, going slowly

with the undressing, stealing some kisses and some licks when the mood struck. If they stayed in bed as long as he suspected they would, he was also going to have to be very, very tough.

Chapter Twenty-five

Two weeks later they were married at the Little Church at La Villita in downtown San Antonio near the River Walk. True to an earlier promise, once Sam got her agreement, he hurried the wedding along.

Louise was her maid of honor and Uncle Joe was Sam's best man. Charlotte asked Sam's father to walk her down the aisle. His mother sat in the first pew crying and sniffling when she wasn't smiling from ear to ear.

The women wore pastel silk dresses, Charlotte's a melon pink. The men were in dark suits. Uncle Joe looked tall, disguished, and very handsome. Sam, of course, was dynamite.

His sister made it in from California for the

wedding, along with her husband and two sons. Ellen Blake kept glancing at the boys as if saying, *See here? This is what I expect of you.*

Charlotte found it very nice having people expect things from her, especially things she could provide. They made her feel needed. They made her feel loved.

Stella, Walter, Ada, and Irene were also there, along with her office staff and a dozen other patients she wouldn't have expected to care. They all had such big smiles on their faces, she saw she had been wrong.

The residents she knew from CC Condominiums showed up at the church, everyone but Blondie. When she had a chance at the reception, which was held at Bistro Tea, she suggested to the architect Justin Naylor that he get in touch with Felicity Ryan about starting projects on improving the city's parking lots.

"I'll put in a word for you. At least I'll get her son to do so. He owes me."

And so he did. If it hadn't been for her, he would not have met Louise.

Roger declined an invitation to the wedding, which was probably just as well. Sam might not think he was a bad guy, but it would take her a few years to agree.

A large contingent from the newspaper was also in attendance, along with a couple of newspeople from the television station. The wedding was much bigger than either she or Sam planned, but after Ellen Blake got hold of the invitation list, the thing just grew.

Joe made a startling announcement at the reception.

"Stella and I are entering the Senior Olympics as a team. We're in the ballroom dancing contest, and we plan to kick some big butt."

"Kicking butt," Stella said with a wry expression on her face, "is one step we haven't practiced yet. Personally, I don't know if I'm limber enough for it."

In her flowing blue pantsuit, she looked capable of anything.

Charlotte and Sam flew down to Mexico for a five-day honeymoon, all the way to Oaxaca, far south of Mexico City, where she could indulge herself in searching for Mayan artifacts and art treasures. They stayed in a Spanish-colonial inn in the heart of town. They seldom got out of the room.

"What about the Mayan ruins?" he asked one morning over a breakfast he had ordered served in bed.

"They've been here for a couple of thousand years, dear heart, and they'll be here awhile longer. We can return, can't we?"

He handed her a tortilla filled with egg and Oaxacan cheese.

"Sure. But why wait?"

He was pushing her for a compliment. She gave it to him.

"Because you're at your best in bed."

"That sounds like a sexist remark. Or maybe it's just sexy."

She ignored him. "You have absolutely no interest in Mexican art or artifacts, and, frankly, I don't care. That's not why I married you. But when we go back home, I'm going to get back to work and so are you, and when you aren't working at the newspaper, you'll be writing your book."

"Sounds like we won't have time for each other."

"Play that one again, Sam. We will have time, we will make time, and when we can't, we'll know the other one is there in support. I can make this marriage work. You told me I could, and when have you ever been wrong?"

He thought that one over. "You have a point."

She finished the breakfast taco, drank down the freshly squeezed orange juice, then set the breakfast tray aside, all the while he sat propped up in bed, his pillow against the massive dark oak headboard of the wide honeymoon suite bed.

At her request, he was wearing the white pajamas decorated with big red hearts. She hadn't laughed any of the times he had made the hearts jump.

"Now, then," she said. "My energy level is up, baby. I'm fortified and motivated. You told me last night you got so much sex from me, you didn't know if you could ever have sex again."

"Did I say that?"

"Maybe you were teasing, maybe not. All I know is that it's such a serious matter, you need a second opinion concerning your condition. Since I'm the only doctor in the room, you'll have to get it from me."

Throwing back the covers, she launched herself at him. It was way past lunchtime before she came up with her diagnosis.

"You're fit, Sam. All you need is exercise. You're going to get all the workouts you need from me."

THE FOREVER BRIDE — Evelyn Rogers

"Evelyn Rogers delivers great entertainment!"
—*Romantic Times*

It is only a fairy tale, but to Megan Butler *The Forever Bride* is the most beautiful story she's ever read. That is why she insists on going to Scotland to get married in the very church where the heroine of the legend was wed to her true love. The violet-eyed advertising executive never expects the words of the story to transport her over two hundred years into the past, exchanging vows not with her fiancé, but with strapping Robert Cameron, laird of Thistledown Castle. After convincing Robert that she is not the unknown woman he's been contracted to marry, Meagan sets off with the charming brute in search of the real bride and her dowry. But the longer they pursue the elusive girl, the less Meagan wants to find her. For with the slightest touch Robert awakens her deepest desires, and she discovers the true meaning of passion. But is it all a passing fancy—or has she truly become the forever bride?

_4177-4 $5.50 US/$6.50 CAN

EVELYN ROGERS

TEXAS EMPIRES: Crown of Glory

It is nothing but a dog-run cabin and five thousand acres of prime grassland when Eleanor Chase first set eyes on it. But someone killed her father to get the deed to the place, and Ellie swears she will not leave Texas until she has her revenge and her ranch. There is just one man standing in her way—a blue-eyed devil named Cal Hardin. Is he the scoundrel who has stolen her birthright, or the lover whose oh-so-right touch can steal her very breath away?

___4403-X $5.99 US/$6.99 CAN

Golden Man
Evelyn Rogers

Steven Marshall is the kind of guy who makes a woman think of satin sheets and steamy nights, of wild fantasies involving hot tubs and whipped cream—and then brass bands, waving flags, and Fourth of July parades. All-American terrific, that's what he is; tall and bronzed, with hair the color of the sun, thick-lashed blue eyes, and a killer grin slanted against a square jaw—a true Golden Man. He is even single. Unfortunately, he is also the President of the United States. So when average citizen Ginny Baxter finds herself his date for a diplomatic reception, she doesn't know if she is the luckiest woman in the country, or the victim of a practical joke. Either way, she is in for the ride of her life . . . and the man of her dreams.

___52295-0 $5.99 US/$6.99 CAN

Dorchester Publishing Co., Inc.
P.O. Box 6640
Wayne, PA 19087-8640

Please add $1.75 for shipping and handling for the first book and $.50 for each book thereafter. NY, NYC, and PA residents, please add appropriate sales tax. No cash, stamps, or C.O.D.s. All orders shipped within 6 weeks via postal service book rate. Canadian orders require $2.00 extra postage and must be paid in U.S. dollars through a U.S. banking facility.

Name_____
Address_____
City_____State_____Zip_____
I have enclosed $_____ in payment for the checked book(s).
Payment <u>must</u> accompany all orders. ❑ Please send a free catalog.
CHECK OUT OUR WEBSITE! www.dorchesterpub.com

Paradise

MADELINE BAKER,
NINA BANGS,
ANN LAWRENCE,
KATHLEEN NANCE

The lush, tropical beauty of Hawaii has inspired plenty of romance. But then, so have the croonings of a certain hip-shaking rock 'n' roll legend. In these tales of love by some of romance's brightest stars, four couples put on their blue suede shoes and learn they don't need a Hawaiian vacation to find paradise. Whether they're in Las Vegas, Nevada, or Paradise, Pennsylvania, passion will blossom where they least expect it —especially with a little helping hand from the King himself.

___4552-4 $5.50 US/$6.50 CAN

A Case Of Nerves

Angie Kay

Standing on the moors of Scotland, Alec Lachlan could have stepped right off of the battlefield of 1746 Culloden. Decked out in full Scottish regalia, Alec looks like every woman's dream, but is one woman's fantasy. Kate MacGillvray doesn't expect to be swept off her feet by the strangely familiar green-eyed Scot. But she is a sucker for a man in a kilt; after all, her heroes have always been Highlanders. Wrapped in Alec's strong arms, Kate knows she has met him before—centuries before. And she isn't about to argue if Fate decides to give them a second chance at a love that Bonnie Prince Charlie and a civil war interrupted over two centuries earlier.

___52312-4 $5.50 US/$6.50 CAN

Dorchester Publishing Co., Inc.
P.O. Box 6640
Wayne, PA 19087-8640

Please add $1.75 for shipping and handling for the first book and $.50 for each book thereafter. NY, NYC, and PA residents, please add appropriate sales tax. No cash, stamps, or C.O.D.s. All orders shipped within 6 weeks via postal service book rate. Canadian orders require $2.00 extra postage and must be paid in U.S. dollars through a U.S. banking facility.

Name_____
Address_____
City_____ State_____ Zip_____
I have enclosed $_____ in payment for the checked book(s).
Payment <u>must</u> accompany all orders. ❏ Please send a free catalog.
CHECK OUT OUR WEBSITE! www.dorchesterpub.com

Virtual Heaven
Ann Lawrence

The warrior looms over her. His leather jerkin, open to his waist, reveals a bounty of chest muscles and a corrugation of abdominals. Maggie O'Brien's gaze jumps from his belt buckle to his jewel-encrusted boot knife, avoiding the obvious indications of a man well-endowed. Too bad he is just a poster advertising a virtual reality game. Maggie has always thought such male perfection can exist only in fantasies like *Tolemac Wars*. But then the game takes on a life of its own, and she finds herself face-to-face with her perfect hero. Now it will be up to her to save his life when danger threatens, to gentle his warrior's heart, to forge a new reality they both can share.

___52307-8 $5.99 US/$6.99 CAN

Dorchester Publishing Co., Inc.
P.O. Box 6640
Wayne, PA 19087-8640

Please add $1.75 for shipping and handling for the first book and $.50 for each book thereafter. NY, NYC, and PA residents, please add appropriate sales tax. No cash, stamps, or C.O.D.s. All orders shipped within 6 weeks via postal service book rate. Canadian orders require $2.00 extra postage and must be paid in U.S. dollars through a U.S. banking facility.

Name_____
Address_____
City_____State_____Zip_____
I have enclosed $_____ in payment for the checked book(s).
Payment <u>must</u> accompany all orders. ☐ Please send a free catalog.
          CHECK OUT OUR WEBSITE! www.dorchesterpub.com

SEVEN BRIDES
LEIGH GREENWOOD

LILY

Refusing to bet her future happiness on an arranged marriage, Lily Sterling flees her Virginia home to the streets of San Francisco. In the best saloon in California, she meets handsome proprietor Zac Randolph, and when the scoundrel refuses Lily's kindness, she takes the biggest gamble of her life.

___4441-2 $5.99 US/$6.99 CAN

Dorchester Publishing Co., Inc.
P.O. Box 6640
Wayne, PA 19087-8640

Please add $1.75 for shipping and handling for the first book and $.50 for each book thereafter. NY, NYC, and PA residents, please add appropriate sales tax. No cash, stamps, or C.O.D.s. All orders shipped within 6 weeks via postal service book rate. Canadian orders require $2.00 extra postage and must be paid in U.S. dollars through a U.S. banking facility.

Name_____
Address_____
City_____ State_____ Zip_____
I have enclosed $_____ in payment for the checked book(s).
Payment must accompany all orders. ☐ Please send a free catalog.
CHECK OUT OUR WEBSITE! www.dorchesterpub.com